"You city fellers are all alike. You just don't understand our western ways."

# HOW I COVERED SAM BASS

A Novel Based on the Adventures of an Intrepid Reporter Who Trailed the Famous Outlaw

By Sid Hoskins

Senior Press

Hilton Head Island, South Carolina

Copyright © 1994   Sid Hoskins
All Rights Reserved


No part of this book may be reproduced or transmitted in any form or by any means, electronic, mechanical, including photocopying, recording, or by any information storage and retrieval system, except in the case of reviews, without the express written permission of the publisher, except where permitted by law.


Library of Congress Catalog Number 94-66190

ISBN Number  0-96368457-4


Published by SENIOR PRESS

Cover Art: Scott Deming


Professional Press
Chapel Hill, North Carolina 27515-4371


Manufactured in the United States of America
96 95 94                10 9 8 7 6 5 4 3 2 1

## DEDICATION

To my grandson, Ian Rowan Fitzpatrick, who spent many nights in my subconscious as I revised, adapted, changed, altered, manipulated and fiddled with the final drafts.

And to my wife, Leslie.

*To Mickie*
*It's been grand sitting next to you all these years. Now you have something to remember me by.*
*— Sid Hodkins*
*December 1996*

## ACKNOWLEDGMENTS

I want to thank Frank Gaspar, David Lipton and all members of the Novel Writing and Fiction Writing classes at Long Beach City College, Long Beach, California. Also, my appreciation goes to the group at the Aspen Writer's Conference in Colorado, especially Cyra McFadden.

## AUTHOR'S NOTE

This is a work of fiction. Sam Bass and members of his gang really did enjoy a great run as leading desperadoes of their time and became famous. However, details of some events and settings of the period have been changed in our book which is the journal of one Nolo Blunt, a New York City greenhorn reporter who found adventure, romance and his big story in the Old West.

# Chapter 1

My name's Nolo Blunt and I'm sitting on this stuffy slow moving train because I'm after a story. My editor in New York sent me out here to the West to find some action, some robbers and cutthroats to write about. It certainly wasn't my idea to leave a cozy Manhattan apartment on Cortlandt Street and venture into this scarcely populated region of America.

Why would anyone in his right mind be sitting here in this noisy mechanical contraption, undergoing all kinds of privations, just to get closer to where some desperadoes choose to shoot up the countryside? The answer is money. There are several stacks of newly printed 1877 greenbacks waiting for me back home. It won't be long before I telegraph my first article back to New York and titillate my editor with on-the-spot descriptions of the ride out west. Besides, my transportation is being paid to make this hazardous adventure so I might as well enjoy it, even though I hate riding trains.

My job could be loading kegs of fermenting beer onto horse drawn wagons in Brooklyn or teaching English in a small upstate New York college, but I've chosen this new life. Nolo Blunt is a writer, all six feet of me. I will be one until someone unwraps my fingers from around my ever moving pen and sends me on my way to meet the final deadline of that great editor in the sky.

You're wondering how I got the name Nolo. My daddy was an avid poker playing man. His favorite betting game was five card stud and he hated low ball. His friends started calling him "No Low" and that's how I got my name. It sounds foreign and doesn't match my all-American ruddy complexion, but I don't mind it much. It's kind of different and looks good when it sits there just beneath the title of one of my articles on the front page of Frontier magazine, the New York publication for which I write.

Lucky to find a job at the magazine. My dad knows the editor and the two of them kind of talked it out. Suddenly I was offered a chance to join the staff. I'd done some writing for a newspaper and I attended the University of the City of New York at Washington Square in Manhattan. Took classes in composition and rhetoric. Got my degree too. Maybe that's another reason why the magazine hired me.

But this Nebraska country is a little too wild even for me and I've been almost everywhere, at least on the east coast. I spied a mass of meandering, fierce-looking buffaloes yesterday. The herd completely covered the low brown hills and moved along like a huge ocean wave. If I'd had me a rifle with good sights, I'd have been able to shoot any number of them without missing a beat I understand they do that out here. Haven't really seen anyone shoot a buffalo from a train, but I could see how it would be possible.

We left the train station early this morning and should be passing through Ogallala in western Nebraska early this afternoon. My ultimate destination is the Promontory in Utah. That's the place where they drove the glittering gold spike back in '69, linking the rails of our great nation for the first time.

From there I'm going to be nosing out a story about cowboy gangs who rob banks, stagecoaches and trains. That's not an easy assignment.

The ride is rough, but improvements in railroad equipment are being made every day. The Union Pacific attached a Pullman car onto this train and I'll stay aboard the line until we reach the new frontier out west.

They call this car the "Emigrant," a good name. It's filled to capacity. The seats are arranged so that two people fit comfortably side by side facing two others. It makes for a good arrangement and gets travelers to talk with each other.

Tucked overhead are slatted boards folded up in the daytime to give headroom for the riders. As night comes, these flat frames are lowered and become the upper berth. The seats we sit in all day are pulled together to become the lower berth. Everyone who has paid for a Pullman seat is entitled to stretch out in a none too comfortable bed and try to sleep. The rhythmic movement of the train does help create a feeling of being rocked. Of all the parts of this ride, I like the sleeping the best.

There are some mighty brave souls traveling with me. Looks like they've packed every last thing they own; of course, they brought the kids too. Across from me is a family of four. Even though the seats are not too wide, mom and pop fit nicely side by side with the kids who run up and down the aisles talking to folks. In the process the youngsters get some needed exercise. It's a long day for them being cooped up in this passenger car. They're wiry rascals, both with red hair and freckles. They must get it from their mother. She looks just like them.

The family's been with me for a while and I've kind of gotten to know them. Their name is Thomas and they want to settle down in Salt Lake City. Maybe they're Mormons. I really don't know and don't want to ask. But they act kind of religious like and talk in Bible-like sentences sometimes.

Sitting next to me is a brown-haired young woman named Joline. I don't know her last name. All she goes by is Joline. Maybe she doesn't want to get too familiar so she hasn't told me her family name. I haven't asked. Joline really is a pretty girl. Her nails are well manicured and she's wearing a blue frock with medium length sleeves. Her high neck collar is starchy and stiff.

She must be about 25. Her skin has the glow and youthfulness of women about that age. She's on her way west to meet her older brother in Utah. I've been talking to her a lot just to pass the time of day and I've learned quite a bit about her. Guess it's the reporter in me. Anyway, she's chatty most of the time. Must be some reason why she won't tell me her last name.

I'm getting kind of hungry. It's almost lunch hour and I've been waiting for the time when I can unpack the sandwiches I put in a bag this morning. Eating a sandwich is a good way to break up the monotony. Sitting in these seats is no fun. Biting down on two good slices of homemade bread with something tasty in between, like maybe roast beef, is my idea of relaxation. Always have liked to eat.

Miss Joline's been extra quiet. I've been watching her when she's not looking at me. She stares out the train window most of the time. When she isn't staring, she's reading a small book about life in the west. I looked over her shoulder to see the title. There's no adequate handbook for folks who travel west, but lots of my fellow writers have tried to tell settlers what they're in for. Might be a good idea for me. I could write one about the experiences I'll have out here.

"Miss Joline, you seem to be mighty quiet. Anything bothering you?"

Her answer was about what I expected.

"No, Mr. Blunt. I've just been gazing out the window and wondering about what it's going to be like in Salt Lake City. I've had letters from my brother, but he always was one to paint a rosy picture of things. You been there?"

"Well, ma'am, can't say as I have, but the magazine I write for ran a story about Salt Lake and driving the spike on Promontory. Salt Lake sounds like a pretty place to live. Lots of salt water, seagulls and religious people. You going to stay there long?"

She poked around in her bag for something. She pulled out a dog-eared picture and held it out for me.

"This is a picture of my third brother Henry. He's not married, but he sure has an eye for the ladies. I know exactly why he wants me to join him in Utah. I have a lot of questions about that. We're close to each other. Ma and Pa taught us that. My younger brother Billy's still at home and going to school."

I took the picture and studied the image. The man was then about 20 years old and had a good head of thick dark hair, maybe brown, like mine. His beard was middle length, mine was shorter, like a goatee. Henry had thick eyebrows a body would always remember after seeing only once. His pose was stiff-like. That's how they take pictures. Always have to hold steady while the photographer counts, then there's that bright flash of igniting powder and for minutes your eyes see the flash.

I leaned over and studied her face. This was one lovely young woman sitting beside me, big eyes with long brown lashes and eyebrows to match.

"He's a handsome brother you have there. What kind of work does he do?"

"He's a miner. He tells me all about how hard it is to find gold in the hills around Salt Lake, but he hopes to come across enough nuggets to set himself up in a mining supply business. He wants to sell shovels and other hardware to the gold diggers. What do you think, Mr. Blunt?"

Well, personally, I thought it a hard way to make a living. I also wondered why he wanted his sister to come all the way out there to help him. What I said was, "He'll have himself a business all right. There must be thousands of miners all needing tools to do their panning. But how are you going to fit in, Miss Joline?"

She was maybe embarrassed by my question. She nervously twisted the strap on her purse. I could sense she was getting edgy.

"My brother said something in the letter about me being expected to go with him to the mining camps and cook and wash up for him. He's going to be busy running his tent store and won't have time to do the housekeeping things. I really don't mind doing it. I've been cooking and cleaning since I was 10. Ma was a good teacher. Only thing I worry about is all those men. They may be quite different from the boys back home in Dallas County. I expect they might even be rowdy at times. I've been reading about them in this."

She held up her guidebook.

"You're probably right about those men. I've read some about them too. To tell you the truth, Miss Joline, I think it'd be mighty dangerous for you to be out in a mining camp with a bunch of rough men like gold diggers. It just isn't the place for a refined young lady. Maybe you should stay in Salt Lake and find yourself a job. Then your brother can join you there."

I could see her deflating like a balloon stuck with a pin. She looked at me with a pained expression, her eyebrows arching.

"Mr. Blunt. You may be right, but I can't rightly believe my brother would lead me into any kind of danger. I'd be much obliged if you'd keep your opinions to yourself about what's good for me. We don't know each other that well."

With that she turned her back to me and resumed looking out the window, her long hair falling straight down her back. Figured she just wanted to be alone for a while.

I heard a rustle behind me. When I turned, it was a passenger making his way down the aisle. But I noticed something else too. Sitting directly opposite me was a gent clad in cowboy clothes, a blue checkered piece of cloth tightly knotted at his throat and a six-gun strapped to his right hip. I thought he might be a character I should get to know.

Joline interrupted my thoughts. She stood up.

"Excuse me, Mr. Blunt. I wish to get by. Would you mind pulling in your knees so I can do so?"

Her slim body was silhouetted against the train window. Always wondered how a woman could have such a tiny waist. But her hips swelled out nicely even though they were hidden beneath yards of blue sateen.

Just at that moment the train lurched and Joline fell against me. I grabbed her to steady her. She sat down on my lap rather suddenly. I could tell she was embarrassed by what had happened. But what really bothered me was why the train had made such a sudden jolt in the first place. Then the train stopped. Trouble? There surely wasn't any station out here.

"Excuse me ma'am. Maybe you better get off my lap and sit next to me again. There may be something happening. The train's not moving. I'll go look."

She sat down and I arose to walk down the aisle toward the vestibule.

When I reached the end of the car I heard gunfire. It sounded like it was coming from where the engine would be. Being a nosy reporter by nature, I stepped out onto the metal grating and stuck my head around the corner of the car to see what was happening.

PING, PING, PING. Bullets ricocheted off the side of the train. I dropped to the floor. Was someone trying to kill me?

But there was no loud explosion. No more bullets. Instead there was the sound of hoofbeats disappearing into the distance. I chanced a look and saw a cloud of dust forming along the top of a small hill beyond the tracks. Figures on horseback, riding with abandon, their mounts charging away as if to catch the wind.

What had happened? The train had stopped suddenly. There was shooting. Then all was quiet again. A holdup? Was this how it was in the west?

I got up and clamored back to my seat. Miss Joline was there and obviously excited.

"Are you all right, Miss Joline? I think we've had a holdup. There were shots, some at me, and then everything stopped. Did you see anything?"

She shook her body as she answered. Her face registered her emotions, strong facial wrinkles on her cheeks outlined her mouth.

"I watched the whole thing from this window. There were five of them. They were shooting at you as they went by. I don't think they got anything. They had no mailbags or heavy sacks. Someone must have thwarted them. I wish I knew what was happening. Oh, Mr. Blunt. I'm so scared now that it's over."

She reached for me, quivering, and I held her close. Then she released her grip, smoothed out her dress and sat back in her seat as if nothing had happened.

"Mr. Blunt. I thank you for the availability of your shoulder just now. I needed someone for a moment and you were there. Please don't get any ideas about anything else."

"No, ma'am. I know that. I'm only glad I was here to help."

While still thinking about the warm feeling of Joline in my arms, something else came into my mind. I looked over where the cowboy had been sitting. He wasn't there. I turned toward Joline.

"Ma'am, excuse me. Did you see where that gentleman across the aisle disappeared to while the shooting was going on?"

She looked toward the empty seat.

"I saw him get up and go to the opposite end of the car from where you were. He jumped off to join the others. At first I thought maybe he was going to chase them, but then when he rode off with them. I was sure then that he was part of the gang. Oh, my goodness. He **was** one of them. And he was sitting across from us."

Joline looked faint, but I thought I detected a small smile creeping up on the corners of her mouth. Now why would she be smiling? My arm slipped around her shoulder and I held her for a moment, then let go.

"I was wondering about him, ma'am. He did look edgy just before the train jerked to a stop. He was wearing a mighty big gun. I've heard tell of some robbing gangs who plant a lone member in the coaches so they can rob the passengers. I think we were lucky. Something or someone cut short the robbery. Maybe we'll find out when we get to Big Springs. It's not far."

The train started moving and I could sense the relief that was shared by everyone in the car. The Thomases were chattering again and their young sons were now firmly seated directly between mother and father. If anything more was to happen, mother wanted her young ones within reach.

# Chapter 2

Big Springs was just ahead. I could barely make out some railroad shacks in the distance. There was a road that wandered beside the tracks. What would happen in Big Springs when the train conductor announced the attempted robbery to the proper authorities?

Miss Joline was quite calm now.

"What are you going to do, ma'am? Are you planning to get off at Big Springs? That was my idea too. I think I've found the beginnings of a good yarn and I don't want to lose it. Maybe we could find a hotel. I'll help you all I can, ma'am."

Joline looked up at me. I could see she was trying to make up her her mind. Tiny wrinkles appeared on her forehead.

"Mr. Blunt, I'm getting off at Big Springs, but it is only because I want to send a telegram to my brother in Salt Lake. I will be staying overnight in a hotel and I would appreciate your assistance in helping me find lodging. Don't get any ideas about anything else. However, I do find you to be a most dependable person on whom I can rely in times of need. Now if you'll help me put my things out into the aisle, I'll get myself ready for our arrival at Big Springs."

And that's all there was to it. The train slowed down. I looked out the window just in time to see the small Big Springs station come into view.

A number of people got off the train when it stopped. I'm sure they weren't all originally headed for Big Springs, but the excitement must have cured them of riding trains for a while. No doubt they'd continue on in a few days.

I was after something else. Now I had a lead and it could help me get my first story. I'd have to be on the lookout for that cowboy who had sat across the aisle.

Joline got her suitcase from the baggage room attendant as I spotted mine. I grabbed hers, shouldered my own, and we started walking toward what appeared to be the only hotel around.

It looked to me as if Big Springs had just grown like Topsy in "Uncle Tom's Cabin." Main street ran the length of the town. On each side of it were the stores that offered services to the pioneers from the area.

The Elkhorn Hotel wasn't really much. It was nothing but a false-fronted, two-story building that had stood too long in the Nebraska weather. It surely was a sorry looking place. Inside, the appearance changed. A huge stuffed elk's head greeted us as we entered the lobby. Potted plants were everywhere. Wicker sofas were arranged for easy conversation. Behind the check-in counter stood a gentleman who glared at us. His black string tie stood right out.

I set down my luggage and Joline's bag. We probably looked like a married couple, but the hotel clerk had no way of knowing. Maybe that's why he was glaring.

"I'd like a room for the night. I believe my friend here, Miss Joline, would like a room also."

I could see the man change his attitude once he knew we weren't trying to settle into one room like we were pretending to be married.

"Sign here, sir and you, miss, sign just below. How long you folks expect to be staying in our hotel? Need to know. We've got a lot of business this time of year."

"You can sign me up for seven days. Maybe I'll stay longer. Can't speak for Miss Joline. Don't know how long she'll be staying."

Joline looked at me in a strange manner, signed her name on the register and peered up at the man behind the desk.

"I'll be here just about as long as Mr. Blunt. I plan to travel on to Salt Lake City in about a week." I smiled. She had changed her mind.

I was just picking up the bags when I happened to glance out the front window. A reflection from outside caught my eye. There was the glimmer of something, something in the sunlight. I squinted and could just make out the figure of a cowboy ambling along, his shiny spurs flashing in the noonday sun. Damn, it was the same man who'd sat across the aisle on the train. He was in town. That could mean other members of his gang might be there too. I hurried Joline up the stairs. When we reached the upper level, I told her what I'd seen.

"Mr. Blunt, do you think we are in any kind of danger? That man may try to harm us. What can we do?"

Again she made that neat little smile of hers. Why?

I stopped in front of Joline's room, took her key and opened the door.

"You stay inside until I can get to the sheriff and tell him what I know. Lock your door and prop a chair under the door handle. If I want to talk with you, I'll knock three times and you'll recognize my voice."

Joline nodded and then closed the door. I thought she would be safe until my return.

The main street of Big Springs looked just like all the other frontier towns I had seen in Frank Leslie's Illustrated Newspaper. There were saloons, two cafes and a combination blacksmith shop and livery stable. The Big Springs Commercial Bank stood on the corner of Nebraska and Sentinel Streets.

I waited for a rickety carriage to pass and crossed over to the sheriff's office. A man with a star on his jacket sat smoking a long black cigar, leaning his chair against the grey boards of the office front.

I climbed the three steps to the timber walkway that stretched along in front of the town's stores. The lawman opened one eye and glared at me.

"Well, stranger. You want somethin'? We don't get many dudes like you in town. Notice you ain't packin' a gun. Be wise for you to get yourself one. This town's no place for any city feller."

"Excuse me sheriff. It is sheriff isn't it? I may have some news for you about the train robbery."

The lawman kicked his chair to an upright position, stood up, faced me and motioned for me to enter his office.

"Sit down young feller. My name's Richfield P. Tatum."

"Mine's Nolo Blunt."

We shook hands.

"I'd be mighty interested in knowin' about it. Railroad people put up good reward money for anyone catchin' train robbers. Tell me about it."

"Well, Miss Joline and I were on the train. We saw the whole thing happen. There was a fellow sitting across the aisle from me. I think he was part of the gang.

He got off the train car when the other robbers fled and rode off with them. Just now I saw him in town. He passed right by the hotel window when I was checking in. You think we're in any danger?"

The sheriff chuckled. I began to wonder if my telling him about the robbery was a mistake. But I had to. He spoke before I could say anything else.

"Sorry, mister. We don't get many folks 'round here who want to tell about a train robber bein' on the street. Most folks just keep it to themselves. Much obliged that you want to tell me about it. What was this desperado dressed like? You get a good look at him?"

"Sure did, sheriff. He was sitting right across the aisle from me on the train. He had on cowboy clothes. Looked to me like they had been laundered quite a bit. He had a blue cloth at his throat and carried a large gun with a barrel about this long."

I help up an index finger on each hand and measured out about eight inches.

Once again Tatum laughed. He sat down heavily into his desk chair and clutched his stomach tightly. He continued to roar with laughter. I began to feel uneasy.

"Excuse me, sir. What's the big joke. Is it something I said?"

Again the sheriff roared. I began to worry about his mental state. Then he calmed down.

"You say, young feller, this cowboy had on well-washed clothes and had a blue bandanna around his neck? And he was packin' a six-gun? That could be a thousand different snaggle-toothed cow punchers in these parts. Here, take a look at these wanted posters. I got a stack of 'em in my drawer."

Some artist had worked hard to capture the profiles of these wanted men. I thumbed through the dozens of posters and was just about finished when I noticed one face that matched the man on the train. I read the name. Joel Collins. There was a reward of $100 for his capture, dead or alive.

"This is the man, sheriff. I saw him in town not more than an hour ago. If you hurry, you can catch him before he has a chance to leave town."

Once again the sheriff let out a roar of laughter. I was getting used to it now. But the reason for the guffawing left me confused.

"What's so funny about that? I try to help you catch a crook and you just laugh out loud."

The sheriff stopped laughing, looked at me kind of funny, and grunted.

"You city fellers are all alike. You just don't understand our western ways. That ain't how you do it out here in Nebraska country. When I go after this here Joel Collins, I got to have me a plan. These badmen got pistols in their belts just like I do, but I've got only one life to give. Lawmen ain't no different from anyone else. They die when a bullet goes through their heart. May be different back in the East. Out here you got to use some trickery and have a bunch of deputies waitin' behind you with their guns drawn. You just be patient. We'll catch this Collins character. Seems to me he works with Sam Bass. You ever heard of Sam Bass?"

"Can't say as I have. Is he famous around here?"

"Bass was a stagecoach robber who's now turned to stoppin' trains. It's rumored this Joel Collins met up with him down Texas way. Cow herders, that's what they were. Ended up here in Nebraska after a cattle drive and stayed on. Wish they'd gone back to Texas. Half the country's up in arms about these two. They got a gang. Reckon they're holed up in Robber's Roost out west of here. Bad country. All kinds of places to hide. Never find them just trackin'. Need a lead. Just maybe you've given me that. Now you go on back to your hotel and wait. I'll get a hold of you when I need you."

With that, Tatum pulled out his pistol, snapped it open to check the bullets, flipped it shut and put it back in his holster.

I walked out of the office and headed down the boardwalk. It made a kind of crunching sound as I went toward the hotel. I was just getting ready to cross the dirt street when I noticed a sign in one of the windows. It said, "BIG SPRINGS CLARION." Suddenly, I had an idea. Who knows more about a town than the local editor? I needed information about this Joel Collins character.

A familiar odor of printer's ink greeted me as I entered the newspaper office. Standing behind the counter was a tall man, grey haired and wearing an ink-stained blue apron. Resting far forward on his head was a green visor like most printers wear when setting type. He was looking me over pretty good as I approached.

"Hello, my name's Nolo Blunt. I'm a writer for Frontier Magazine and I'm on my way to Utah. But the train I was riding on was stopped by a gang of outlaw cowboys and I need some information. That is, if you'll help me."

The man just stood there for a moment, continued to look at me before he spoke.

"Heard about that. There's a small story about it in tomorrow's paper. You want to read it? Got it right here."

He walked over to the press and picked up a proof sheet. I noticed he was limping as he returned to the counter, handed me the paper and went back to what he was doing.

The article told pretty much what I already knew. The train had been stopped by a bunch of armed men. They were thwarted by some Pinkerton's men who were riding in the engineer's cab. When the desperadoes stopped the train, they hadn't counted on any opposition. After shots were exchanged, the cowboy gang rode off.

I put the paper on the counter and looked up. The man glanced my way. I wanted to tell him about what I'd seen.

"I might have some news about the attempted robbery. Maybe we can make a swap. I'll tell you what I know if you'll help me get some background information about one of the gang members."

I watched him closely. There was something strange about the way he looked when I said gang members. I didn't know whether or not he was hard of hearing or just thinking. Finally he spoke.

"Might be able to do that. What do you know?"

"A man across the aisle from me on the train was Joel Collins. I identified him from a poster in the sheriff's office. I just saw that same Joel Collins in town when I arrived. The entire gang must be around here somewhere."

The man listened with interest. Then he said,

"Joel Collins. Yes, I know about Joel Collins. He came up from Texas with Sam Bass. Last year I think. They were pals on the cattle trail, sold a herd, pocketed the money. Now they're outlaws. It's a fact that Collins and Bass have held up more than one stagecoach. Didn't get much, nothin' more than a few dollars. Bass is a strange one. Always gives back a dollar to the person he robs. Says it's for them to get breakfast on. Ain't heard of the Bass gang tryin' to rob trains. You might just be on to somethin' there."

I thanked him for the bit of information and walked out onto the sidewalk once again. Then I thought about Joline being shut up in her room all this time.

I hurried back to the hotel, walked up the stairs and knocked on Joline's door. There was no answer. I knocked again and still there wasn't a sound in her room. I tried the door. It was open. I walked in half expecting to find her lying in a pool of blood, but worse, she wasn't even there. I looked around. There was no evidence of a fight. A note was propped up on the table next to the bed.

"Dear Mr. Blunt,

I have gone to the telegraph office to send a message to my brother. I want him to know where I am and what I am doing. I will return shortly. Wait for me."

It was signed, Joline.

I left the note where it was, walked out of the room and headed downstairs. Joline was taking chances by walking around Big Springs in the daylight. She obviously had a mind of her own and there was nothing I could do to keep her from doing what she wanted. My only hope was that Joel Collins didn't find her before I did.

I pushed open the front door of the hotel and looked up and down the street. There wasn't a sign of Joline.

# Chapter 3

Telegram! The telegraph office! Must be by the train station.

A thick, clay-colored dust piled up on my once cleanly polished shoes as I headed down the street. I'd have to get myself some western clothes and boots.

Soon I found the rough wooden steps that led to the telegraph office. Even before I opened the door, I had a sinking feeling. Somehow I knew Joline wouldn't be there.

A neat middle-aged balding man was seated at his roll top desk tapping out Morse code, his right hand on the key.

"Excuse me, sir."

The man kept sending without looking up. I waited. Finally, he stopped, turned his head toward me and gave me a look.

"Be right with you, young feller. Gotta finish this wire to Salt Lake City. Hold your horses a minute."

Salt Lake City. Joline's brother Henry lived there. It must be her telegram he was sending. She had been here.

The operator's fingers tapped evenly on the key, the clattering sound echoing against the bare wooden walls. Then he finished, stood up, took off his eye shade and approached me.

"Got a wire to send?"

"I'm looking for a young lady, short, with brown hair. Name's Joline. She was sending a wire to her brother in Salt Lake City. Maybe you've seen her?

"Sure have. In here 'bout an hour ago. Had a long telegram. You looking for her?"

"Can you tell me which way she went?"

The man scratched his head, then looked at me squarely.

"She left here with someone. Cowboy came in while she was waiting. Acted like he knew her. Kinda took her by the arm and led her out the door. She went right along. I watched them double up on his horse. Ain't easy for any gal to ride that way, but that lady had class. Just pulled together her skirts, let the cowboy help her up and settled herself behind him kinda sidesaddle like. They rode off down Main street toward the Elkhorn Hotel."

I thanked him for the information. Joline was in trouble. That cowboy must have been a member of the Bass gang and Joline was headed somewhere with him. How did he know about her? Poor Joline. Poor me.

I knew nothing about this country. I was a greenhorn when it came to tracking or shooting. That would have to change.

I thought back to the Clarion. Jim Copley, the editor, might be the way to my finding Joline. He could know more about this gang than he told me. I headed in his direction and before long found myself in front of the office. He was still there, hunched over, visible through the large front glass window.

The door closed with a bang behind me. The man looked up, shock spreading over his face, then he recovered.

"You surprised me," he said, and went back to setting type.

"You mind if we talk while you work? I need some help. My friend Joline's been kidnapped by a cowboy. You got any idea where the gang stays or how I could find them? I've got to get her back. She's innocent of anything."

He didn't even look up, just kept working with the metal type. Finally he said, "Buck Redwing."

I was confused. "What's a Buck Redwing?"

He looked up. "Indian. Best tracker around these parts. Find him at the livery stable. Always there. He knows this country. Born in Kiowa country in Texas but knows this part of Nebraska. Seems to me he came north on the cattle drive with Sam Bass and Joel Collins. Kind of stuck around here when the drive was over. Reads the prairie like a body reads this newspaper. Find Redwing. He'll help you."

With those words he went back to work.

Buck Redwing. I wondered what he would be like. I'd never even talked to an Indian before. I'd read many stories about them, but it didn't seem possible all the stories could be true that cast the Indians in a bloodthirsty image, taking scalps and killing settlers.

I found him at the stable. He sat against a wall near the entrance door. His dark black hair hung down his back in one long braid. Matted eyebrows hovered over gleaming black eyes. A handmade cigarette rested in his wrinkled fingers. I approached him with caution. He wore a gun.

"You Buck Redwing?"

He looked me over.

"Might be. What's it to you?"

But Joline was in danger and I had to get this man to help me find her.

"Might need your help. Want someone to do some tracking in the hills, help me find someone."

His expression changed. He warmed to the subject.

"You need some tracking done? Do you pay good? I need money, a hundred dollars."

I could just see myself putting an item on my expense account.

***"Secured the assistance of a tracking expert, $100."***

My editor would have me skinned alive and fried. No one had said it would be easy to write about a gang of desperadoes.

I put my hand out to his and said, "Done. Let's go."

The Indian just sat there without saying a word or shaking my hand. He put the cigarette in his mouth and lit it. In a moment he took it out of his mouth and turned toward me.

"You are a real greenhorn."

I chose my words carefully. My success in finding Joline depended on what I said now.

"I believe the Bass gang has kidnapped my friend, Miss Joline. A cowboy tricked her into going with him on his horse. I think they've gone to Robber's Roost. I want to get her back. You'll take me there so I can talk with this Mr. Bass?"

This was no ordinary man. I could tell that. He put his head back and let out a whoop of laughter. Then he doubled over like he was in pain. Soon he straightened up and looked directly at me.

"You made a big joke. You're funny. Find Bass. If Bass wants to see you, he'll find **you**. Just wait. He'll come or send someone. You don't need me."

With that he stood up and pushed past me shouldering his way inside the stable, the glow of his cigarette growing dimmer.

I followed him. He wasn't going to get away that easily. I called to him through the darkened open door. Dimly I saw him pause and turn.

"What do you want with me? Are you crazy?"

Maybe I was crazy, but I knew what I wanted.

"I want you to track for me, teach me, help me find Joline and the Bass gang. I'll give you a hundred dollars like you asked, fifty now and the rest when I'm safely back here."

My heart pounded as I thought about all I had said. A lot of things were involved. It meant learning how to shoot a pistol and wear cowboy clothes. Riding a horse was no problem. I'd done plenty of that back east. But more than that, it meant following tracks in sandy soil, becoming a cowboy myself so I could locate the Bass gang. Maybe this was the real story of my adventure in the west.

I had hooked him. I knew it. He needed money.

"We will meet tomorrow, Big Springs Cafe, end of street. Find you a horse, then go to the general store to get you blankets, a mess kit, clothes, boots, a shootin' iron, bullets. Yes, I'll teach you. You give me enough money and I'll teach you all."

He turned and disappeared from my view.

I woke up early next morning. All night long I had a nightmare of Joline being tied up, tortured, whipped and violated. I bumbled as I got out of bed, washed my face in the cold water in the basin and headed through the hotel lobby to find the cafe.

The smell of frying bacon mixed with tobacco smoke greeted me as I stepped through the open cafe doorway. I wished someone had opened a window. I looked around the room. A dozen tables were spread in a scattered pattern on the bare wood floor. I stepped into the room. The boards squeaked under my feet.

Over in the corner next to a potted palm was Buck Redwing. He sat straight up, unmoving. He gazed at the opposite wall. I approached him.

"You're an early bird. Mind if I join you for breakfast?"

I took his grunt to mean it was all right. I sat down.

"You're late. The sun came up a long time ago. You slept while I waited for you here. That's no good. Pay me my money. Let's get started. We have much to do. Greenhorns. Ugh."

I handed over fifty dollars and ordered breakfast while the Indian just sat there occasionally grunting to himself. I tried to carry on a conversation with him without success.

"I guess all Indians get up before the sun. What kind of horse do you think we'll find for me? Any ideas about western clothes? I need some boots and a pistol. You'll have to teach me how to shoot it. Have you tracked many horses in your lifetime? Can we find the track of the horse that carried Joline out of town?"

I stopped, picked up my fork and shoved egg into my mouth along with a piece of sourdough toast.

The Indian just sat there and stared like he was in a trance. Then he opened his mouth.

A strange noise came out. It was a high-pitched noise, barely audible. I stopped eating and watched him. He turned and looked at me.

"You really are a greenhorn. You talk too much. Keep your mouth shut unless you're eating. I know what to do. It's quiet on the prairie. Eat faster. We have much to do."

He was right of course. I was excited. Joline was in danger. I finished my breakfast quickly.

"We can go now."

I mumbled those words as I chewed on the last bit of bacon.

He crouched slightly, rose quickly from the table and was gone. Buck moved with speed for a man over six feet tall and maybe weighing 190 pounds. He had the look of a hungry animal. I watched as he crossed main street. He headed for the only general store in Big Springs.

I dumped my napkin on the table and rushed out the door, trying to follow him. But he was gone. He just disappeared.

A noise behind me made me look around.

A scroungy looking cowboy tapped my shoulder. He wore a gun and his clothes reeked of prairie dung and body sweat. As he opened his mouth to speak I could see yellow stains on his rotting teeth.

"You Blunt?"

I shook my head up and down.

"I've got a message for you. Keep your nose out of our business or your lady friend will be missin' for a long time. You done talked to Sheriff Tatum and Jim Copley over to the Clarion. Ain't nothin' goes on in this town without one of our boys knowin' it. You just get your stuff together and get out of town. When we hear you've left, your lady friend goes free."

His fist was faster than my reaction. The blow landed in my midsection and for a moment I couldn't breathe. I doubled over and fell down with my head spinning and my lungs gasping for air. The pain in my stomach was something fierce.

My head finally cleared. As I opened my eyes I could barely make out the shape of the man who'd hit me. He reached his horse, mounted and rode off down main street.

The Indian stood beside me again.

"I overheard that cowboy. Do you still want to find your lady? It'll be dangerous."

He was right. If I continued to hunt for Joline, I could be endangering her life and mine. But the choice came easy. I had to be sure Joline was all right. Who could trust an outlaw? It was only his word that she wouldn't be harmed. I had to find Joline.

"Let's go, Buck. Let's get on with it. The quicker we get started, the quicker we find Joline."

I stood up and dusted myself off. My stomach still felt like I'd been kicked by a mule, but I had a new determination. I would save Joline at all costs. Now I needed supplies and clothes.

The general store was open. Together Buck and I stepped through the front door, his broad shoulders touching mine. I'm sure the merchant must have thought we were a strange pair and we were. Buck stood much taller by a few inches and was beefier than I. His stringy tasseled grey deerskin jacket contrasted greatly with my simple eastern tailored black cloth coat. But more than that, his feet were much larger than mine. I didn't understand how he could move so quietly on such big feet.

The clerk strode toward us, a broad smile crossing his face.

"What can I do for you? Looks like you just stepped off a train from back east and done fallen down in a pile of dust. That's a mighty fine tailored piece of material you're wearin' even if it's all smeared with Nebraska dirt. Can't find anything like that around here. Couldn't sell it if I had it. Well, what'll it be?"

I looked around and Buck had disappeared. I wondered what he would be like on the trail. Could I trust him?

The clerk cleared his throat. I looked at him and remembered why I stood here.

"I need an outfit. Rugged clothes. Pair of boots. I'll be on the trail soon. Can you fix me up?"

## Chapter 4

All I required now was a gun and a horse. And where was that damned Indian? Just when I needed him he wasn't here. I'd have to do something about that. What if he disappeared when I was in danger? Would he do that?

My new outfit fit loosely, the coarse denim pants tucked casually into the tops of my hand-tooled leather boots. I felt like a part of the west. My image reflected in the hotel room mirror confirmed my suspicions. I was filling out around the middle and there was just the trace of a budding beard on my chin.

I needed a six-shooter to complete my image, not that I would ever use it. But what was a man to do without a "shooting iron," as the men in the west called it.

The worn carpet on the hotel stairs muffled my steps as I tried out the new boots. They squeaked and the spurs jangled. I liked the sound. It made me feel like I was part of the Big Springs scenery.

Where was that damned Indian? Had he left town with my fifty bucks in his pocket?

My questions were soon answered as I rounded the base of the stairs. There he was, standing tall like one of those wooden statues I'd seen back east in front of a cigar store. His eyes followed me as I strode toward him.

"You look like a greenhorn with new clothes. Maybe your eyes shine like a greenhorn too. Your hair's parted in the middle. Never let an Indian on the warpath see you. Tomahawk, chop, chop. Hate greenhorns."

That was all he said. Just like that. He had sized me up. And I thought I looked like a seasoned westerner ready to herd cows or hunt outlaws.

His sudden presence piqued my curiosity.

"Where have you been? I couldn't find you anywhere. What kind of tracker are you? You're never around when I need you."

Buck just stood there looking at me with those dark cutting eyes.

"I'm here now. You need me. I'm here. I'll be here. I know where you went. You didn't see me, but I was there."

With that he turned and rushed out the front door. I followed, but didn't know where we were going.

I reached the boardwalk and looked around. He was nowhere in sight. Once again he had eluded me. I'd have to find out how he did that.

The sky clouded over as I looked toward the east. I could see threatening flashes of light, a warning that I might need that new poncho before the day was over.

I started toward the livery stable, but something made me stop. It was a sensation, a feeling that I was being watched. Someone was near me. I looked around quickly, but no one was there.

I headed for the stable.

The odor of manure greeted me as I walked through the partly open double door that separated the animals inside from the rain that was now beginning.

"Anybody here?"

I heard something behind me. I glanced around and saw a hunchbacked man, approaching. His dark red hair was disheveled. Bits of straw stuck out over an ear.

"I need a horse. Can you fix me up? Need it for a week or more. I'll pay you good for a gentle steed that doesn't buck."

The man stopped, adjusted the top button on his stained blue shirt and looked right at me. He chewed tobacco and the brown spittle ran down his chin.

"You want a horse, do you? Just like that, you want a horse. Ain't no way you can get a horse without me knowin' who you are. Strangers ain't welcome in this here stable."

A soft scratching sound made me turn suddenly. Buck stood next to me. How did he do that?

"I say give him a horse. I work for him. He'll take good care of it. I'll see to it. You know me, Dewey."

Dewey was thinking. There was a wrinkled-up look to his forehead and his eyes stared into mine. Finally he shook his shoulders as if making up his mind and moved past me toward a rear stall.

I followed and found where Dewey was headed. A chestnut mare stuck her head out over the top of the bare wood gate and looked me over. I must have passed inspection. She extended her muzzle toward me. I patted and rubbed her white-blazoned forelock.

Horses. How many times had I been nipped, kicked, scratched and bruised by a horse? They could be mean and nasty. But then they could be like this gentle mare. A man could fall in love with a horse, especially one who would be true. This mare was one of those horses. It didn't take more than an instant to determine it.

I couldn't wait.

"Lead her out of the stall, Dewey. I want to see how she looks when she moves."

Dewey must have thought I was touched in the head.

"You goin' to buy her or just ride her? You said somethin' about renting a horse. This here mare's about as gentle as they come. I can let you have her for five bucks a week. You buy the oats and feed her. I'll warn ya. She's got a mountain-sized appetite. That's why her name's Big Mama."

Dewey handed me the halter and I turned Big Mama around. She danced some, but followed my lead. I could see she was all class, smooth back, sturdy legs and a chest cavity built for endurance. This would be a horse to match a man's spirit and catch the wind. She might be gentle, but I sensed that she could break through that gentleness and become a spunky girl, kind of like Joline. Yes, there was a parallel there.

Dewey brought a blanket and saddle. I helped him spread the woven wool horse pad neatly on Big Mama's back. I didn't want any lumps or creases to cause her discomfort.

The saddle fit snugly against her sides. Reaching under her belly, I grabbed the cinch and pulled on the worn leather strap. This was a western saddle, much different from the ones I'd known back in New York. I knew I'd get used to it before long.

"Now, now old girl. Just let out some of that breath for me so's I can make this belt a little tighter. Don't want me to fall off out on the prairie, do you?"

I had learned to talk softly to a horse and amazingly enough, the horses I had ridden seemed to respect me for it. They always responded as if they fully understood what I was saying.

Anyway, Big Mama did what I told her to do. She blew out once and I cinched up on the strap.

Buck stood nearby while I saddled my horse and only when I finished did he speak.

"You're a greenhorn, but you know about horses. Maybe you'll even make a good tracker. We'll see."

I led the mare out of the stable. The two men followed.

Dewey approached me with his hand out.

"You got the money for this horse? That'll be five bucks payable in advance. I'm only doing this 'cause I know Buck here and trust him to get this mare back to my stable if somethin' should happen to you, greenhorn."

I didn't like the way he emphasized the word "greenhorn," but decided to let it pass. These western folks had their funny little ways of showing their distaste for strangers. I wouldn't be a greenhorn long once I could get on my horse and ride out of this town.

"Here's your money. I want a receipt. Got to keep things straight with my editor."

I don't know why I added all that about my editor, but it was true. Without verified expenses, I'd be hard up to prove what I'd spent.

I led Big Mama along the muddy street. The rain slanted down in sheets, soaking me to the skin. The horse didn't seem to mind. For at least a few moments she would be rid of those pesky galling small black flies that seemed to attack every horse in every stable I'd ever visited.

My poncho was back in the room. I'd just have to brazen out the storm and put Big Mama under a protective overhang of the hotel roof.

My once shiny new boots were now caked with sloppy grey-colored mud as they sloshed along making a slurping sound.

Buck was nowhere in sight. He must have found his own place away from the slashing rain.

There were only two other horses tied to the rail in front of the hotel. I tied up Big Mama between them.

The upper porch of the Elkhorn jutted out just enough to give the animals some shelter from the weather. Big Mama would be all right there for a while. I'd have to return her to the stable if the storm kept up.

I stomped my mud-caked boots a few times on the wooden steps. It didn't seem to do much good. Found a small stick and scraped off what I could. I didn't want the hotel clerk to hassle me when I walked across the lobby.

The wind began to blow harder. It felt good to step inside the warm, dry lobby, away from the rain that began to beat against the porch roof. This storm might slow me down. What would happen to the tracking that Buck and I needed to do? There couldn't be any tracks left. Maybe Buck knew the answer.

The clerk stood behind the counter, his eyes on me and then he looked at my boots. He smiled, then motioned me toward the desk.

"Mr. Blunt. I have a note for you. A cowboy just put it in your box no more'n ten minutes ago."

He reached behind him where the keys were kept and handed me an envelope.

I looked long and hard at the writing on the outside. It read "Mr. Blunt" in a woman's delicate hand.

I tore it open, extracting the piece of paper.

> Dear Mr Blunt,
> I am all right. Don't try to find me. You could get hurt. Leave town on the next train. No harm will come to you. If you try to find me, there could be trouble.
> Joline

There could be trouble. Did the gang force her to write the note? It didn't seem that way, but I couldn't tell. She wanted me to leave town. I wouldn't be harmed if I did. The cowboy told me **that** on the street just before he punched me. Why did they want me out of the way? What was there about Joline that made my heart sing?

I folded the note, put it in the envelope and started for my room. I had just reached the bottom step when I heard a grunt from behind me. My head swiveled. There was Buck.

"Are you ready? We go. We'll leave now. I found you a gun. Here."

He handed me what looked like a left-over pistol from the Civil War. It was well-worn, but it had been recently oiled. The barrel must have been ten inches long making it a blunderbuss of a weapon.

"What do I do with this? It won't fit in my holster. Do you have bullets to match? How do I load it? Is it accurate?"

Buck screwed up his face again. His mud-streaked forehead wrinkled.

"You talk too much. Let it be. You'll learn. I'll teach you. Get your poncho and bed roll. We'll go. We want to get moving before the bad weather stops."

I didn't argue. I just followed directions and went to my room. Hurriedly I pieced together my newly acquired outfit. I threw my sausage-shaped blanket pack over my shoulder, stepped through the door and strode toward the steps.

Buck was at the bottom of the stairs, his eyes glaring at me as if to tell me that he wasn't certain if I could make it through the first day of our ride. I could. I was tough. Maybe I hadn't served in the army, but there had been some tight spots in my life. Reporting news stories from the Bowery wasn't exactly an easy way to make a living. New York streets were different from these in Big Springs, but just as deadly.

Enough of those thoughts. Joline needed me. I'd find her and bring her back and maybe I'd get my story too. The Bass gang. They sounded almost like they were daring me to find them. Warnings. What did they mean?

Big Mama watched as I undid the reins. I patted her nose then nudged her away from the other horses. She backed out and stood still while I tied my pack in place, checked the saddle and made ready to climb on.

One foot in the stirrup. Now up and over, sitting on top of the world, sixteen hands high. What a good feeling. Once again I controlled my universe. This horse would take me where I wanted to go. Feeling her muscles beneath me, my knees sensed Big Mama's energy, her need to run.

The rain stopped. I looked around. Where was Buck? That was my most frequently asked question. I didn't need to worry. I had learned by now to start out in one direction and Buck would be there. And sure enough, there he was just ahead of me, his pinto pawing the muddy ground, its head bent forward and twisted slightly toward me.

Touched Big Mama with my spurs; she responded with a burst of speed that threw me back in the saddle. I grabbed the pommel and held onto it, the reins dropping toward the ground, flapping in the breeze.

## Chapter 5

We rode out of town, Buck and his pinto in the lead. There was a scent of freshness in the air. I had an experienced guide and a horse just now beginning to realize what I required of her.

A man could have no better life. How could I have let myself be trapped, living in the regimented canyons of New York City, Broadway and the apartment over J. Gallet, Swiss watch merchant. The west, that's where life still responded to the primitive rhythm of basic urges. Survival involved a keenness of the senses and a heightening of mental processes.

Joline. How I wanted to see her again. On the surface she seemed so prim, so naive, so untouchable. But there had been that note. It moved me on. It flashed a signal within me, *"Save Joline, Save Joline"* and all would be right with the world again. Where was she? How could a greenhorn hope to rescue her from the Bass gang? I didn't even know how many men were holed up somewhere in those low rising brown hills just ahead of us.

I pulled up alongside Buck.

"You know exactly where the gang is hiding out?"

Buck shifted in his saddle, turned his massive head toward me and looked at me. Tiny wrinkles formed at the corners of his mouth, his forehead grooved into lines.

"Why do you think we are riding this way? Maybe you have a better idea?"

His answer caught me off guard. Of course I had no idea which way to ride. He could leave me out here on the prairie and I could die.

"No, I haven't any better idea. Just making conversation. Maybe you can tell me the names of places around here. After all, I am writing a story for my magazine in New York. It's paying the bill for all this."

For once I think I made sense to Buck. He looked ahead again, his horse picking up speed as we came to the crest of a small grass-covered rise. Then he reined in sharply. I did the same. We sat there for a moment without talking. I could sense something in the wind, that tingling feeling again, as if someone were watching. Buck was motionless in his saddle, only his head now moving right and then left. He looked down.

In one graceful motion he was on the ground, bending over, looking at something, something that made sense only to him.

I was curious. What could there be down there that was so important? And how had he spotted it while riding along at a fast pace? I was beginning to gain respect for Buck not only as a tracker, but as someone who had extra senses, perhaps even mystical senses. He was an amazing fellow.

"What'd you find down there, Buck?"

He didn't make a sound. Just stood there motionless, listening, staring, sensing the wind, his eyes moving slightly, his gaze centered on the hills ahead.

Finally, he looked up at me and whispered, "We are not alone. Riders. They've been through here in the last few minutes. Danger. Is your pistol loaded? You know how to fire it? Keep it handy."

With those words, Buck swung into the saddle, his toughened leg muscles doing all the work. I saw him pull a rifle out of its bag and place it across his lap. One hand was on the reins, the other on the trigger piece of the long weapon.

I checked my handgun. Although it hadn't been fired yet, I knew the general principles of how it worked. I had read about guns in my early years. Deep down, guns fascinated me.

I took out five bullets from my pouch and put them in my jacket pocket.

Buck disappeared over a low hill ahead of us. Big Mama was ready to move and a touch of my foot on her flank got her going real quick. She jerked toward the direction Buck had taken. The Indian was nowhere in sight. I reached the rise where I had seen him last and looked into the gully that separated me from the next rise in the ground. He was not there.

But there were tracks. I'd learned that much already about reading signs on the prairie. It was almost like the old game we played on the sidewalks of New York. It was called follow the arrow. Someone would chalk arrows along the concrete walkways and a youthful city detective like me would come after, searching ahead for the next mark that would lead toward the hidden treasure. The treasure I searched for now was Joline.

Buck's horse must be moving faster now. The hoofprints were farther apart. I stopped to listen and couldn't hear anything except the Nebraska wind on this almost flat land.

Where was Buck? There was a sound behind me. I turned in my saddle to look. No one there.

Darkness crept in over the prairie. I was getting worried and spurred Big Mama on. There was just enough light to see the tracks, but it wouldn't be long before I'd have to give up and find shelter.

A sixth sense made me turn my head and there was Buck next to me. He had ridden up, silent as the stars, his horse making no snorting noises or sounds. It was as if the animal were part Indian and knew how to do what Buck wanted him to do.

I was glad to see him.

"You're here." He cut me off without another word. Finally he spoke, his voice soft and his head next to my ear.

"We are not alone. Follow me. Keep still."

Squinting, I could see Buck easier by looking off to one side. Natural sunlight was failing, but there was still enough reflected glow for me to make out the big Indian as he rode ahead of me. Then I remembered Buck's warning.

We rode on. Finally, Buck stopped, smelled the wind, listened and dismounted. I pulled on the reins and held Big Mama tightly, ready for anything. Evidently we had reached our campsite. Buck took down his sleeping roll. No words were exchanged. I got down from my horse.

There were no trees, just grass and prairie dog holes.

I unfolded my blankets and went to work with the saddle. I staked out Big Mama and she immediately started pulling up bunches of sweet grass.

My hat came off quickly and it was soon filled with water from my canteen. I held it out for her. She drank it all and more.

Buck spread his bedding opposite mine. I waited for him to speak.

"No fire. We'll chew jerky and go right to bed. I'll watch first, then you'll watch. We must be ready for tomorrow."

With that he headed off over a small hill in front of us. I watched him as he crouched low to the ground, his head moving slowly from side to side, his nostrils always sensing.

My body ached from all the riding.

I stretched out on my blankets and looked at the sky. A thousand stars shone down through the clear air. Off in the distance a coyote howled.

My thoughts turned to Joline. Maybe I would see her again. I hoped Buck had a plan for her rescue.

I felt a punch on my shoulder and looked up into Buck's face. There was a full moon. Its light reflected off the sandy soil giving Buck's image an eerie glow. Where was I? Why did my back ache? Why was I sleeping on the ground?

"Time for you to watch. Keep your eyes open. I'm going to sleep."

I remembered now. It was my turn to stand guard. My knees ached as I pulled my legs out from under the blankets.

Strapping on my pistol, I caught a glimpse of Big Mama and Buck's pinto. They were still busily eating grass. Did they eat all night?

There wasn't much to see, but there were sounds and smells that I had never experienced before. I scanned the horizon. Only bright moonlight in a cloudless sky. My vision seemed amazingly keen.

There were shapes there, other small hills, a tuft of grass silhouetted against the skyline. Nothing moved. A slight breeze blew into my face from the west and then I caught the faint smell of smoke.

My eyes became accustomed to the light. Looking off to the right, I could see a flicker of light, a campfire out there somewhere. Other riders. Who were they?

Now there was sound. I could smell dust. Then I heard it. Loud hoofbeats pounded and suddenly I was surrounded. No time to warn Buck. Men were all around me, armed men with bandannas over their faces.

I put my hands up in the air to make sure they wouldn't think I was going to shoot at them. Suddenly, I knew what it felt like to be afraid.

"Drop that gun belt a yourn, Blunt. You don't need that thing strapped to your leg. We got ideas for you."

I reached down with my left hand and unbuckled the belt. The holster dropped to the soft earth with a thud. My heart pounded madly. Finally I found my voice.

"What are you going to do with me? All I want to do is find Sam Bass and Joel Collins. I want to write a story about them. I want to see Miss Joline again too if you haven't done away with her."

The men laughed loudly.

"You done found Joel Collins," one of them said. "That's me, you greenhorn. Saw you the first time you were ridin' the train sittin' next to my sister."

Next to his sister! Joline had sat next to me. Did he mean that Joline was his sister? It couldn't be. But maybe it was.

"I'd be obliged to know that Joline is safe."

Again there was laughter. I felt something metallic sticking in my back. The person holding it urged me forward.

Collins talked again.

"Get your horse saddled. We got a bit of ridin' to do before sunup."

I moved toward Big Mama and glanced toward where I'd last seen Buck. No one was there. The Indian was gone. When I looked for his pinto, it was gone too.

Big Mama greeted me with a snort. As I finished cinching the strap under her belly, Collins yelled at me to hurry up. I tied my bed roll behind the saddle and stepped into the stirrups.

We rode at a pace that apparently would get us where we were going in short time. I could see the sun just beginning to peek up over a low hill behind me. I knew we must be close to where Sam Bass and the rest of the gang were holed up. The pace didn't slacken.

Then I saw it, a bigger hill. A trail wound through many gullies until it reached a jagged cleft in a rocky formation. My gaze strayed to the hilltop and a slouching man peered down at me. A lookout! We were close. Joline was near. I knew it.

Then a shout. Collins hailed the lookout.

"All clear, Eakins."

The other man's voice was high-pitched.

"Hurry along. Sam's waiting."

The cleft in the rock turned out to be the entrance to the hideaway. I guided my horse through the opening into darkness. Old feelings returned, feelings of being locked up in the basement of the apartment on Cortlandt Street when I was young, all alone. The beginnings of a scream started at the base of my throat, but I held it back and continued riding.

We came out into a large basin where campfires smoldered. A crude shack was in the middle of the compound and next to it stood a black-haired young man. He was dressed like every other cowboy I'd seen since I'd been in the west, but there was something distinctive about him, a sense of importance that the other men didn't have. I took him to be Sam Bass.

Collins pulled back on his reins. He was off his mustang's back in a slippery move and then the rest of the riders dismounted leaving me the only one sitting on a horse.

"You can get down offen that mare, greenhorn. Ain't nobody goin' to give you a prize for sittin' on a horse."

It was the man with the dark hair who was speaking, the one I thought must be Bass. His words were drawled and his voice low-pitched with a touch of a nasal twang.

"We been waitin' for you to get here. Thought you'd never make it. What took you so long?"

"Are you Sam Bass?"

There was laughter.

"Yup, I'm Bass. Be sure you spell it right when you send your story back east. We been waitin' for you to get here so's you could write one of them stories about us. Joline done told us about how you're one of them fancy reporters from New York."

"Joline. Where is she? I haven't seen her since yesterday. I thought she was kidnapped."

Bass threw back his head and let out a war whoop.

"Kidnapped. Miss Joline. Hell, man, we been expectin' her for a month. Me and the boys sure enough escorted Joline's train into Big Springs just so's nothin' would happen to her. You done stuck your nose into our business by steppin' out on that vestibule at the wrong moment. One of the boys just dropped some lead above your eyebrows to chase you back. You'd been a dead man if'n he'd wanted to kill you."

"You boys play rough. Why didn't you tell me you wanted me to write something about you. I'd have been willing to join you. That's why I'm here."

Bass moved closer and grabbed Big Mama's bridle and held her steady while I slid to the ground.

"If we'd made it easy for you, you'd have lost interest and gone on to find someone else for your stories. Always like to add a little mystery to make things more tasty. Joline had the idea of leavin' the note for you. She knew you'd follow her."

Sam pushed back a shock of his black hair.

"Uh, where is Joline? I'd like to see her," I said.

Just then I heard a female voice, one I'd heard before. It was Joline. I felt a tap on my shoulder, turned and Joline stood before me. She was as pretty as ever. A plain calico dress fit her snug figure and around her neck was a gold necklace.

I didn't quite know how to greet her. I wanted to take her in my arms and hug her. Reaching for her hand, I looked longingly into her eyes.

# Chapter 6

A reporter is supposed to know what to do and say at all times. Words are his life. Expressing himself in comprehensive sentences is his profession. But at that moment, standing with my hand in Joline's, my heart pumping wildly from the simple contact, I was almost at a loss for words.

"Are you all right? I worried about you when you weren't in your room. Traced you to the telegraph office and discovered you might have been kidnapped."

I looked into her brown eyes and my knees started to shake. When she answered, her voice was like a bit of sunshine on the rainiest of days.

"Mr. Blunt..."

"No, please call me Nolo."

Her voice came back with a softness that reached the very center of my spine and made me shudder.

"Nolo. I certainly didn't want to inconvenience you in any way. My brother Joel insisted that I ride off to camp with him. I always do what my brother tells me. You can let go of my hand now."

Embarrassed, I dropped it.

"Excuse me ma'am. Or may I call you Joline?"

The beginning of a smile appeared at the corners of her mouth. Her eyes closed some as if she were feeling mischievous.

"That will be just fine. You must be starved after all that riding you did yesterday. Come along. We'll eat."

I looked around the camp as we walked. It wasn't much. There were shacks made out of tree limbs covered with sod. Tufts of grass sprouted from the tops. Wagons filled the spaces between the shacks. The wagons looked as if they had crossed the prairie several times, the muslin covering sagging and the metal hoops sticking up like so many ribs of a skeleton. The spoked wheel rims had rusted. Some of the rolling stock lacked tongues and sideboards.

In contrast to the wagons I noticed a healthy looking collection of horses all busily munching the plentiful yellow-green grass.

"Here we are, Nolo."

Joline put her hand on my shoulder. I wondered if she knew just how much I enjoyed being near her, feeling the touch of her hand, watching her eyes. And to have her call me by my name. That was beyond belief.

"I am hungry, Joline."

The camp cook, in mud-stained trousers, tattered grey shirt and a confederate artillery cap worn backwards on his big head, stretched out a hairy, grease-encrusted arm in front of me. He held a ladle in his right hand and dipped it into a mixture of what looked like beef chunks and greens. My stomach growled as the odor rising from the kettle reached my nose. I **was** starved.

"Here you go, cowboy."

He called me cowboy. Progress! From greenhorn to cowboy in one day. Not bad.

The cook handed me a dappled tin plate.

"Grab a chunk a my fresh-baked sourdough and slap some cow butter on it. Ain't no better grub 'round here for miles. No extra charge for the coffee."

Joline pointed toward a flat rock where we could sit. I found it hard to juggle the plate and my coffee cup, one in each hand, settling myself on the rock. Joline sat beside me.

"Nolo. There's something I've been meaning to say. Since we met on the train a lot has happened to me. I still want to go to Salt Lake City to visit my brother Henry, but it's going to be a while. Joel needs me here and I rather like living with the gang. They're really gentlemen. They never bother me. 'Course Joel would kill anyone who even looked at me in a wrong way. That includes you."

A piece of stringy beef caught in my throat and I coughed. Joline was quick to pound me on the back to free it.

"Hope your brother understands that my attention is sincere. Wouldn't want him to have any confusion about my intentions."

"He knows. I told him you were an honorable man. He saw what happened on the train when I accidentally sat in your lap. He noticed your reactions and decided at that moment you were a gentleman. But be aware that he is watching us at this very moment. You spoke of intentions. Just what are they?"

I stared into Joline's eyes and saw there a sincerity in her questioning. I also saw what I thought was a flicker of feeling toward me. It stirred my emotions.

I couldn't hold it in any longer.

"Joline, I love you."

Suddenly, it was out. I felt embarrassed. I'd never said that to anyone. Joline might laugh. It would destroy me, completely.

But she didn't laugh or say anything for a while. We just sat there, my food getting cold, flies darting around over the lumps of grease-caked beef. I didn't care. All I wanted was for Joline to love me.

She took my hand.

"Nolo, I love you too. What can we do about it?"

The hard Nebraska sun was almost overhead. It cast a shadow from my plate that made a round spot of darkness over my leg. Looking toward the horses grazing in the distance, I listened to Big Mama's jaws crunching noisily as she made her way through a green patch of prairie grass.

I felt like leaping in the air, grabbing Big Mama by the mane, springing astride her and riding circles around Joline.

Instead, I returned the pressure of Joline's hand and matched her gaze.

"Will your brother understand? Don't want to end up buried because of some misunderstanding."

"He'll understand. He knew that some day the right man would come along. We've even talked about it. It's nothing new for him."

I felt better. At least I could now write about the gang without waiting for a bullet in the head from a jealous brother.

Writing about the gang. My mind was so filled with thoughts of Joline that I had forgotten why I was here. Somehow I had to get the story about Joel Collins and Sam Bass and their cattle drive from Texas that landed them here in Robber's Roost. I could ask Joline about it, but first, I needed answers to some questions in the back of my mind.

"And who is the right man for you, Joline?"

She reached across my lap and took the empty plate. She stood up, held the dish in one hand, straightened her dress with the other and turned to walk away. She took a step and looked back over her shoulder.

"You should know the answer. There's been no other man in my life, not since I met you on the train."

I watched as she disappeared behind the cook's shack.

Where was Buck Redwing? I last saw him out on the prairie early in the morning before the gang took me.

I looked at Big Mama. She still pulled up bunches of grass and ground it between her jaws. Beyond her was a pinto. It looked like Buck's, but that couldn't be. Buck was somewhere out on the prairie trying to find me.

There was a breeze at the back of my neck. Turning my head, I found myself staring at the knees of a large man. They belonged to Buck. My jaw dropped.

"You're surprised to see me?"

That was an understatement.

"Buck. Buck Redwing. What are you doing here?"

"I'm a member of the Bass gang. Have been since Bass and Collins drove the cattle up here from Texas. Came with them from down Denton way. Bass hired me to bring you out here."

"It'll take a moment to get used to this. You're part of the gang? Makes some sense. You did take me right to them."

Other things crossed my mind. The editor of the paper, Jim Copley. Maybe he was their contact in Big Springs. And the sheriff! He could even be tied in with the gang. It wouldn't be the first time lawmen looked the other way when strange things happened outside their territory. No wonder the sheriff laughed at me when I tried to tell him about Joel Collins. He probably knew everything the gang was doing and where they had made camp.

Buck sat down and stared off in the distance toward the grazing horses.

"You need to get Big Mama back to town. No sense paying for her when you can saddle up a spare pony. We'll leave for town in a day or two."

With those words, Buck stood up, stretched and was gone.

At last I was alone. There was much to think about.

Joel Collins called. He motioned for me to join him.

He stood next to his horse, the reins loosely held in his left hand, his mount pulling just a bit as if it was ready to go. Joel's battered broad-brimmed hat sat jauntily on his head. His blazing blue eyes had a matter-of-fact look.

"Blunt, let's get some things straight. I've given Buck Redwing the job of looking out for you. You do what he says. If I hear you giving him trouble, there'll be parts of you missing in the morning. You write what you want, but show it to me before you send it. Just for your information, I'm the head of this here gang. Sam Bass is my friend, but he ain't got no brains for runnin' this outfit. And somethin' else. Stay away from my sister. Saw you makin' eyes at her and holdin' her hand."

I wanted to say something, but couldn't. Collins had a mean look. He meant what he said. Best not to mention anything about me and Joline and my intentions.

"The Indian said we'd go into town. I'll have time to write my first story by then. You'll want to see it when you get back."

"I'll be back this afternoon."

That's all he said and with a quick movement, he was in his saddle and riding toward the tunnel.

I stood for a moment just watching the dust cloud created by his horse. Now was the time to figure out what to write and soon.

I found my saddlebags and flipped open the strap, took out a pad and pencil and looked for a place to work.

The flat rock where I'd eaten lunch appealed to me. I sat for a moment gathering my thoughts and then heard Joline's voice calling from one of the wagons. Squinting against the sun, I saw her shape silhouetted against the dingy canvas cover of the nearest wagon. She motioned to me.

I climbed over the tailgate and found Joline sitting in a rocking chair, her gaze fixed on me.

"You think you can make it, Nolo? Thought you might need some help getting over that tailgate."

I smoothed my trousers and buttoned my shirt.

"You wanted to tell me something?"

Looking around inside, I could see there was a lot of room. I'd never been inside a prairie schooner, but had always wanted to. Our magazine had printed stories about the Conestogas and their use in crossing the great plains of Kansas and Nebraska.

In one corner was a chest, obviously handcrafted by a skilled workman. A line of finely carved rosebuds outlined the rectangular shape.

There was almost enough room for me to stand, but I had to bend my head a little. I found a three-legged stool and sat.

"Joel's gone," Joline said.

"I have to write my first story before he returns. Maybe you can help."

With a toss of her head she reached her hand to me and pulled me toward her. Her warm breath blew against my temples as she whispered something to me.

"Later tonight."

That's all she said. With that she rose from the rocking chair, crossed over to the tailgate and jumped to the ground.

Pulling a small table toward me, I found my note pad and began writing the saga of Nolo Blunt, greenhorn, in search of a gang in the west.

Its title: **"Somewhere in the West."** The first paragraph was an account of the attempted train robbery. Action, I needed action, and the perfect place to begin was on the train with shots being fired over my head. That'd grab the readers. My editor back in New York would be pleased. Tom always told me to cut to the chase to catch the attention of the reader.

I had just finished writing about my capture and the ride to camp when I heard someone outside yelling.

I stuck my head out the rear flap and found myself staring into a one-eyed metal monster that loomed in my face. Collins was on the other end.

"What are you doin' in my sister's wagon? Get down from there."

I slid over the tailgate and dropped to the ground. My hands were in the air and my fingers still gripped my pencil, the writing pad in my other hand.

"I was just doing some writing. Joline was here, but she left."

Collins uncocked his weapon and put it back in his holster.

"Don't know why I'm so suspicious of you. You're too much of a greenhorn to try anything funny. Hand me your story."

I let him take my note pad. He sat down on a water barrel and began to read.

My heart pounded.

# Chapter 7

Collins looked up finally and a slight smile crossed his sun-wrinkled face. I knew immediately he liked my story.

"Hey, greenhorn. You're some writer. I was right to bring you here. Now let's get some things straight."

Collins shifted his weight on the barrel, pulled one knee under his chin and looked me in the eyes.

"You understand this is a most dangerous game. If you got to know too much about this gang, you could be hanged along with the rest of us. Best you don't know what we're doin' until after we done it. I've decided to send you into town. Take Joline with you. Buck will ride shotgun on you."

I just stood there thinking about what he'd said. The gang must be planning a robbery or Collins wouldn't have wanted to get rid of me so fast.

I watched as he slid off the barrel. He handed me the pad and walked off toward the mess shack.

Editing is always necessary. I read the first part of my story again.

SOMEWHERE IN THE WEST
ABOARD AN IRON HORSE
By Nolo Blunt

> A violent desperado wearing cowboy gear and a faded blue bandanna over his face mounted his high-stepping roan horse and fired several rounds from his six-shooter at this reporter in a recent attempted robbery of a train nearing the station at Big Springs in the newly admitted state of Nebraska.
>
> Lawlessness and senseless wild behavior mark this part of our United States as an untamed, uncivilized region. Only the stout of heart need travel here. Danger lurks behind every bush and near every watering hole. Life is cheap in the west.

As I finished reading the last line something bumped against my shoulder. It was Big Mama. She had worked her way over. She gazed at me.

I stroked her muzzle with my free hand. She jerked her head back. She was ready to go.

I heard a yell, turned my head and saw Buck Redwing waving. I grabbed Big Mama's halter and walked toward Buck.

"You ready? We will go to town now. Miss Joline will come with us. Here's your loaded pistol. There may be trouble."

The trail to Big Springs seemed different. How strange this country looked. All flat land covered with yellow-green grass. Wedges of brown clay-like soil made a pattern of bald spots between clumps of green. A prairie dog village was off to my right and the tiny animals were standing atop their mounds. When we got too close, one would thump his tail and his friends would seek the safety of their holes. It was a warning system that worked. No coyote, bobcat or wolf could sneak up on those wide-awake creatures.

I guess I'd never get used to carrying a gun on my hip. There was too much of a New York City boy in me.

Buck and Joline were getting away from me. They had chosen to ride ahead. It was what Buck wanted. He probably thought that if he kept Joline with him, I'd always follow and not get lost. He was right.

It was time to catch up. I prodded Big Mama and she responded.

There were some rises in the ground and also places where a herd of buffalo had wallowed. These were modest depressions in an otherwise level land.

I could barely make out the figures of Buck and Joline ahead. Then I noticed something else. The weather was changing. A circular dark cloud trailed us, like a funnel. The tip touched the earth. Now I could see it pick up the prairie grass and strew it around. I'd heard about such clouds.

Buck and Joline stopped. They looked at the cloud too. I booted my horse in the flanks and she picked up speed. Soon I caught up.

"What do you make of it Buck? Is there any danger?"

Before I could say anything more, Buck dismounted and motioned for us to do the same. We slid off our horses. Buck grabbed the reins and pulled the animals toward the largest hole he could find. Joline and I followed.

"What's happening, Nolo?"

Joline's voice shook.

"It's a twister, Joline. Never seen one, but I know about them. It can be dangerous if it touches down where we're standing. The odds aren't great. Let's get on with Buck and drop down into one of those wallows. We'll be safe there."

We found a deep hollow and scrunched down. Buck sent the horses galloping off in the opposite direction from the approaching cloud. I could make out Big Mama with her lengthy stride, her nostrils flaring, her mane streaking backward in flight. She was no stranger to twisters.

Looking over the edge of our wallow I saw the cloud racing toward us and gaining strength as it scooped up brush and grass as if to feed a monstrous unseen mouth.

I backed down to the bottom and joined Joline. We stretched out on the ground. I covered her with my body. If the funnel struck, we might be killed.

I whispered in her ear.

"Stay calm, Joline. It'll pass over. We're safe in here."

Her body twisted against me as she fought to find all the protection she could.

Now the fury of the storm grew. An ear-shattering sound reached my ears as the descending cloud drew nearer. I buried my head in the back of Joline's neck and hugged her tightly.

Dust began to pull up in waves around me. The cloud must be near. Would it pass over or would we just be travelers caught on the prairie by a storm, no obituary to be written, no mark left on earth of the place where we had died?

The crashing sound of the vortex chilled my insides as I heard what must be the cloud overhead. A sucking sensation surrounded us. I could feel myself being pulled upward. Only the weight of our bodies, clinging to each other, prevented us from being drawn into the circling cloud above.

Joline whimpered.

"We'll be all right, Joline. The worst is over. We're safe. The cloud is moving on."

The ear-blasting sound continued, but the twister had done its worst.

I chanced a look toward the sky and could make out the funnel moving away. Growing braver, I left Joline's side and crawled to the top of the wallow. Big Mama's shape loomed ahead. It looked like the cloud would miss her.

Joline moaned.

"Are we safe, Nolo?"

"We're safe, but we should stay here a few moments longer, just in case."

Lying down next to Joline, I put my arms around her as before. Her face was next to mine and my lips sought hers in our first embrace.

Buck's voice echoed above us.

"You two lovebirds can get up now. The tornado's gone. I'll go get the horses. You get ready to ride. We want to leave here as soon as we can. That cloud could come back."

Joline stood next to me. She dusted off her clothes. Her hands moved swiftly over her denim skirt as she brushed away twigs and pieces of grass.

I looked into her eyes. She still was frightened. I put my arms around her and pulled her body next to mine. She melted against me and then her face tilted upward. I kissed her again, a hard kiss that told her I was her man, her warrior, her protector, her rescuer. She returned the feeling of my kiss. I knew then that we would be together forever.

The snort of a horse surprised me. I broke off our kiss and turned my head. Big Mama shoved her nose up against my neck. Buck hovered nearby and looked unhappy.

"You found them, Buck. It would've been a long walk to Big Springs."

He just stood there, the reins of all three horses trailing behind his massive fist.

"The storm moved on. We'll move on too."

Buck handed Joline her reins, stooped next to the stirrup and meshed his fingers together. Joline placed her foot in his hands and pushed herself into position on her sidesaddle.

Buck turned toward me.

"You're next. Big Mama is ready. What do you have with this horse?"

I didn't think I had anything special with horses in general. But Buck was right. There was a magical bond between me and Big Mama. It was as if fate had meant for us to share this ride. There was something about these western horses. They had spirit and they had big hearts too.

Buck helped me to mount.

Settling myself on Big Mama, I had a better view of the prairie. In the distance was the twisting cloud. It moved slowly toward the eastern horizon. Big Springs would be spared.

The town was much the same as when I had left. Nothing changed. The same mangy grey dust-streaked dog lay in the same place, one eye drooping and the other watching us as we walked our horses toward the stable.

Dewey stood out front, his blue cambric shirt stained in exactly the same places. His hair was still uncombed and pieces of straw still clung to his matted curls.

For some reason, Dewey looked agitated.

"It's about time you got that horse into town. Been worryin' about you. Heard there was a tornado out there. I could see you and my horse bein' blown sky high. Could have lost a lot of money on you. Horses ain't cheap."

I pulled on Big Mama's halter and whisked her past Dewey, turned and handed him the reins.

"You treat her right. Rub her down good and give her some oats for dinner. She's a damn good horse and I want to buy her."

I'd been thinking about Big Mama for a long time. I didn't see any way I was to stay out here in the west without a good horse. I'd just put her purchase down in my expense account under *"transportation charges."*

Dewey stooped, grabbed the reins and led Mama into the stable. I knew he would take good care of her especially if he thought I would buy her.

Joline and Buck had already tied their mounts to the railing along the entryway to the barn. Joline looked fatigued. Our brush with the twister had affected her more than I thought.

She took my hand and we walked off toward the Elkhorn.

"You tired?"

Joline turned toward me.

"Nolo, I can't remember when I've been more tired. Dodging that storm cloud sapped my strength."

I agreed. It hadn't been easy for me either. My back still itched from all the twigs and pebble-sized rocks I'd collected while lying in the wallow. A good night on a hotel mattress would be just right for me too.

I put my arm around her waist. There was something about her that brought out the best in me.

We passed the Clarion office. I stopped in the middle of the street.

"You go on to the hotel. I want to see that newspaper fellow. Get some rest. I'll meet you later."

Joline nodded and kept walking toward the hotel. She sure had a trim figure. Was I ever lucky.

Entering the office, I noticed something different about the place. Jim Copley wasn't there. I stood at the counter for a moment. A young woman approached.

"May I help you?"

Her black hair was piled up on top of her head and she wore a lacy red ribbon in it. Her eyes looked directly at me. A pair of rosy lips formed into a smile.

"Yes, ma'am. I was in here a few days ago and spoke with Jim. He gave me some information about Joel Collins. I'm a writer from New York and I'm doing an article about Bass and Collins. Do you have any information I could use?"

She adjusted the ribbon in her hair and looked past me to the door. I heard a noise behind me. Someone else must have entered.

"Mornin' Sheriff Tatum. This here dude's been askin' about the Bass gang. Maybe you have news."

"Nope, ain't heard nothin'. So where you been, Sonny? Ain't seen you around town here. Looks like you been really ridin' the range in that grimy outfit."

This was a tense moment for me. How much should I tell these two? I could end up getting hanged or shot if I said too much.

"I've been out on the prairie. Twister came following me and if it hadn't been for a buffalo wallow, I'd have been done for. Just got into town. Had to file my first story about the train ride here to Big Springs. Wanted to get started writing about the Bass gang."

I was starting to talk like these people. It was easy. Tatum looked me over closely.

"Like I said, ain't heard nothin'. Been long enough. They must be plannin' somethin' though. Heard they was seen ridin' west of here. Most likely there's somethin' in the wind."

With those words he turned toward the young lady.

"Miss Nancy, where's old Jim? Ain't seen him for a few days. Drunk again?"

"No, sheriff. He packed his bags and took the mornin' train out of here. Said he'd head toward Ogallala. I think he's on his way home. He used to live somewhere out that way. I'll miss him. He was a good typesetter even though his gimpy leg sometimes got in the way of his workin' longer hours."

That was a piece of information I could use. Jim could be tied in with the gang in some way. He was the one who directed me to Buck Redwing who was a member of the gang.

"Well ma'am, sheriff. Must be on my way. Got to check in at the Elkhorn. It's been a tough day after dodging that twister. You hear anything about the gang, get word to me."

I left the two standing at the counter. I'm sure the sheriff was watching me as I crossed the street. I could feel his eyes burning into my back. I'd have to be careful around him.

# Chapter 8

Morning came. A bright ball of sunshine rose in the east with its rays unmolested by the shape of a tree or bush. The light suddenly awakened me as something haunted me from an uncompleted dream. The gang. That was it. Had they robbed a train or stagecoach? Had I missed the big event?

I hurried into my trousers and boots, slipped on a shirt and scrambled downstairs. The dining room was open. Through the doorway I could make out Joline sitting primly at a table, her hair tousled up in a most casual way. I hurried to sit next to her.

"Good morning. Sleep well?"

She smiled warmly.

"Good morning, Nolo. Yes, I slept well. Never slept better. You hear the news?"

I could hardly wait to find out what she would tell me. The gang had struck. I just knew it.

"No, I haven't heard."

"The gang held up the eastbound train last night. They got over $40,000 in newly minted gold, Wells Fargo coins headed for New York. They held up the passengers too."

"Anyone hurt?"

"I haven't heard. Sheriff was by a while ago and asked for you. Oh, Nolo. If anything's happened to Joel, I'll go to pieces. He means so much to me. Now that I've found him, I may lose him."

I put my arm around her.

"It'll be all right, Joline. I'll get over to the sheriff's office and find out as much as I can."


Sheriff Tatum was in front of the jail. He was saddling his horse.

"Heard about the train robbery last night."

"Well, if it isn't our late rising reporter. You missed all the fun. The Bass gang's been busy."

I got out my notebook and began writing.

"Can you tell me what happened?"

The sheriff tilted back his sweat-stained hat and looked at me.

"You mean you don't know what happened?"

I had to be careful. The sheriff's question implied that I knew what the gang was going to do before they did it.

"No, sheriff. At the Elkhorn last night. Never slept better. That twister yesterday really wore me out. You tell me what happened. I've a story to write."

He pondered for a moment.

"Get your horse. You can ride out with me."

I jammed my notebook into my shirt pocket, slid the pencil into my pants and hurried over to the stable. Dewey stood out front as if he knew I'd be coming.

"Looks like you're in a hurry there, Mr. Blunt. Goin' somewheres?"

"Got a story to write, Dewey. Get Big Mama ready to ride. Sheriff's waiting."

"Kinda thought you'd be ridin' out a here this mornin'. Your horse is already saddled. Told her you'd be takin' her out. She's rarin' to go. Wait here. I'll fetch her."

Got to buy that horse. She's just right for me and it's impossible for me to get my story without transportation. I took out my wallet and counted the bills. Dewey would settle for a hundred bucks, but I held a hundred twenty in my hand just in case.

I looked down the street. The sheriff already had mounted his horse and was staring back at me.

Before I could turn around, I felt a sloppy wet nudge on my shoulder and knew it was Big Mama.

Dewey held the horse while I mounted. It felt good to be in the saddle again.

"Dewey, make out a bill of sale for Big Mama. I want to buy this horse. How much?"

"Well, seein' as you have some bills in your hand, I'll take what you offer as long as it's over a hundred."

"Sold. We'll shake on it and you have that bill of sale ready for me when I get back. I may be riding fast soon."

Booting Big Mama, she responded with a jump and then smoothed out. Soon we were up with the sheriff.

His glove-covered hands were holding the reins lightly, his knees pressed against his horse's ribs. He sat erect in his saddle. I could tell he meant business.

"Best we get started Mr. Blunt. I've got witnesses to question. Asked them all to meet me down by the station. I'd appreciate it if you'd keep yourself out of my way when we get there."

I nodded and both our horses broke forward.

The sun now blazed. After the terrible experience yesterday, a few days of sunshine would make things right again. There wasn't a cloud in the sky.

I followed Tatum who set a good pace. No conversation, just steady riding.

Up ahead was a cluster of people. They stood in a group next to the dun colored timbers of the train depot. "Big Springs" was spelled out in large letters on a sign atop the building. A water tower loomed nearby, the refill spout still dripping, probably used last to fill up the engine of the train that was robbed.

The sheriff was off his horse and already had selected two women to interview. I hurried Big Mama and soon was able to dismount, tie off the reins on the railing and get out my notebook.

Don't know what it is about reporters. We look for the unusual whenever we can. I spotted something right away, a one-armed man standing off to one side.

I approached him, but he backed off.

"Excuse me, sir. My name's Nolo Blunt and I'm a reporter from New York. I'm writing an article about this robbery. Will you give me your impression of what happened last night?"

"Can't tell you much. Train stopped. We thought maybe there was trouble on the tracks. We heard some noise and a couple of cowboys sportin' guns shoved their way into our car and started robbin' the folks. This black-haired thug kinda stooped over and took twenty dollars from my pocket. Then he noticed my arm and handed back my money. Told me he didn't want it and told me to sit down and be still. I did just that. Didn't want to get shot."

The man had said the robber was black–haired. It could have been Sam Bass.

"Did he say anything else?"

"Nope. Just kept on walkin' down the car. Noticed him and his partner were gettin' a bit nervous and them guns were shakin' a might when they reached the door. I just scrunched down in my seat and did a little praying."

I looked at the sheriff. He was talking with a man who had been wounded, a makeshift bandage covered his upper left arm. I walked over and stood where I could overhear the conversation.

"And you say you recognized one of the bandits."

"Yes. Joel Collins. That's who he was. I rode with him and Sam Bass over the cow trail to Deadwood. It's been a year since I seen 'em, but I'd recognize those two anywhere. Damn. Sure hate to be shot. Guess I'm lucky, just a scratch. Scares the bejesus out of a body to come that close. You mind if I find my way back to the hotel?"

The sheriff inspected the man's bandage, looked him over and wrote something in his book.

"Got your story Mr. Brown. Stay around town for a few days. I may need your testimony."

I had to find out what the lawman had learned about the gang. Joline would want to know about her brother.

"Sheriff. Any idea where the gang was headed after the holdup?"

The lawman looked up from his notes.

"You mean you don't know? Only reason I brought you with me was to have you lead me to the hideout. Heard you was with the gang, you and that filly you been hangin' around with."

He knew all about us. How was I going to convince him otherwise?

"Sheriff, I'm a reporter. Reporters get into all kinds of situations and I'll admit I was kidnapped by the gang and held captive. All they wanted was for me to write about them."

Tatum looked at me. I kept talking.

"Wrote a story, then I was sent to town with Miss Joline and Buck Redwing. We were almost killed by that tornado. You know the rest. I'm not a member of any gang. I'm just a reporter trying to do my job."

Tatum straightened to his full height.

"What you say may be true, but I still need to know where that hideout is. You got to show me."

My mind raced ahead. What would happen if I showed the sheriff where the gang had holed up? Would they still be there?

"I'll show you where they took me, but do you really think they're back in the hideout? If I had done the train robbing, I'd hightail it for the Kansas border or somewhere else. Too many people know where the hideout is."

The sheriff rubbed his face and spit out a gob of tobacco, a portion of which dribbled down his chin and ended up on the collar of his shirt.

"Well, maybe you're right. Guess it'd be better to track 'em from the scene of the robbery. I may want you later. Stay in town."

With those words, he walked over to another group of people and started taking notes.

I had to find out what had happened to Joel and Sam. The only person I knew who could track them was Buck Redwing. I decided to get back to the hotel, find Joline and Buck and set out on my own hunt for the gang. The sheriff be damned if he wanted me to stay around town.

Tying my horse to the railing outside the Elkhorn, I hurried inside and ran up the stairs to Joline's room. I tapped at her door and could hear someone stirring inside. The door opened and Joline fell into my arms looking as if she'd seen a ghost.

"Nolo, you're here. I've just seen Joel. Told me to stick with you and the Indian. Oh, Nolo. I'm so worried. Something dreadful is going to happen to Joel. I know it."

With my arm around her shoulder, I walked her to the bed and gently sat her down.

"Did he say where he was headed?"

"No, just that the gang was going south and then would split up. I just know the sheriff or someone else will catch up and then..."

"Now, Joline, only thing we can do is follow them. Get your things. I'll find Buck and we'll track your brother. The Indian'll know where to start."

I ran down the stairs to the door and there he was. Once again he stood out front like a cigar store statue, his feathered hat still covered with the prairie dust of the tornado.

"You looking for me? I saw you come into town on your horse. Can we go now? Got your bill of sale from Dewey. Knew you wanted to buy her. Stopped by the stable and Dewey told me."

I had no idea how Buck knew we were going anywhere or why he went to the stable, but I was glad he did. Saved me some time. He had a sense about him, a sense that told him just what I was about to do or say. Perhaps it was natural for him to think ahead. Whatever it was, I was grateful that Buck had it. It saved a lot of time if nothing else.

"We're going after Joel and the gang. Joline's coming. Are you ready?"

Buck nodded.

Joline came out of the hotel. She had crammed her possessions into two saddlebags carried over one arm. An oilskin-covered roll of blankets draped her right shoulder. She looked like she was prepared for any emergency.

We rode out of town toward the place where the train had been stopped the night before. Buck led the way and when we reached the scene, he dismounted and scouted around the area. Suddenly, he bent over, inspected marks on the ground and motioned for Joline and me to follow him. I knew he had found something because he was smiling just slightly. And then we were off at a more rapid pace.

Joline rode next to me.

"I think he's on Joel's trail. I don't know how he does it," I said.

She turned toward me.

"If anything happens to Joel, I'll just die."

"Joline, you know Joel is strong. If he wanted to do something, nothing you could say would stop him. He picked his way of life. All we can do is follow him and find him before the sheriff does."

The Indian moved rapidly. I think he wanted to find the gang as much as I did. If anyone could find the fugitives, Buck could.

Far up ahead there was a dust cloud. Buck had seen it too.

I turned to Joline.

"He's spotted something."

"You think it's my brother?"

"May be. Lots of dust up ahead like there are many riders."

The sun beat down on me as it can do on the Nebraska prairie. Our horses began to tire and I knew we'd have to slow down. But it was tantalizing. If the dust cloud meant we were near to Joel and the gang, we could join them soon.

We got closer. Then Buck stopped and turned his horse to the left. He motioned for us to follow him. Joline and I made the same maneuver, but when we reached the peak of a low ridge where he had ridden, the Indian was gone. Vanished! I was dumbfounded again. How could a man on a horse disappear so easily? There must be something magical about Indians, especially this one.

Joline caught up. She looked frightened.

"Where's Buck?"

"He's gone somewhere."

"Nolo, I'm scared. Suppose those riders aren't the gang."

I'd thought about that too. If it were the sheriff's posse, we might be in trouble. I was supposed to be back in Big Springs minding my own business.

"We'll stay here. Let's find some water for the horses. Buck'll get back to us when it's safe."

I looked and could see the dust cloud getting larger. The horsemen were heading straight for us.

# Chapter 9

The sheriff had chosen a motley crew of town thugs as his posse. I had seen a few. They were mostly the ones who hung around the Elkhorn bar. A posse member didn't make much money. I wondered why the sheriff wanted to ride the range with such a crowd of misfits in search of desperadoes.

"So it's you, Blunt. And your lady friend is with you. Where's the Indian? He's the one I want to see."

This would take some fancy talking, but I had to protect Buck and Joline.

"Buck was with us sheriff, but we lost him. He just disappeared. Joline and I are headed for Kansas and are searching for the Bass gang just like you. I've got my story to write."

I hoped a forthright approach would keep the lawman from arresting me for disobeying his order about staying in town.

The sheriff looked down as he leaned forward in his saddle.

"You and your lady friend are in great danger out here. We'll all water our horses and then you'll join us. Maybe you can help us find those robbers."

He drew his right leg over the back of his horse with great ease, put all his weight on his left foot and swung down to the ground.

"I ain't forgettin' that I told you to stay in town. Only way you can keep from gettin' arrested is to help me find Bass and Collins."

He certainly had me in a bind. I nodded in agreement. What else could I do? Tatum had all the aces. Like my poker-playing dad always told me, when you can't beat the other guy, cut your bets and wait for the next hand.

Joline looked frightened. She was probably thinking about her brother.

"Joline. We have to go along."

"Yes, Nolo, but I'm scared. If they find Joel..."

"Don't worry. He has a head start."

"I know. But the sheriff is persistent."

Joline was right. Tatum had set out to find the gang and wouldn't stop until he did. There must be reward money involved. Why else would he be in such a hurry?"

The horses had been watered. I found Big Mama grazing on bits of grass near Joline's mare. Grabbing the reins of both horses, I led them to where Joline stood.

"I'll help you up."

She put her foot in the stirrup and was about to throw her right leg over the mare when her horse jumped. I held tight to the reins, but it was more than I could do to keep the animal from bolting. Something must have spooked the horse. Joline was in danger. I could see she was barely hanging on. At any moment she might slip and tumble to the ground.

Big Mama's head was up now. I was on her in a flash and prodding her into a full gallop.

Joline fought to keep herself in the saddle. Then the horse slowed and she was able to push herself into an upright position and gain control.

Big Mama caught up and pulled alongside. Joline was trying to tell me something. I leaned over as far as I could without falling off. I could just make out her words.

"Buck Redwing taught me that trick while we were at the hideout. He's up ahead. I saw him. Sheriff's men are still standing and watching us."

What a woman! We were a good distance from the posse. No one had tried to follow us. Evidently they thought I would stop Joline's horse and bring her back. Well, they figured wrong. Now that we were free again, we'd be more careful about riders we saw in the distance.

Far up ahead was Buck. His pinto loped along so we could catch up. He must have known what Joline would do and waited. He turned in his saddle and looked at me.

"We must hurry. The sheriff will figure soon you have escaped. Come on. Follow me."

I wasn't thinking about following anyone but Buck.

With the sheriff well behind us we were on our way.

We made good time. Buck knew right where the trail headed. He kept an eye to the ground, but from time to time he'd gaze over the horizon, one hand placed on his forehead to shade his eyes from the sun.

Far behind I could see that familiar dust cloud, the posse in pursuit. I could envision the look on the sheriff's face, his deepset eyes squinting to make out our shapes on the prairie, his mouth set in determination.

Or maybe he had let us go. We would lead him to Joel and the rest of the gang.

I rode harder and caught up with Buck.

"You see the sheriff coming?"

"Yes, I saw him. The Big Springs Sheriff Tatum is like a coyote. He hangs on with tight teeth," Buck said.

"What can we do?"

"Keep riding. We'll reach the Kansas border in a few days. The sheriff can't cross."

I relaxed and let Big Mama drop back. Joline was even with me and I looked at her. In my mind she was a woman of the west, tall in the saddle, her hair caught by the wind. She was a jewel. Fate brought us together!

"Buck says we'll lose the sheriff at the border."

Joline looked back.

"He's still coming. You think the sheriff figures we'll find Joel?"

"Maybe. Buck seems to know where the gang is headed."

"Oh, Nolo. This whole thing has me so worried. If we find my brother, so does the sheriff. What'll we do?"

"Just keep riding. Something will happen. I have faith in Buck Redwing."

As night approached, I began to wonder how Buck could follow the track in the dark.

Again I caught up with the Indian.

"Are we almost there?"

He held his horse in stride, shifted in his saddle, but still kept his eyes on the horizon.

"Not far. Tatum is still coming. We must lose him."

I agreed.

"You have any plans?"

"Keep riding. Soon it will be dark. Frenchman Creek is ahead. I know a way. You and Miss Joline follow me closely."

I didn't have to be told twice to keep my eyes on Buck. He was our only hope for staying out of trouble on the prairie. My article depended on getting first-hand statements from the robbers. The sooner I got them, the better.

We reached the creek and Buck plunged his horse into the water. Joline and I followed. Big Mama took to the water and relished the cooling effect after a long day's ride. I felt spray on my face as we pushed ahead, trying to keep our guide in sight.

Riding along in the creek would leave no trail. At least we'd be safe until dawn.

Midnight came and still we sloshed along in the shallow creek. Buck went slower. Then he veered and rode up the bank. We followed.

He stopped, listened and smelled the wind.

All I heard was rustling of cottonwood trees that grew next to the water. A gentle breeze blew from the north.

Buck dismounted. I was soon off my horse and helping Joline down.

"We'll camp here. Get some sleep. I'll guard first, then you, Blunt. If trouble comes, wake me quick."

Buck led our horses toward the creek so they could be watered.

Joline stood by my side. Her hand slipped into mine.

"Hold me close."

My body responded. I held her tightly. She whispered in my ear.

"It's all right Nolo. I won't break in two if you hug me hard. I like your arms around me."

We stayed like that for a long time. Only when I heard Buck returning with the horses did I let go. Joline continued to hold my hand. I felt the gentle pressure of her fingers on mine.

"I'll spread out your blankets near mine Joline."

"That'll be fine. I want you near me in the night."

Nothing more was said. The Indian went off to the high ground. Joline and I slipped into our blankets, our hands joining for just a moment before sleep came.

I opened one eye. Buck's big hand was on my shoulder. He shook me, hard. I sputtered.

"What are you doing? Are you crazy?"

"It's time for you to watch. I need sleep."

I pulled back the blankets. It was cold. The freezing air whistled around my middle even though I was dressed. I shook out my new boots and fitted my feet into them.

My eyes gradually became accustomed to the grey early morning light.

I leaned over to kiss Joline on her forehead. She slept on.

Climbing to the top of a rise near our camp, I looked out over the prairie. I could see our horses. They still grazed, their picket line giving them enough room to move to new clumps of grass.

Then another sound. It was nothing like our horses. I tried to focus to see what made the noise. The prairie in front was moving in an undulating rhythm. Buffalo. Maybe a thousand shaggy heads bobbed up and down. They just kept coming. Water. That's what they were after. We were between them and the creek.

I raced to Joline, shook her awake.

"Get up. Buffalo are coming. I must warn Buck."

I charged toward where I'd seen Buck prepare his bed after midnight. He wasn't there. His blanket roll was neatly prepared and on the ground next to his saddle.

I turned when I heard his voice.

"We go. Heard them far off. They won't stampede yet, but we'd better go."

There was time to water the horses.

The buffalo posed no harm for us now, but it wouldn't take too much to set them off. Rain clouds settled in over the flat land.

Far off on the other side of the creek I could see a familiar dust cloud rising. It could mean only one thing, the sheriff and his posse were on the move. I pointed toward what I'd seen. Buck looked and so did Joline.

"Sheriff's coming. What now?"

Before the words were out of my mouth, Buck swung his horse around. Yelling and shooting his pistol, he charged the buffalo herd. They responded. Oh, did they respond! It didn't take much to get them started.

That was some sight. A massive herd of buffalo all crashing across the creek. Buck had turned them so they'd miss us. Everyone of the herd headed straight for Tatum and his posse. A little surprise for our pursuers.

Buck returned now and motioned for us to follow him. I felt Big Mama take in air, her massive lungs expanding until I thought she'd burst. Then came a snort of her nostrils. She was ready for the day.

Joline rode beside me, her mare snorting too and blowing out steam on the morning air.

"Sleep well?"

She raised her head, ran her hand through her hair and looked my way.

"I really needed sleep. And you?"

"Not much. Buck woke me for guard duty."
"Maybe today we'll find my brother."
"We should."
After that we rode on in silence, the Indian far up ahead.

The gang had been here. Buck found their campsite. Rocks around the fire were still warm. Home-rolled cigarette butts littered the ground. Empty sacks labeled *"Wells Fargo"* were scattered next to the fire and horse tracks were evident. Many had been here. Buck read the prints.

"The horses are carrying a heavy load. Two went this way. Two others went the opposite. Two headed toward Kansas. Others follow the creek."

I knew Buck could read horse signs better than anyone.

"Which way did Collins go?"

The Indian looked down and studied the turf.

"He and one other went toward Kansas, toward the rising sun. His horse has a bad shoe. We'll follow them."

Joline started to shake. She fell against me. Sobs welled up inside. Tears began to flow down her cheeks.

"Now, now Joline. We'll find him. Buck's a good tracker. It won't be long. We'll find your brother."

But it was going to be harder than I thought.

Several days later we reached the Kansas border and crossed over into much the same kind of country through which we'd been traveling. Beaver Creek was just ahead and as we prepared to ford the small stream, the trail we followed ended. I couldn't see a thing on the ground, but Buck kept plodding ahead, his eyes sifting every shape, every blade of grass, until he knew exactly which way to go.

I looked back the way we had come. No dust cloud, no riders. I thought about the sheriff trying to outrun a stampeding herd of wild-eyed buffalo.

# Chapter 10

Frenchman Creek and Beaver Creek were far behind us now as Buck Redwing followed the trail of Joel Collins and his companion. We were nearing Buffalo, Kansas, where I knew there would be a telegraph office. We followed the railroad tracks. Off to one side there were the bare-topped poles of the telegraph line. They were no more than young trees, cut down, stripped of their branches and replanted upright to hold the wire that would carry my message to New York.

My story of the robbery grew in length. It was time to send the editor another chapter. I read over what I'd written two nights ago.

> COLLINS-BASS GANG
> HOLD UP EASTBOUND TRAIN.
> ESCAPE WITH $40,000 IN GOLD COINS.
> WELLS-FARGO OFFERS REWARD.
> By Nolo Blunt
>
> The Collins-Bass gang struck again. This time it was the eastbound train stopped for water at Big Springs, Nebraska. Two bandanna-masked desperadoes drew down their weapons on the engineer and forced him and

the fireman from the locomotive cab. Once that was accomplished, the gang members used a ruse to break into the mail car. Thoroughness marked their activity as they searched the bags and boxes contained therein. Only by accident did one bandit, suspected to be Sam Bass himself, kick off the top of a box and to his surprise, newly minted gold dollar coins fell out. There were 40,000 of them and the robbers scooped them up and passed them to their confederates outside who stowed the loot aboard their steeds.

Meanwhile other members of the unholy group passed through the passenger cars and forced the travelers to cough up cash and jewelry to fill bags the looters held in their greedy hands.

It is reported that Sam Bass, having finished in the mail car, was identified by one of the passengers. Bass robbed a one-armed man not knowing at the time that his victim had only one upper limb. When he discovered the fact, Bass allegedly told the man, "Hell, boy. You need this money more than I do. Sit back down and stay calm." The one-armed man obliged and added a few prayers while staying calm.

I bundled together my material and stuffed it in my shirt.

Up ahead the Indian was searching for something on the ground.

"What's happening, Buck?"

"Collins stopped here. Maybe he didn't leave."

"What do you mean?"

"The trail shows that Collins crossed the railroad tracks here."

Buck pointed down. Joline looked over his shoulder.

"Do you think my brother's in this small town?"

"We'll find him Miss Joline. We're almost there."

There were so many horse tracks that Buck couldn't follow Joel's horse.

In the distance was the Buffalo train station. We rode toward the brown frame building next to the tracks. A sign on the wall identified it as a telegraph office. My story could be sent.

"I'll stop here."

Joline and Buck watched me.

"You two go on into town and get something to eat. Join you later."

I dismounted and tied Big Mama to the railing.

Inside, a man with a visor sat at the telegraph key tapping out a message. His shoulders pushed forward as he concentrated on what he was doing.

I stood at the counter for a few minutes, got out my story, read it over once again and looked up in time to see the telegraph clerk staring at me. He had stopped sending and was now waiting for confirmation from the other end. Our eyes met.

"You want something?"

"Sure do. Want you to send this to my editor back in New York City. Send it collect."

The operator looked at my story, wiped his brow and read the first part out loud.

"You're a reporter."

"Sure am. Name's Nolo Blunt as you can see on the copy."

"You're writin' about the Bass gang, heh? Collins is dead. Layin' over at the barber shop. Shot it out with the soldiers and sheriff yesterday. He and his sidekick, Heffridge."

"Are you sure?"

If it were true, Joline would be grief stricken.

The visor on the man's head slipped forward. His steely-grey eyes were framed by the piece of green celluloid.

He answered my question.

"I'm sure. Collins and his partner rode into town yesterday 'bout noon. He saw me and asked where he could buy some provisions. I told him it was hard to get food in this small town, but he kept after me. Finally, I pointed him in the direction of Jim Thompson's store. Thompson keeps a few food items for the folks around here. I took the two of them to the store and went inside with them. Thompson wasn't there, but the hired girl was. While Collins was buyin' goods, an envelope fell out of his pocket. Saw his name plain as day. Got myself outa there and slipped down to tell the sheriff. He alerted the soldiers and when Collins and his buddy left town, the army surrounded the two of 'em. There was some shootin' and I saw the two drop down off their horses, not movin' a bit after that. Sheriff told me Collins had said, 'Pard, if we have to die, we might as well die game.' Them's the last words Collins uttered. Soldiers let go with their carbines at close range. I saw the bodies riddled with holes. Both must of died instantly. Sheriff found ten thousand in new Eagles. He'll get a reward from the railroad."

Thanking the clerk, I left quickly. Big Mama was at the rail. I mounted and rode toward the only restaurant in town.

Joline's sorrel stood next to Redwing's pinto at the rail.

Telling Joline about her brother would be difficult, but it had to be done.

They were seated at an oilcloth covered table in a quiet corner of the cafe. An empty chair leaned against the wall and I grabbed it, hauled it over near Joline and sat down. I was tired, not only from all the riding of the last few days, but also from the emotional pressure of knowing that Joel was dead.

"Telegraph man had some news."

Joline looked up.

"Your brother and Heffridge came through here yesterday about noon."

Joline leaned forward. Her eyes were clear and she stared straight at me. She must have known what I was going to tell her."

"He's dead, isn't he, Nolo?"

"Yes, Joline. He's over in the back of the barber shop. The sheriff will ship the two bodies to the city of Ellis, here in Kansas, this afternoon. You want to see him, we better go now."

Barbers in western towns sometimes served as medical men. At least they knew some tricks on how to stop bleeding especially if they happened to nick one of their customers with a razor. The barber in this town also served as mortician, because he needed the money.

"He's in here, Joline."

We went to the back. Light from a high window inside allowed me to see the two men lying side by side. They were still clad in their dusty cowboy clothes, their hats lying on their chests, covering their folded hands.

Joline walked to the bodies and looked down.

She saw her brother and bent over to kiss his forehead. She stood up straight, looked down at him again for a moment, then walked outside.

I stayed for a few minutes to take notes and make a few sketches. I had no emotional ties to Collins. My story would be a first-hand account of a famous western robber and this kind of article was popular back east.

The other man was supposed to be Bill Heffridge. As I stared at the corpse, I suddenly realized who Heffridge really was, the limping printer from the Clarion in Big Springs. His name there was Copley, Jim Copley. So that's what happened. Copley must have quit his job to take a seat on the train that the gang planned to hold up. Maybe he was the inside man when it came time to rob the passengers. Seemed logical. He could watch the other passengers to see if any were carrying a lot of cash. When it came time for the robbery, Copley was on board to quell any would-be six-gun heroes. No matter what, he sure was dead now.

Joline waited outside and when she saw me walk through the doorway, she moved toward me and collapsed, sobbing my arms. I held her tightly.

"Joline, it's all over."

She continued to cry, but I could sense her struggle to regain her composure.

Gradually she calmed and pulled away, but held onto my hands.

"Nolo. He was my brother. They shot him so many times. Did they have to?"

Wrapping an arm around her waist, we started walking away from the barber shop. We reached the horses without saying a word and as I untied Big Mama, Joline stood at my shoulder.

"What are we going to do? Joel's dead. I feel so lost."

"Got my job, Joline. Sam Bass is probably still alive. I have an idea he'll be heading for Texas, probably Denton. Read an article in a newspaper about him and that's his home town. I'm going to find Buck and we'll search him out. I want the whole story of this robbery and especially the part about Bass. Come with us."

I hoped she'd agree. Leaving her now would bother me greatly. I loved Joline. She must feel the same way about me.

Joline unhitched her mare and led her horse over next to mine.

"I've got to follow Joel to Ellis and see him properly buried. My folks will want to know about him. They knew nothing of his life as a bandit. I'll go home to Texas and stay there with them for a while. When I finish, I'll come on to Denton."

It was a risk I had to take. She **would** follow me.

"Check general delivery at the post office in Denton. I'll send you a message by mail," Joline said.

I caught a glimpse of Buck riding toward me. He'd been busy rounding up food for our trip. His saddle bags were full.

It was time for me to say farewell. Pulling Joline to me, I kissed her. My heart pumped wildly, my knees nearly buckled and a wild feeling developed in my stomach. I pushed back.

"Joline, you must come on to Denton."

"Don't worry Nolo. I'll be there."

Big Mama nudged my shoulder. I dropped Joline's hand, squared my horse around and slipped into the saddle. Joline looked up, tears forming at the corners of her eyes.

"We're off, Joline. Make it soon."

With those words I laid the reins against Big Mama's neck. Buck and I were on our way to Texas. I looked back once. Joline still stood in the middle of the road, a handkerchief at her face.

After more than three weeks of hard riding, heading south, Buck and I reached the Texas border. The small town of Denison was only a few miles ahead. We'd stop there for the night. I didn't know what it was about Texas towns being named the same or almost the same as other Texas towns. There were two Dentons, a Denning, a Dennis, and the town we now approached, Denison.

I was hoping for a good hotel, even a lumpy straw mattress would feel good under my punished body. Sleeping on the flatlands might be all right for some prairie creatures, but an easterner like me needed some basic comforts once in a while.

It would also be good to see a newspaper again. I'd lost touch with the Bass gang and what had happened following the train robbery. Also, I wanted to know how Sheriff Tatum had made it through the herd of buffalo near Frenchman's Creek.

Buck tried to tell me something.

"Good hotel in Denison. I know. This is my country, Kiowa land."

"How long will we stay? I need a bath, a newspaper and a good meal."

"We'll stay overnight. We must get to Denton. We'll see if Bass is there. He owes me money."

"All right with me. You'll stay in the hotel too?"

"No. I'll stay with friends in town. I'll rise early. We'll ride out in the morning. It's a long way to Denton."

Simple shacks and tents appeared on either side of the trail. We passed through the outskirts of Denison. A few people stopped to look at us. We must have made quite a sight, a feather-decorated Indian on a pinto preceding a white man, maybe looking like a greenhorn, a Civil War pistol sticking out of an undersized holster.

Up ahead was the Longhorn Hotel. Buck pointed to it so I moved Big Mama between two other horses, dropped to the ground and tied my reins to the rail. We'd been traveling light. I didn't have much to carry inside.

A bright-eyed aging clerk with balding head, big ears and a string bow tie greeted me.

"Welcome stranger. Saw you tie up your animal. Fine piece of horseflesh. Not from around here. No mares like her in Denison. Strange brand. You goin' to stay long?"

I had to admire his reasoning.

"No. One night. You have a room with a soft mattress? Been on the range for a while."

"Got just what you need. Up one flight and down front. Davy Crockett room. Fifty cents a night. Pay in advance. Sign here."

This man wasted no motions or words.

"I need a newspaper. You got one for sale?"

I signed the card the man had placed in front of me.

"Sure do."

He reached down below the counter and brought up a dog-eared edition of the Denison Star. He handed it to me. It was a month old, but as I glanced at the headlines, I saw one small article about the train holdup in Big Springs. I'd read that later.

I thanked the clerk as he handed me a key. When I turned to gather up my saddlebags and blankets, I heard a scraping sound. A pair of dirty, scruffy boots met my gaze and inside them was a giant of a man, maybe six feet four inches. He wore a star.

"Greetings, stranger. Like to get to know all the new folks in town. Name's Sheriff Benson. Been the lawman here in this town nigh onto ten years. Keep this place in good order. Saw you and that Indian ride in. Where you headed?"

This was some welcome. First the hotel clerk and now this lawman giving me personal attention.

"Riding to Denton. I've been up Kansas way. I'm a reporter for a New York magazine. Been following the trail of Sam Bass. You have any information?"

When I mentioned the name of Bass, I saw him draw back a little.

"Sam Bass. Well, I done heard of him. But ain't seen him though. Didn't pass through here far as I know. Seems like he lives down Denton way. Newspaper says he robbed a train in Nebraska and I've been keepin' my eyes peeled. Might be some reward money offered for him and wouldn't mind collecting that."

I left the lawman standing at the counter. My back ached and I had to get my things in the room, then find a place for Big Mama to spend the night. She needed rest too. A bag of oats would give her the energy for our ride to Denton.

# Chapter 11

Next morning there was a rapping at my door. Getting out of bed, I staggered toward the sound and turned the handle. Buck stepped inside.

"You are ready. Morning is here and almost gone. The horses are ready. I paid for you at the stable. Big Mama looks for you. She saw me, but she whinnied for Nolo."

That was a lot of information for me to take in so suddenly. My brain was fogged. I was still wiping my eyes and trying to gain some sense of reality, but here was this dark-skinned man in my room telling me about my horse. I was still several hundred miles away at Joline's side in my dream.

"Give me a minute. Need coffee. You get it and I'll be right down."

Buck knew it was a lost cause to try hurrying me. During the trip from Nebraska he hadn't been successful in making me move faster about anything. Maybe it was my eastern ways, but rushing to dress or wash was not my style.

The pitcher standing next to the porcelain basin brimmed with cool water. I splashed some on my face and felt immediately better. Maybe there would be a place in Denton where I could at least get a decent bath with hot water and soap. Real scrubbing would have to wait. Now that Joline was no longer traveling with us I could let my personal hygiene slip.

The image of myself in the mirror told much about what I'd gone through. My hair was shaggy and needing cutting. My eyebrows and beard could stand a trim too. But it was the deep lines on my face that told me of the hard riding we'd done. I would even call my face "weatherbeaten" in cowboy terms. My eyes were clear though and seeing that made me feel better.

Sure enough, Buck waited for me in the hotel restaurant. He had a cup of coffee sitting at an empty place. Sliding into the wire-backed chair, I began breathing the delicious aroma of the coffee before me, tempting me to drink it. I put the cup to my lips, slurped and spat it right out.

"You don't like the coffee? I asked the cook to make it extra hot for you," Buck said.

My eyes met his. There was the least little smile curling up from the corners of his mouth.

"No, Buck. It's not too hot. I always like to burn my mouth when I drink coffee."

As I spoke, he smiled again.

"Forget the coffee. We'll ride long time today. You'll spend the night in my village. You'll meet other people of my tribe, Kiowas. I have a squaw there."

Well, this was something new. Buck Redwing, a man with a squaw. No wonder he was in such a hurry to get to Texas. Not only did Sam Bass owe him money for taking care of me and Joline, Buck had a woman waiting for him.

"You have children?"
"Boy and girl."
"They're young?"

"Boy's not yet a man. The girl is older."

My coffee had cooled now and I gulped it down quickly. I wanted to see Big Mama and get on the trail.

"Let's go, Buck."

That's all it took. Buck got up from his chair and headed for the door. I followed more leisurely. When finally I stepped outside, Buck was in his saddle and had his horse headed south. I began to realize how he could disappear so easily.

"Morning, Big Mama. You sleep well? Good oats last night?"

I rubbed her down along the flanks. Her hide felt smooth and warm. The stable boy had brushed her and removed all the trail mud from her coat. These western people really treated animals well, often better than they treated each other.

I glanced down the street toward the town jail. Sheriff Benson sat outside, his chair leaning back against the wall, his eyes staring straight ahead, his eyelids closing from time to time as if he were about to take a nap. Nothing like a wide-awake sheriff in a wild Texas town where gunfire could erupt any moment. Benson must know some secrets. Maybe some day I'd find out how he did it.

My horse moved around as I mounted, but that was her usual way. It kept me on my toes trying to figure out what she was going to do next.

Buck was now at the end of the mud-rutted street. He turned in his saddle, looked for me and when he saw me coming, started off at a slow pace.

"Did I tell you about my greeting from Sheriff Benson back at the hotel last night?"

Buck eyed me cautiously.

"No. You didn't tell me."

"Well, he looked me over very closely and told me Sam Bass hadn't passed through Denison. He knows about Bass."

Buck thought for a moment and then said, "Bass is too smart to come through Denison."

I had to agree. He must have entered Texas through Red Rock or some other border town where no one would know him.

"Hey, Buck. Do you think Bass is in Denton right now?"

"I know he is. He told me a long time ago. If he struck it rich, he'd go to Murphy's ranch."

"What about Murphy's ranch?"

However, Buck didn't say anything more about it and I figured it wasn't a good idea to press him for information. Things would just have to develop by themselves. He had given me something to think about. Who was this Murphy and why would Bass stop there?

The morning air was cool. It looked like rain. The ground was still dry and this was Texas. It could rain a gully washer or it could be as dry as the Sahara desert in summer.

Glancing back the way we'd come, I saw someone in the distance.

"Buck, take a look."

The Indian turned around, studied the horizon, then caught my glance and held it.

"Knew someone was following us."

There wasn't anyone in Denison who would follow us unless it was...

"Sheriff Benson. That sly codger. Leaning back in his chair so innocent like. He knew we're hunting Bass. His nose smelled reward money."

Buck looked back again.

"He's not smart. We fox him later."

I'm sure Buck had a plan. Didn't need to know it. He'd fill me in later.

We rode on in silence. Being followed nagged at my brain. This was no child's game. I was sure the guy had a six-gun in his holster and a rifle stuffed in a scabbard next to his knee.

The dusty miles went by. Big Mama reached her ground-eating stride. Her long legs stretched out over the uneven prairie ground in an almost hypnotic movement. Riding was monotonous at times and this was one of those times. I yawned.

The horseman still followed us, but we had gradually gained some distance on him. It had to be Benson. Maybe we'd find out by night time.

Buck motioned to the right. I'd already noticed a body of water in the direction he pointed.

"Lake Kiowa. We're near my home. We'll soon be there."

That was good news. My back ached from the pounding I'd taken in the saddle and I could use a hot meal. I wondered what Buck's squaw would be cooking. I'd heard stories about Indian meals. The best thing for me would be to keep my questions to myself.

Buck gazed toward the horizon and then looked back.

"Maybe two miles more."

I got a second wind and felt like I could make that far even if I had to walk. Big Mama could use the rest also. Fresh water and Texas grass would get her ready for the days ahead.

"Is your woman a good cook."

The Indian once again turned toward me.

"She's the best. She cooks squirrel stew. Mixes in corn and acorns. You like it?"

"I don't know. Never tried it. "

I smelled the camp odors before we arrived. There was the scent of meat braising over an open fire. And then there was the fainter odor of boiling corn.

As we drew closer I could see the skins of small animals pegged to the ground.

A scraggly one-eyed dog barked incessantly as we rode down the dusty trail through the middle of the encampment. The Indians were all out now. This must be a festival. Buck was home and he had brought a white man with him.

We were surrounded by dark-haired, dark-skinned men and women, their hands pawing at my trouser legs and pulling me from the saddle. I floated down to earth supported by strong sinewy arms that held me securely and kept me from falling.

Finally, I stood upright in the dirt, hands still holding me, brushing my clothes. Someone wiped my boots. A gourd dipper full of cool sparkling water was raised to my mouth. I drank deeply, then took it and poured some over my head. Someone behind me laughed. When I turned around, no one was even smiling.

Buck disappeared into a buffalo skin tepee. A woman held his hand and led him inside.

The design on his tent interested me. Along the border was a drawing of a running buffalo being chased by a lone hunter. Above this were the moon and the stars, a solitary sun higher up casting its rays down on earth.

I stood amidst a group of people who were alien to me and spoke a language I knew nothing about, but their eyes glowed and reflected an inner joy at seeing me. At least I hoped it so.

A stately man wearing a necklace with rattlesnake fangs and a pair of buffalo horns approached. Fear grabbed me.

"I am chief of Kiowa. You are my friend."

That's all he said.

"Yes, I am a friend."

I made the sign by raising my right hand, palm forward. It was something I'd learned from Buck. He did the same.

Then he turned and headed for a tepee that was much larger than the one Buck had entered. Hands gently pushed me toward the skin-covered opening.

Once inside, my eyes adjusted to the dark. The smoke from a lazy fire drifted toward the open flap at the top, its acrid smell blending with human odors of sweat, unwashed hair and decaying food.

A pair of hands came out of nowhere, the owner clamping them firmly onto my shoulders. I was seated on a patterned woven blanket facing the fire.

Other men were there, all sitting up straight, hands folded across their chests, eyes staring directly into mine. I crossed my arms and stared back, looking at each one as I moved my head to see all of them around me.

"Welcome to my tepee, noble Blunt one. Brother Redwing tells us of your bravery."

Buck must have been talking.

But bravery? When had I been brave?

"Redwing tell us how you rode to save the white-skinned woman. A man who rides like the wind may one day sit at the fire ring of the great Father in the sky."

I didn't know what he meant by that, but it must have been a good sign. The others around the fire grunted loudly.

I finally found my own voice.

"I'm happy to be here. Buck Redwing is my friend. We have ridden many trails together. I respect him for his knowledge of the wilderness."

Nothing more was said. The chief reached toward the fire and brought back a yard-long filthy looking tube with a rounded portion at one end. As I watched, he put it in his mouth, drew in deeply and held the smoke, then passed the pipe along to the next man. I was fascinated. The chief's face puffed out as he held his breath. Then he expelled a cloud of bluish smoke that drifted upward.

There must be some meaning in all this. Maybe it was the blending of man's exhalations with that of the smoke produced by nature.

I realized it would soon by my turn. I needed to follow the example of the chief.

The pipe arrived. Looking at it carefully, I fondled the squirrel tails that dangled loosely from one end, put it to my lips, drew in deeply and coughed loudly. It was too much. The tobacco was rancid. It made me choke.

My eyes watered and I began to feel light headed. I could sense all those warrior eyes watching. I couldn't show any weakness. Sitting there, I tried to regain my composure, tried to breathe in fresh air to replace the smoke that had entered my lungs.

The chief spoke.

"First time is hard."

"Strong smoke," was all I could say.

And then the ritual was over. The men rose and paraded out of the tent. Only the chief and I were left.

He motioned for me to move closer. I seated myself next to him.

"You'll stay with us Blunt man?"

I didn't know quite how to respond. Just how long?

"I'll stay one night. Buck and I leave for Denton tomorrow, early."

The chief looked hurt.

"We'll make you one of us. You'll write our tribal history. You'll make me famous. Teach my tribe to read your language."

It was out. The chief was after exposure himself.

"I'll come back later and write your story. I'll teach your people to read English. Now I must find Sam Bass and write about him."

He didn't answer. Then his face changed. He smiled again.

"Redwing say you are a real smart writer. He says a big man in the New York City pays you to write. We'll make agreement now."

He put me on the spot.

"I must go early tomorrow. I'll return. My sacred pledge."

I crossed my heart because that's all I could think of doing to seal our bargain.

Once again the chief looked downcast but then he rose, dusted off his clothing and offered me his hand. I stood next to him.

"You return when Bass story is written."

He held up four fingers. Then he departed, leaving me standing next to the fire, my eyes finally adjusted to the darkness. A young woman in a doeskin dress threw back the skin flap that served as a door. She came toward me, stopped, then began removing my clothes. She placed a basin of water on the ground.

# Chapter 12

The woman rubbed me down with some dried moss, handed me a loin skin, and led me by the hand out of the tent. I blinked as the sunlight reached my eyes after the dark. Gradually my eyes came back to normal. I saw for the first time where we were headed. A large skin-covered shelter stood before me, steam rising out of the top. She pulled me through the opening and once again we plunged into darkness.

It was so hot inside I was glad I had few clothes on. Other men were seated around a pile of stones, their bodies glistening with sweat, their ebony hair stringing down over their faces. What kind of place was this?

The answer came quickly. I began to perspire as I had never perspired before. Sweat began to roll off as my body reacted to the sudden change in temperature.

The girl was gone. She had disappeared almost as fast as Buck.

I never had liked the steam rooms in New York. I didn't like this one either.

I stayed. The Indians looked at me carefully and then motioned me to join them. I found a spot near a fierce-looking man who was blowing on the fire, heating the rocks piled in the center of the tent. He reached behind him for a dipper of water, kept blowing on the fire, then poured water over the stones. Clouds of steam rose, circled, and floated through the vent. Heavy vapor now engulfed me and blurred my vision.

I sat quietly.

The sound of Indian conversation filled the air. I just nodded occasionally. A happy-looking fellow sat next to me. His stomach pushed on the bounds of the animal skin sash he wore about his middle and a river of sweat cascaded down his chest. He kept talking to the man on his right. Then he stopped and turned toward me.

I didn't know if he understood English, but I'd give it a try.

"Do you really enjoy sitting here and sweating?"

He muttered something in the Kiowa language, turned back to his friend and resumed his conversation.

So much for small talk.

My eyes cleared and through the mist I made out the face of Buck Redwing. He was looking my way. I moved closer to him.

"Buck, haven't seen you. What have you been doing?"

There was no need for an answer. Buck's big smile told me exactly what he had been doing.

"Buck, we must be on the road. Need to get my story. Are you ready to ride?"

Buck twisted his body at the waist and faced me.

"We'll go. Me satisfied for now. Leave before dawn tomorrow."

The sun wasn't up and we were packed and ready to go. Big Mama knew we were riding and she snorted in the crisp morning air and pawed the ground.

"How far do we go today, Buck?"

"Day's ride, no more. We'll go now."

He was into his saddle and away before I could gather my thoughts. The rest had done wonders for me. Big Mama moved as she always did when I was ready to mount, but soon we were moving off behind Buck.

How long had it been since I'd seen Joline? I wondered what she was doing. I needed to see her, feel her touch, take her in my arms and hold her. I loved her so.

Buck was getting far ahead of me. With a slight kick of my spurs, Big Mama caught up with him.

Out of habit I glanced back. Even though it was just getting light, I could make out the figure of a man on horseback far off behind us. Was it the sheriff from Denison?

"Hey, Buck. Looks like the sheriff is on our trail."

Redwing turned half way around in his saddle and stared off toward where I had pointed.

"Sure looks like the same man. He wants to find Sam Bass bad. He follows us. That's no good," said Buck.

"He knows we're headed for Denton. Why didn't he just ride on ahead while we were in your village?"

"Must be a reason. Sheriff Benson doesn't ride the trail and follow us without a reason. He smells money, a reward."

I had to agree. But the sheriff must know we had seen him. He wasn't trying to hide himself. And what had he been doing while we were in the Indian camp?

"Should we try to lose him?"

After a moment Buck eased up his horse and swung his pinto close to Big Mama.

"Don't pay any attention to the sheriff. We'll ride on to Denton, then we'll lose him."

That satisfied me. The less I dealt with sheriffs the better.

We reached Denton late in the afternoon. As we rode into town I could see why Sam Bass might like to live here. The muddy streets were rutted and the rude wood buildings needed paint. But there was something about Denton that made me feel welcome. The people walking along the wooden sidewalk looked at me and smiled. In other towns some of the folks had frowned at me as if I were a stranger coming to rob them.

Buck slowed his horse to a walk.

"The people know me here. I've spent much time in town with Bass. They are smiling at me, not you."

So that was the reason. Buck Redwing must have made quite an impression in town to get a reaction like that from these frontier Texans.

"Where's the post office, Buck? I'm waiting for a letter."

The Indian nodded, then pointed down the street toward a small store. An American flag flew from a pole over the entrance.

"Right there," said Buck. "I'll meet you at the Gideon Hotel. I'm thirsty. Be quick. We have much to do."

We approached the main intersection of town and Buck split off to the right. Sure enough, down the side street was the hotel. It didn't look like much. I hoped the beds were soft.

I slid off Big Mama's back at the post office, excited at the prospect of a letter from Joline.

Mama was tied to the rail and I glanced up the street toward where Buck had turned. Nothing was stirring. Across from me was the Bon Ton Cafe. Next to it was one of those saloons with swinging-doors. Foot-high letters on the front spelled out the High Stakes Palace. This must be a gambling town.

I stepped up onto the walkway and opened the door.

There was more inside than just a post office. Tools were piled up in one corner and in another part of the room were bolts of calico. A window with bars was at the back of the store.

No one was there. I yelled and there was no answer. I called out again, and louder.

A door shut somewhere inside the building and there were light footsteps. A woman came into the room and saw me standing at the window.

"What's all the rush? Can't a lady do her housework without bein' bothered by some dusty cowboy?"

From the appearance of her face, smooth skin and all, I judged she was about 30. Her hair was tied up with one of those bandanna things. She had on a homemade apron with the initials JDB on the pocket.

"Well, JDB, I'm expectin' an important letter from a friend of mine, Miss Joline Collins by name. I'd be very pleased if you could find it. It'd be addressed to me, Nolo Blunt. General Delivery."

She opened a drawer, took out some envelopes, shuffled through them, put them down, rearranged them, then looked through them again. She separated a brown envelope from the others.

"This might be what you're lookin' for young man. 'Fore I give it to you, how'd you know I was JDB. You some kind of wizard?"

I smiled.

"Saw your initials on your apron. Now, may I have the letter?"

She handed it over after I'd signed the register and convinced her I was truly Nolo Blunt.

My hands shook as I tore through the flap of the envelope. I flipped out the pages of the letter, found a ladderback chair next to the pot-bellied stove and sat down to read.

> Dearest Nolo,
>
> I do miss you and will be with you again soon.
>
> We buried Joel in Ellis. Mom and Dad are still not convinced that Joel was a train robber. Maybe it's best that way. They'll remember him as he was when he was back home.
>
> I am staying with them and we are still grieving. I plan to leave for Denton and will be reunited with you soon. I plan to arrive in Denton on the afternoon stage, on the 30th. I hope you will be there. If you are not, I'll get a room at the biggest hotel in town and wait for you to find me. I think you will find me.

My heart skipped a beat or two as I finished the last paragraph.

> Well, my darling, we'll meet again and maybe this time we can stay together forever.
> Lovingly,
> Joline

I folded the letter and put it in my pocket. There was work to do and I had best be getting to it.

The post office lady stared at me.

"Must be good news. You've got a smile on your face a mile wide."

She was nosy, but there was something likeable about her.

"Yes, it's from my girl and she'll be here soon. You know where I can find a preacher?"

"Well, now. Ain't that somethin'? We're goin' to have us a weddin'. Folks around here really like to see two young people get hitched. Means they might stay in town and settle down."

"Ma'am, we aren't planning to settle down here, but I would like to spend more time in Denton. I'm a writer and have a job to do. Speaking of that, what's happening in this town?"

"Presbyterian Church burned down last night. Seems the District Court was sittin' temporarily in the church on some cases. New courthouse is being built. Cases were mostly cattle stealin'. Records were destroyed. Everyone hereabouts suspects Henry Underwood. Some folks say he's part of the Bass gang."

Her words registered in my brain and I suddenly became interested in what she had said.

"You know where to find this Henry Underwood?"

She looked at me with a sideways glance. Her eyebrows raised.

"You say you're a writer. If I help you, will you spell my name right?"

"Ma'am, I'd be glad to spell your name right if I knew what it was."

"Josie Donna Baines. That's my handle and you spell the Baines with an 'i' in the middle."

She kept talking as I wrote her name into my notebook.

"Henry Underwood's a no account robber who threatens people with a knife. He has the meanest looking eyes I've ever seen. But I hear tell he's good to his family. Don't know where you'd find him right now, but won't be long before the sheriff locks him up. Body can't burn down a church around here without anyone knowin' who done it."

I asked her if she knew Sam Bass.

"You interested in Underwood or Bass?"

"Well it's really Sam Bass I'm lookin' for. You know him?"

"Sure do. He's been in here recently lookin' for mail. I see everyone in Denton from time to time."

"Where might he be found?"

Again she angled her eyebrows and gave me a looking over.

"You just a writer or maybe a lawman too?"

"Ma'am, I'm just a writer."

I pulled a copy of Frontier Magazine out of my shirt and let her see the front page where one of my articles appeared with my byline.

"Well, guess it's all right to tell you. Everyone around here knows where Sam Bass hangs out anyway. You maybe got a right to know too. He's up around Cove Hollow. Ask Jim Murphy where to find Bass."

I thanked her and left. This had been my lucky day. A letter from Joline and a lead to finding Bass.

Looking down the street past the Bon Ton Cafe I saw Buck Redwing racing toward me. I had never seen Buck in such a wild state.

# Chapter 13

"Sam Bass is at Cove Hollow. We'll go," said Buck, pointing down the road.

So that's what he was so excited about.

"I know. The lady in the post office told me. She also mentioned a Jim Murphy. You know him?"

"I know Murphy. Get your horse."

I hurried down the dirt street walking next to Big Mama, grabbed the reins and while Buck left for his pinto, I mounted. Once again we were off. Finally, I would be able to talk with Sam Bass and get his story.

Buck came riding up.

"Follow me. I know the way to Cove Hollow. We gotta move fast."

Big Mama was ready to go. She moved into her speeding pace. We soon were galloping out of Denton.

Ahead was a forest of pine trees which looked like a good place for an ambush. In times past there may have been bandits who lived in these woods, robbing passersby and escaping the law by riding off through the trees. Bass knew what he was doing by making his headquarters in this countryside. The fellow named Jim Murphy must have some reason for joining forces with Bass.

Buck, as always, was getting far ahead of me and my horse sprinted, with a nudge from my knee, to catch up. Big Mama hit a good pace and soon we were once again even with the Indian.

"How far now, Buck? Is it hard to get to Cove Hollow from here?"

Buck's head turned and made a sign for me to be quiet.

"Buck, do you know how far it is?"

Once again Buck made a sign. Whatever the reason, the message got through to me and I shut up.

The timber thinned out as we rode along the trail. Up ahead was a ranch. It looked like a two-story house and outbuildings where the cowboys and horses must be quartered.

Buck slowed. He motioned for me to ride alongside.

"Here's where Murphy lives. He's a good friend to Bass. We'll stop. He knows me."

Buck reached the railing first and was off his horse in a flash. Big Mama sidled alongside the pinto. I slid off, tied her reins to the rail and followed Buck to the front door of the house.

"What's Murphy like, Buck?"

"He goes for action. Likes to have Bass around 'cause Bass always tells stories. You'll like him."

The front door opened and a tall man stepped out on the porch. His tanned and wrinkled face reflected the hardships of living in the west. His dark hair fell to shoulder length and a drooping moustache rounded the corners of his mouth.

"Buck, Buck Redwing, you son of a gun. Haven't seen you since you left for Nebraska. What you been doin' you rascal? And who's the slicker with you?"

Buck looked at Murphy, then at me.

"He's Blunt, Nolo Blunt. Writer. He's following Sam Bass. Wants to write about him. Have you seen Sam lately?"

"He's here. He did say something about a New York feller up in Big Springs who was stickin' his nose into the gang's business. So you're Blunt."

Murphy looked me over good.

"Name's Nolo. Writing about the adventures of Bass. Saw Joel Collins up Buffalo, Kansas way. He'd been gunned down. His sister, Joline, is coming to Denton and we're going to be married."

Murphy raised an eyebrow, put his hand on his chin and eyed me once again. What was he thinking?

He started to speak.

"Heard about Joel. I knew Collins well. Also knew about his sister. Didn't know she was gettin' married. You must be some smooth dude. Joline's not the one to take to just any feller."

Murphy looked away, then spoke again.

"You fellers must be tired after your ride from town. Come on in and sit a spell. I'd like to hear some more about how Joel met his end."

I told him about our arrival in Kansas when we found out Joel and his sidekick had pulled their guns on the sheriff and how almost an entire army opened up on them. Murphy winced when he heard about all the bullet holes in Collins.

"You say Joline stayed with the body. Hope she had someone to help get Joel underground."

I told him about the letter I'd received and assured him that Joel had been properly buried.

Buck and I bedded down at Murphy's ranch.

In the morning at breakfast we found out how we were to meet Sam Bass.

Murphy poured my coffee.

"Bass will come by the ranch today. He's headed for town, but he'll stop in. He can size you up and decide if he wants you around."

My breath deepened. If Bass didn't want me to write about his exploits, I'd have to start all over again and find some other desperado. That wouldn't be easy.

Buck sat at the table, his eyebrows meeting in the center of his forehead, wrinkles rippling just above them.

"What do you want to do Buck?"

He gave me a look of concern, but didn't respond.

Murphy left the room. Buck turned toward me.

"Bass will come."

That's all he said.

I finished my coffee and sat staring at the kitchen wall. It was papered with a bright design. There were roosters and hens overlaid on a barnyard scene.

Copper-bottomed pots hung next to the wood-burning stove. Many ranchers did their own cooking mostly because they lived alone. When they were out on the range with a herd of cattle, they butchered a beef and cooked the meat. But here at the ranch there were vegetables to vary their diet.

Buck had gone outside and I was left alone. It was an opportunity for me to get to work.

> ON THE TRAIL OF SAM BASS
> SOMEWHERE IN TEXAS
> By Nolo Blunt
>
> Bass and his gang are nearby. The exact location can't be revealed. There's a Texas

sheriff trailing me and my Indian friend. To give away Bass's hideaway would mean certain death for the two of us. But today we'll meet Bass again. Last time I saw him was at the gang hideout in Nebraska and there's been a lot of water along the river since our paths crossed.

I put down my pencil and thought for a minute. The newspaper from Denison must still be in my saddle bag. Maybe there would be something in it about Collins being caught and shot.

I rummaged around in the bag and found the crumpled paper. Turning to the inside pages I noticed a headline I hadn't seen before. It blared out "BIG SPRINGS TRAIN ROBBER CAUGHT."

Loud voices and laughing came from the front of the ranch house. I put the newspaper down, rolled up the sheaves of paper I had been writing on and stuffed them inside my shirt. The voices got louder.

Sam Bass burst through the kitchen door. Quickly I stood up to meet him.

"Well if it isn't my old friend, Nolo. How're things goin'? Ain't seen you since Big Springs. Heard you had a bit of trouble with a twister out on the prairie. Glad you got Joline to Big Springs in good shape. Tell me about the lawman who's been chasin' after you. May be serious."

Bass still had that downcast look, the same as when I first saw him. His black hair was slicked back now and he wore a red bandanna around his neck. His shoulders sloped forward and gave him the appearance that he was leaning on a post only there wasn't any post there to lean on.

I put out my hand. Bass took it.

"Glad to see you again, Sam. Lot of water under the bridge since we last breathed the same air."

He cocked his right eye at me, scrunched up his eyebrow and then a broad smile spread across his hairy face.

"Writers, hell! You guys talk like one a them there giraffes I seen pictures of in a magazine down to the barber shop. Stuck up high off the ground. Big neck. No wonder all you got to keep you company is a bunch a words. Now tell me about this here sheriff from Denison."

Come to think of it, I hadn't noticed anyone following us when we left Denton yesterday. But Buck Redwing must have told Bass about the trailing lawman who'd dogged us from the Indian camp.

"Name's Benson. Talked to him back in Denison when we crossed over into Texas. He seems to know you and suspects there will be a reward for your capture. Trailed us to Denton. Think he knew you lived here and would probably head for home. Didn't see him in town. Only talked with JDB at the post office."

Bass threw back his head and gave out a throaty cackle.

"JDB. Boy you can pick 'em. She's my girlfriend. She tell you where I was?"

Things were getting delicate. I had to tell the truth.

"Sure. Asked her questions. That's my job. Didn't get any invitation from you. Had to find you and get the story of your life. JDB didn't tell me anything Buck and I couldn't find out from anyone else in town."

Bass's expression changed. He seemed to relax a bit. Maybe my words had been the right ones.

"Well, you done found me, boy. Get that there pencil out from behind your ear and start writin'. Ain't got all day. Got me a few trains to rob. You're with me now for better or worse. You get ideas about leavin' and a bullet's goin' to find its way into your heart, lover boy."

Shaking, I reached up and pulled my pencil down, retrieved my notes from under my shirt and began to write.

## Chapter 14

Big Mama stood next to the railing in Murphy's corral. She looked well fed and rested. Her head was held high and she faced in my direction, sniffing the wind, her ears up. She whinnied when I approached. As I opened the gate, she trotted over to greet me, rubbing her nose against my neck.

Redwing saddled his mount and led it through the gate before I had a chance to get a bridle on Big Mama.

Bass had a new partner in crime, Frank Jackson, a skinny light-haired metalworker from a tin shop in Denton.

They were waiting for us at the edge of the forest near Murphy's ranch. Bass had kept an eye on me the whole time I was putting the saddle on my horse. I began to feel like a criminal who was being guarded by the local constable.

That made me look around to see if the Denison lawman was here. There wasn't a sign of him. I hurried toward Bass and Jackson.

As I rode up, Sam greeted me.

"Well, now, aren't you the one. All saddled up and we been waitin' here for you. You keep this up, maybe I'll just shoot you out a meanness. Let's get goin'. I done seen somethin' I don't like out there mid those two tall pine trees yonder. Keep close up. The goin' gets mighty rough to Cove Hollow and if some lawman is tailin' us, he'll think twice about gettin' to our hideout."

The trail was difficult to follow. As we neared the turn from the main path, Bass said,

"Don't you be gettin' any ideas, Blunt. You bring that flop-eared mule of a horse up here next to mine. Goin' to keep you in my gun sights."

Flop-eared mule of a horse! This man was trying to make me mad. How could he say that about a mare worthy of respect and devotion. He'd pay for those words one day. Didn't even know him yet and already I disliked him.

We entered the woods. The trail was mud, sloppy, sticky and chunky Texas mud that stuck to Big Mama's hooves and made a sucking sound when she pulled her legs up to take another step. Why would anyone want to live in a place like this when he had all that gold from the train robbery? This man should be bedding down between clean sheets in a hotel suite in town, eating at the Bon Ton Cafe three times a day and drinking nothing but the best whiskey at the High Stakes Palace in Denton.

And Bass had a girlfriend. So that's what Josie Donna Baines meant when she told me she sees everyone in Denton from time to time. No wonder when she told me where to find Bass, she was really cautious.

The trail was rougher now. Elderberry vines were everywhere. Stickers caught at my clothes as Sam led us through what must be the most unholy place on earth. There was a foul odor of swamp gas. It reminded me of rotten eggs. Somewhere in the distance a loud belch broke the surface of the swamp. I heard it again and looked at the top of a brown-scum pond where the ripples from the gas explosion spread toward the shore. What a mess. I thought about my editor back in his cool, dry wood-paneled office, smoking a cigar and reading my latest copy. Did he have any idea what I was going through to get the Sam Bass story?

Big Mama began to froth. The heat in this Texas morass was unbearable. She was used to riding free on the plains, not stomping through the underbrush like a pack horse. We'd been descending into a hollow for quite some time.

Bass reined in his horse. I pulled up and asked, "You got some water, Sam? My horse and I are thirsty."

Bass took off his sweat-streaked wide-brimmed felt hat and wiped his hand across his forehead.

"Thirsty you say, boy. You'll know what thirsty is before we get to the hideout. Just keep your trap shut and ride."

He moved on down the overgrown trail. I could understand now why no lawman wanted to follow him. This place would be just right for an ambush. Bass could hold off an army in here.

I dismounted. My boots hit the slushy ground, my feet making a sucking sound as I plodded through the brush. With my hands I pushed away the knots of tangled branches and tried to make it easier for Big Mama to follow. But as soon as the path was cleared, the branches closed together leaving no evidence of anyone having gone this way. Only broken branches marked the trail. It would take an expert tracker to find where we had walked.

We reached an opening in the path where there were piles of rocks and some empty food containers. A tent stood beneath the twisted branches of a pine.

Bass stopped, jumped off his horse and tied the reins to a mulberry bush. I did the same.

"You really are a tenderfoot aren't you? I sure don't know what Joline sees in you. She musta become a bit loco on that train when she met you."

What could I say? I really wasn't a tenderfoot any longer, not after having spent all that time on the trail, dodging a Nebraska tornado, outwitting Sheriff Tatum from Big Springs, seeing Joel Collins laid out at the barber shop in Buffalo Station, sweating in an Indian tepee, and finally finding Sam Bass. And as for Joline, she had good taste in her choice of men.

My mouth stayed closed.

Dinner at the hideout was something else. Never before had I eaten Brunswick stew and never again do I want to eat it. It actually tasted all right until I found out about the squirrels, snakes and lizards that went into its making. Then I got sick. Squirrels were all right. I'd tasted them back at the Kiowa village. But I passed up the slimy lizard meat.

After dinner I spread my bedroll on the ground at the base of a gnarled oak tree. My boots came off without too much effort. I slid in between my blankets and looked up through the matted leaves. The stars were out and shining down. Somewhere they were shining down on Joline too. I thought about our future. What a nice way to go to sleep.

Life in this outlaw camp was different from life in the one in Nebraska. The coffee pot was boiling by the time I awoke. There's nothing like the smell of fresh brewed coffee mixing with the smoke from a wood fire early in the morning. I sat up and looked around.

Bass was dressed and seated on a log across from me. His eyes scanned the woods around him.

Finally, his gaze rested on me.

"You city fellers. Mornin's half gone and you're still in bed. Ain't life out here taught you anythin' about gettin' up and at 'em in the mornin'?"

I decided to take a stand against Bass riding me all the time.

"Hey, Bass. If gettin' up early makes you handsome, you sure spent some long time in the sack."

Bass frowned at first then let out the loudest laugh I had ever heard. He leaned back while he was laughing and fell off the log. I could still hear him roaring even though he had landed in a thick bush. He finally stopped and sat back down on the log.

"That's a good one, Blunt. Been jabberin' at you to see if you had any spunk. Don't want just anyone writin' my story. Got to be someone who's got some spark about him. Everythin's goin' to be all right now."

I sighed. Now maybe we could get started. Lord knows I'd been wanting to write about Bass for long enough.

The dew was thick on my boots so I wiped them off with a saddle cloth and shook them out. Woodland creatures like to hide in a warm place like the toe of a boot. Nothing fell out so it was safe to put them on.

Buck Redwing was out near the horses. He had fed and watered Big Mama along with his pinto.

Frank Jackson rode into camp from along the trail. He cradled a rifle in his left arm and looked tired. His hat was pushed down over his forehead, the leather strip around the brim was covered with sweat. He wore a wool coat lined with sheepskin. Cocklebur seeds dotted the collar of his jacket. There was a smudge of mud on one elbow.

Jackson walked over to me.

I looked into his face and saw kindness despite the two day's growth of beard he was wearing and the weariness in his eyes.

"Didn't see anythin' a that sheriff that's supposed to be followin' you. Maybe you lost him in town. Suspect he be trailin' us though. Won't find this hideout 'less we want him to."

Jackson stepped over to the fire, grabbed a mug and poured a cup of coffee. I watched him as the hot liquid dribbled down the front of his shirt.

Jackson looked toward me. I wanted to talk with him.

"You see anything unusual out there last night?"

He moved closer while gripping the coffee cup.

"No. Nothin' strange. But I got the feelin' there's goin' to be more than one sheriff lookin' around. Lot a gold was taken in Big Springs and the train company wants to get it back. Heard there's a $10,000 reward. I wasn't in on that one but Sam's got some more action planned."

Because Jackson was willing to tell me this, I felt the gang would trust me now.

More action! That's what I came west for.

A mockingbird sang in the trees, its voice sounding out of place in this morass.

My thoughts were broken by Bass's voice. He stood next to me.

"We got some time. Get your pencil, boy."

Bass was planning a robbery. Most likely he'd be stopping a train south of Dallas. At least that was what he was talking about.

Being a reporter and not a member of the gang gave me special status. I could know everything there was to know about the robberies without actually being held to account should the robbery fail and Bass and his men were arrested. But then, how would the sheriff know I was not a member of the gang? That worried me. Didn't want to have my neck stretched with a fine piece of homemade Texas hemp.

Buck Redwing and I were left alone in camp. Bass and Jackson had ridden off after lunch to go into town. They were looking for a man named Underwood to add to the gang before the big train heist. Maybe they would return with more than just one man. It would take more than three for such a venture. This was new to me. It was a once-in-a-lifetime experience, how to plan a train robbery.

Buck approached, smiling.

"Bass gave me gold. It's time for me to leave. I'll return to my village. There's enough money for a lifetime. Tell Bass I've gone."

This shocked me. Buck leaving!

"Buck. I'm sorry to see you go. We've been through a lot together, but I know how much you want to go home."

He looked me straight in the eyes.

"You are a friend also, Nolo Blunt. There were times when I wasn't so sure you would make it in this country. You have great inner strength. I will always be your friend. I hope you will be mine. You and Miss Joline must come and stay with my people. We would welcome you. Never told you. I went to church school when I was younger. Learned the white man's language from a little old lady. I also know Indian short talk. It really saves time in tight spots. I use it because to speak in longer sentences might mean death. My son and daughter will learn the church school way too."

He grabbed me by the right hand and threw his other arm over my shoulder, then stepped back and was gone. The tail of his pinto disappeared through the rough brush at the edge of camp.

I was alone in the middle of a swamp, mosquitoes buzzing around my head, the odor of the swamp gas filling my nostrils. Bass figured I couldn't ride out of the camp by myself. He was right.

# Chapter 15

My reverie was interrupted by the arrival of Bass and Jackson. A new man was with them.

Bass looked around the encampment, pulled up his horse in front of me and dismounted.

"Where's Buck Redwing?"

I looked up at him.

"Redwing's gone. Said he was going home. Rode out of here about an hour ago. You should have passed him on the trail."

My words registered with Bass. He had a confused expression on his face.

"Gonna miss him. Redwing was a good man. Sorry to see him go."

Then Bass changed his posture.

"With him gone, why didn't you run away?"

I thought carefully about that and prepared my answer.

"No need to. Want to write your story. You've given me part of it, but I want the whole story. No way to do that unless I stick around."

My response pleased him. He smiled and then turned to the new man he'd brought with him.

"Henry, Henry Underwood. Step over here and meet Nolo Blunt. Blunt's writin' my life story. Got myself my own writer. Be famous someday. You need to tell him how you burned down the Presbyterian Church in Denton."

Underwood made his way over to where I stood.

"So you're Blunt. Heard about you back in Denton. JDB said you was askin' about me. Well, here I am. What ya wanta know?"

I didn't like this man, and after hearing him talk, I liked him less. He was pushy.

"Sure I'm interested in you. Any friend of Sam Bass is a friend of mine at least until I get their story. A reporter is interested in all kinds of things."

Underwood stuck out his lower lip and sized me up.

"Well, I think you're a nosy writer and I don't wanta have anythin' to do with you. Bass says you stay, it's OK by me, but I'd just as soon see you outa here."

With those words, Underwood dug his boot heel into the mushy earth, turned and grabbed his horse's reins.

Bass was still standing next to me. He smiled.

"Henry don't take kindly to no strangers, but he's all right. Give him time. Right now we be plannin' a little action. You get yourself saddled up. You come along, stay in the bushes, watch our style. Might be somethin' for you to write about."

Excitement gripped me. My first chance to observe Sam Bass and his men while they committed a robbery. Could be dangerous. But the opportunity for a grand story made it worth all the risk.

My saddle still sat on the ground where I'd left it. I picked it up and threw it over my shoulder and headed to where Big Mama was tethered.

Bass and his two men waited for me as I led my horse back through the camp. I mounted and before my right foot was even in the stirrup, Bass moved out. He seemed agitated and nervous. He had a right to be. Robbing someone took a lot of gumption.

The trail out of the hollow was more difficult than coming in. Most of the branches seemed to face the other direction. Every time the three men in front of me urged their horses through the brush, the limbs would swing back and hit me in the head. I soon learned to duck just before the branches reached me. Big Mama had learned how to dodge also. Her giant head bounced up and down in rhythm to the swinging limbs.

Then we were on the wide road to Denton, and I rode alongside Bass.

"Where are we headed, Sam?"

Bass looked over at me.

"Tain't none a your business to know. Just keep ridin'."

I drew Big Mama back.

Henry Underwood had a casual way about him while he was in the saddle. His hat brim was pulled down close over his forehead. His hands rested idly on the pommel. His eyes scanned the far reaches of the surrounding pine forest and his lips spread apart like he was about to say something, but no words came out.

Underwood was about what I expected him to be, a raw-boned man with a pock-marked face and stringy black hair. He looked mean. Anyone who would set fire to a church really was mean. I had no doubt he could do such a thing.

Jackson was calm. He rode easily, like he had been born in the saddle with the reins in his right hand. His left hand fondled the bone handle of his six-gun. That was the only indication of tension he displayed. But tension was there. Robbing a stagecoach must create a thrill. Money wasn't everything. Maybe it was the chance of getting caught. Maybe it was the thrill of getting away, being chased by the sheriff and his posse, eluding them and living to rob again.

We were now about ten miles south of Denton and still riding. What would happen next?

Bass held up his hand and pointed to the woods. We followed his lead and soon we reached a place where the trees were sparse. The others dismounted, tied down their reins and began preparations for something.

I jumped off Big Mama and walked her over to where the other horses were tethered. Bass came toward me.

"Now you just stay calm young feller and you won't get hurt. Me and the boys are goin' to have a little fun. You can watch, but I don't want you nos'n around and mixin' in what we're about to do. You understand?"

I nodded my head. I understood. A chill began at the base of my spine and moved upward. What if the gang was caught and the sheriff thought I was part of it? I could be hanged along with the rest. I certainly **would** keep my nose out of their business. It might mean life or death.

We moved to the bushes next to the trail. Bass stood and gazed off toward where undoubtedly a stagecoach would soon come over the knoll.

The trio pulled their blue-spotted bandannas over the lower parts of their faces. The robbery had to be imminent. Bass and Underwood had their pistols out and Jackson cradled his Sharps rifle. Evidently Jackson would be the cover man.

I heard the rumble of the stagecoach before I saw it and then things happened fast. Looking up, Bass and Underwood stepped out onto the road in front of the coach about fifty yards away. Underwood fired his weapon in the air and Bass took aim at the driver. Jackson, hidden in the bushes near me, covered the driver's sidekick with his rifle.

The coach slowed as the man with the reins pulled back hard. The horses came to a full stop. Bass was the first to speak. His voice rasped as he spit out his words.

"Throw up them props, boys, and ain't nothin' goin' ta harm you."

The two men on the driver's seat put their arms in the air and Bass continued.

"Now get that money box out'n the boot and toss it down here."

Meanwhile, Underwood approached the door of the coach, jerked it open and motioned for those inside to step out.

Three men and a middle-aged woman stumbled down the steps to the ground. Their hands were raised and they sure were frightened. One man had a nervous twitch above his right eye. The woman looked like she was about to faint.

Underwood began frisking the men, but when he came to the woman, he just spoke to her.

"Pardon me, ma'am, but I would like you to hand me that purse a yours."

She looked him in the eyes, saw something there then gave him her purse.

"You ruffians. What's happening to our country? Common robbers accosting a stagecoach and taking our money. Why don't you get yourselves a regular job and especially you, Henry Underwood?"

Underwood looked up, startled. He stared at the woman. I could tell he was trying to determine how she had recognized him, bandanna and all.

"Well, ma'am, might have to put a bullet through that pretty little brain a yours."

Bass came up, the heavy strong box in his arms, but still with his pistol aimed at the driver.

"You drive on now. Get yourself down that road and don't be lookin' back to see where we've gone. You're lucky I didn't plug ya outa meanness," Bass said.

The driver wasted no time. He got the passengers inside and closed the doors. He yelled at his horses. The stagecoach started down the road.

Bass and Underwood came staggering into the bushes. They were breathless and excited. My mouth was shut.

Sam suddenly burst out singing and Underwood joined him in a chorus of "Blue Tail Fly" while Jackson rounded up the horses.

Bass hoisted the strong box onto his saddle, mounted and soon we were riding back to camp just like nothing had happened. But something **had** happened and I was riding along with a trio of crooks who had just robbed a stagecoach. If a sheriff caught us, I would be one of the gang. It made me shudder.

We finally reached Cove Hollow. Bass, Underwood and Jackson dismounted quickly. They were like youngsters at Christmas, eager to see what was in the strong box and count up their booty.

Bass aimed his pistol at the lock. The roar deafened me for an instant, but the bullet did its job. The lid flew back revealing the box's contents. Even I was anxious to see what was inside.

Bass pulled out some bags and papers and put them on the ground. He untied the strings on the first bag and dumped it out.

Underwood was busy inspecting a gold watch he had stolen from one of the male passengers. He opened it up, held it to his ear, listened for a while then checked the stem and wound it. There was a smile on his face.

"Hey, Sam, Frank, look here."

He held up the watch and dangled it by its gold chain.

"Got me a fine ticker here. Even has the picture of an elk on the cover. Runs good too. Ticks along mighty fine."

Bass was too busy with his own search to pay attention to Underwood. But Jackson looked up and stepped over to see the watch.

"Well, Henry. You really got something there. Let me see it."

Underwood handed the watch to Jackson and then joined Bass.

"What'd we get, Sam?"

Bass spread out some folded papers and a few greenbacks on the rock where he sat.

"Not much here, Henry. Looks like we struck out. Some stocks, bonds. Nothin' we can turn into cash. Few pieces of gold. We'll split those even up. What'd you get?"

Underwood dumped out his saddlebag on the ground. He and Bass picked over what fell out.

"Two hundreds bucks. That's all Sam. Ain't enough to buy beans. Maybe we should take up stable cleanin'. Probably more money in that. Could get fifty bucks for the gold watch. You got somethin' else figured out?"

Bass scratched his head and looked over at me.

"Well, Blunt. What ya starin' at? Ain't you never seen a gang a stagecoach robbers up against it. You gettin' all this down?"

I eyed Bass and thought about what he had said.

"Seems to me you'd make more money if you robbed a train like the one in Nebraska."

Bass frowned.

"Don't you be gettin' smart with me, you whippersnapper. I know what I'm doin'. Got me some big plans. Goin' to show you what a real train bandit can do. We'll get me some more men and we'll be off to stop a locomotive or two. Goin' to have me a great time with the South Texas special that pulls through Dallas carryin' a load of gold and passengers with lots of cash."

I watched Underwood's eyes while Bass was talking. He was smiling and looked the part of a robber, cool, mean and dependable.

Jackson was another matter. His heart didn't seem to be in the business. However, he would do anything Bass wanted him to do.

I had a secret about the robbery. While the three bandits were busy, one of the male passengers stuffed a wad of cash into his glove behind his back, casually holding the glove while Underwood made the rounds. Wouldn't tell Bass. What he didn't know wouldn't hurt him.

A rustle in the bushes came from behind me. When I turned around, Big Mama's head nestled under my arm.

Joline was due into Denton tomorrow. Needed to be on my way to get a room and prepare for her arrival. My problem would be in telling Sam Bass about leaving camp.

# Chapter 16

Bass, Underwood, and Jackson still jabbered about the holdup even though the sun had long ago set and the fire had died down. Only a few embers glowed through a covering of wood ash and soot. Bass seemed elated by the events of the afternoon.

"Did you see that driver throw up his props? He thought for sure I was goin' to blast him 'tween the eyes if he even flinched."

Underwood guffawed. Then he got serious.

"Just remembered. That lady on the coach. She recognized me. May be trouble, Sam."

Bass was disturbed.

"Whatya mean she recognized you? How could she? You had a mask over your face. She'd have to know you pretty damn well with just your eyes showin'."

Underwood hung his head a bit, then answered.

"Do know her. She's a distant relative. Lives in Dallas. Had no idea she'd be on that stagecoach. Whatta we goin' to do, Sam?"

Bass didn't answer. He gazed into the coals of the fire.

I approached him.

"I'm leavin' camp tomorrow morning early, Sam. Got to get to Denton and meet Joline. She's comin' in on the afternoon stage. We're goin' to be married within the week and then we'll find you no matter where you move your hideout. I'll be careful in town. Won't talk to anyone about what happened today."

I felt something round and metallic being pressed against my left temple. Turning my head, I stared down the barrel of a .44 caliber six shooter held by Underwood. He seemed agitated.

"I'd just as soon blow your head off as look at ya, but Sam seems to want to keep you around. Just remember this here pistol will find you no matter where you hide if anythin' leads a sheriff onto our trail."

Bass put up his hand and pushed the pistol away.

"Easy Henry. This here man is goin' to be important to us later. He ain't goin' to say anythin' in town. He wants to keep his skin in shape for some fancy humpin' with his bright new bride-to-be. And if somethin' slips and we get caught, I got my ideas about how we might just tell the sheriff how Blunt was with us on that raid and how he's a member of our gang. They'll stretch his neck along with ours."

What Bass said got through to me for sure. But he had other instructions for me.

"Now you get on into Denton and stay a while. Keep your ears open and your mouth shut. Get yourself wed proper like then I'll get word to you where we be hidin' out. Ain't goin' to stay here much longer, not with Henry's lady friend probably spillin' her guts about how we done robbed the stagecoach."

I took off my boots and snuggled down deep between my woolen blankets. I could still feel the metal imprint of Underwood's six shooter against my head.

Riding to Denton in the early morning without Buck Redwing at my side was a new experience. I'd always had the Indian ahead of me leading the way, but now had to go it alone. There was only one trail through the woods so it wouldn't be impossible.

Just beyond Murphy's ranch I noticed a movement in the woods ahead of me. I was wearing a pistol and a Winchester rifle stuck out of the scabbard that was now part of my regular gear. However, trouble on the trail without Redwing would be something new to me. I listened closely for sounds that might tell me about anything moving in the brush.

I had just rounded a bend in the trail when a horse and rider bounded out of the woods and blocked my way. It was Sheriff Benson from Denison, the one who'd been trailing me and Buck Redwing.

His hat was pushed back and his handlebar moustache drooped menacingly over his upper lip. He held up his hand for me to stop.

"Hold on there Blunt. Wanta talk with you."

I pulled back on the reins and Big Mama dug her hooves into the soft dirt of the trail and came to a halt alongside the sheriff. He was talking even as I approached.

"Where're ya ridin' young fella? Been chasin' you halfway 'cross Texas. Bet you didn't even know that."

The sheriff must have thought I was a fool not to have noticed him trailing me.

"What do you want? I have business in town."

"I'll just bet you do. You got any a that Nebraska gold on ya? You been somewhere with Sam Bass, I'll bet on it. Sure would like to get my hands on that man. Nice reward now for his skin."

"Sheriff, my gal is comin' in on the stage today and we're goin' to get married. You're holdin' up a lovesick man. Now if you don't mind, get your horse outa my way so's I can ride on into town."

Benson pulled his horse over.

"You ain't answered my question, but reckon I'll find Bass soon enough. Maybe I'll be seein' you around Denton tonight. Maybe we can have a drink to celebrate your comin' wedding and just maybe you can give me a hint where I can find Bass."

I touched Big Mama in the sides with my boot and we were again on our way.

Denton was dirty and dusty the same as the last time. There were more people on the streets now, not like the day Buck and I rode into town.

JDB was out on the bare wooden sidewalk and waved. I waved back and rode Big Mama over to where she stood.

"Howdy, ma'am."

My Texas accent was improving each time I talked to someone down here.

"You all been takin' care a yourself since I saw you last?"

JDB smiled at me. She wasn't bad looking. Her auburn hair was piled up on top of her head and she was wearing a pea-green apron over a dark dress. She sounded enthusiastic.

"Whatcha doin' in town, big boy?"

"Joline's comin' on the afternoon stage. Goin' to invite you to the weddin'. Only thing I need is a wedding ring. Any jeweler in town?"

"Sure have. His name's Jones. He charges a lot for what he sells, but what he sells is worth a lot. 'Round the corner, two stores down. Stop back here when you get through. Like to see whatcha bought. Ain't never been associated with a writer gettin' married before."

I waved my hat and pushed forward on the reins for Big Mama to move along.

The town jeweler was a sharpy. He greeted me at the door of his shop and shook my hand hard. I almost counted my fingers to see if they were all still there. Bushy eyebrows framed his dark brown eyes. He sported a traditional moustache for the times, twirly ends caked with wax. Didn't believe I could trust him, but what was I going to do? I had to get a ring.

"Come on in young man. You obviously need something for your sweetie. What is it? A diamond broach, pin on lapel watch, or maybe, just maybe you're looking for a gold band so's you can get married."

I eyed him suspiciously.

"How'd you know I needed a wedding band? You can't have talked with JDB. I just left her."

"What me? Talk to JDB? Of course. There isn't anything goes on in this town without JDB telling all she knows. But I just guessed about your wedding. Mostly when a young cowpoke comes in here, he wants a wedding band. Even know you're looking for Sam Bass. Well, I know a bit about that too."

He had me hooked. His was the only jewelry store in town. He had information for me that I could possibly use. I entered the store following the sweep of his left arm. He pointed to a place where we could sit.

"Name's Casper Jones. You must be that writer feller, ah, what's the name?"

"Blunt, Nolo Blunt's my handle. What do you know about Sam Bass?"

"Well, you bein' a city feller you probably don't know nuthin' about the gold business. I do. Been meltin' down gold, makin' rings, foolin' around with the stuff ever since I can remember. Now Bass, he done got himself a lot a gold up there in Nebraska when he robbed that train. Don't make no difference whether it's gold outa the ground or gold from coins. It's all the same to me and if Bass wants to get rid of some incriminatin' evidence, he might just like to know what I can do. Now what was it you wanted? Ah, yes, a pair a gold rings, one for you and one for the new missus to be. Like to do you a favor, give them to you at wholesale cost if you can persuade Bass to get some a them gold coins to me."

I couldn't argue with the man's gift of persuasion. He'd make a lot of money if Bass decided to melt down the gold coins so they couldn't be traced. But I didn't have any idea where Bass kept it.

"Do what I can to help you. However, I'm just a poor reporter for an Eastern magazine. I'd kinda like to get my hands on some a that money too. I'll tell Bass about you if I see him. You say you'll give me a discount?"

"Sure will stranger. Just pick out what you want. I'll make it right by you. Just remember where you got such a good deal and tell Bass."

What I was doing was not exactly legal, but then life wasn't always going to be black and white. I might as well profit from my association with Bass as long as it didn't get me into the town jail.

I chose two simple rings and then thought about Joline and what she might want.

"Mr. Jones, my future wife's comin' in on the afternoon stage. I'd kinda like her to see the rings. You give me a chance to exchange them if she doesn't like them?"

Jones smiled broadly.

"Why sure. You can bring your honey around here any time. Be glad to see her and help her pick out what she wants. Does she know Bass too?"

I had to be careful in what I said. This could be a ticklish situation if Jones found out that Joline was the sister of Joel Collins. I decided to sidestep his question.

"That'll be fine. I'll take them with me. She may want to exchange hers. Mine will be fine. Let me know how much I owe you. Got to hurry. Stage is comin' in."

I dashed out the door as the stagecoach came down the main street. I sprinted to where Big Mama was tied, loosened the reins and climbed on her back. Joline was coming and I wanted to be there when she got off the coach. I'd been waiting a long time to hold her in my arms.

The coach was just pulling to a stop when I reached the stage office. The driver wiped his brow and was about to stand up and jump down from his seat. I watched the passengers begin to descend the steps that the express agent had let down from the coach. A rather portly gentleman wearing a striped suit and dotted tie stepped onto the stairs. The whole coach shook itself like a lady removing her corset. Inside I could see just the top of Joline's head. She would be with me soon.

And then there was gunfire. Two men came running out of the mercantile store. They were firing toward the building they had just left. A window broke and there was the sound of shattering glass. It startled the horses because at that moment they bolted. The driver had forgotten to set the hand brake and I could see him jump down and reach the ground as the heavy coach sped off behind four frightened horses. And then it struck me. Joline was in there!

Big Mama had jumped also when the window broke. Fortunately she was securely tied at the railing. I jumped for the reins, untied them and leaped onto Big Mama's back and was off after the runaway coach. I had no idea what to do, but I'd be there when the coach came to a stop.

I could see Joline's outline in the back window. She saw I was following.

Big Mama picked up speed.

I drew even with the coach now and could see Joline straining to see me out the side window. I waved to her and shouted I would save her, but I was sure she couldn't hear. The coach made such a racket that nothing could be heard over the turning of the wheels and the squeaking of the frame along with the clomping of the horses hooves.

The land was flat and I was able to keep even with the four horses. I decided to jump aboard.

I reached for the metal railing circling the driver's seat and with my good right hand I grabbed it, yanked hard using all my strength and pulled away from Big Mama. I made it topside the coach, untied the reins and steadily brought the frightened horses to a halt.

The remaining passengers shouted with joy. Joline was safe!

# Chapter 17

I tied down the reins on the brake post and jumped down. The coach door was open. A woman was on the floor, her dress spilling over a man who was holding his head.

Joline was in one corner, her hands over her face. I stepped up into the coach, over the woman and pulled Joline to her feet. She looked up at me.

"Nolo, you saved us. I saw Big Mama running alongside. Oh, Nolo."

She fell into my arms and I guided her down the steps onto the ground.

Big Mama was nearby. Grabbing the reins, I passed them to Joline.

"Here, you take Big Mama. Ride her back to town while I get this stagecoach turned around and headed that way too."

Joline put her foot in the stirrup and threw herself over Big Mama's back and into the saddle, tucking her long skirt in between her legs.

By the time I got back to look inside, the other passengers were in their seats. I cautioned them.

"I'm goin' to get this stagecoach back to town. Horses are dead tired but they can make it. Sit tight and don't fret."

With that I closed the door, put up the step, jumped onto the driver's seat, grabbed the reins, let off the brake and said "giddy yap." I held the reins loosely and with a gentle whipping motion, rippled the leather straps along the backs of the horses. They started with a jerk and then I laid the reins over on the right side. They responded. The coach turned around and we headed back to town. I thought to myself that I had done that rather neatly. Never would have been able to drive a stagecoach when I first arrived in the west. Progress!

Halfway back to town I spotted riders coming toward me. One of them was the stagecoach driver so I figured he wanted to take over. I slowed the horses with a "whoa" or two and they settled down real nice and came to a stop just about the time the horsemen got even with the coach.

I hailed them.

"Sure glad to see you folks. Had a bit of trouble stoppin' this stage, but everyone's OK inside and Miss Joline's ridin' my horse back to town. I'll get down and give you the reins."

I said this to the driver. He looked a bit sheepish as he got off his horse and changed places with me. I mounted his speckled grey and waited for him to take charge of the coach. He had the feel for what he was doing. I marveled at the way he gathered in the heavy leather reins and started the horses moving again. He could give me lessons.

When we reached town there was a crowd standing in the middle of the main street. They were waiting for the coach to be returned and eager to find out what had happened.

When they saw me riding the speckled grey, they all cheered. Joline had preceded me into town and had spread the word that I had stopped the coach.

As I dismounted, people crowded around me and started asking questions. Casper Jones, the jewelry salesman, was in the front.

He yelled.

"Hey, young feller. That was some feat. Glad I got to know ya. You coulda been squashed. Got to meet your sweetie pie. Talk to ya later."

A wizened old man grabbed my hand and held it.

"Ain't never heard tell of anythin' quite like what you done, young feller. My wife was inside that coach. Sure owe you a lot for stoppin' that stage. Come on around and see me when you get yourself settled. Name's Tomkins. I own the livery stable."

I thanked him and then pushed through the crowd to Joline. She looked flushed, but she was standing up straight and holding Big Mama's reins. I took her in my arms and kissed her.

Then her lips were next to my ear and she whispered to me.

"Oh, Nolo. I love you so. I've missed being in your arms. Hold me closer, darling."

I was doing the best I could to hold her. This was something new. We had embraced before, but never like this.

The people stood around talking. As we held each other, I noticed JDB in the crowd, smiling broadly.

Joline relaxed. I knew it was time for us to settle down at the hotel. She was tired after her escapade and needed time to relax. So did I. My body was just reacting to the ordeal.

I had rented two rooms at the hotel. Joline was glad I'd made prior arrangements. The hotel was crowded.

She found her room. I left her to be alone. We would have dinner together in the restaurant downstairs.

I sat in the lobby of the hotel and watched the staircase where Joline would descend. It had been three hours and I waited excitedly.

First saw her at the top of the stairs. Her hair was brushed back and she wore a new dress, one I'd never seen. As she came down the steps, she looked at me. Her pace quickened and soon she was at my side.

"Oh, Nolo. I'm so happy to be with you again. Let's never part, even for a moment. I love you so."

I stood up and put my arm around her waist.

"Missed you Joline. When Buck Redwing and I went to his Indian camp and Buck was with his wife, I thought about you and the times we'd have together. Let's get married right away. I've got the rings."

I pulled the gold bands out of my vest pocket and showed them to her. She eyed them and then looked at me.

"Nolo, they're lovely. Just what I wanted. Where did you find them?"

"They're local. Talked to the jeweler, Casper Jones. He picked them out. Told him I had to get your approval before buying them. Since you like the rings, I'll pay him first chance I get. But let's eat now."

Joline gave me her hand. I led her to a table in the restaurant and looked around. The food was simple from what I saw on the plates of the other diners. It had been a long time since I had sat down to a decent meal with linen on the table and real knives and forks.

A waitress appeared.

"Whatcha goin' ta have? Say, ain't you the feller what stopped the stage this afternoon? That was somethin' to hear about. This your lady friend?"

She sure was nosy, but I liked her friendliness.

"Yes, this is Miss Joline. We're going to be married soon and yes, I'm the one who stopped the stage."

The waitress handed us a menu.

"You the reporter from New York, the one who's huntin' Sam Bass and his gang?"

"Yes, I am. What do you know about Bass?"

"We used to live in the same house. My father's the sheriff hereabouts."

Well, that was news. Bass used to live with the county sheriff. What a switch he'd made from traveling the straight and narrow and living with a lawman to robbing stagecoaches and trains.

"You must tell me more about that. For now, we'd like to eat one of your biggest T-bone steaks surrounded with a few boiled potatoes and some garden peas. You think you can handle that?"

The waitress eyed me again and then jotted down our order.

"And whatcha goin' to have to drink with that?"

"I really want to have some fresh cow's milk. Joline, what would you like?"

Joline wasn't looking at me. She was looking past me at a table across the room. I turned around to see who it was she was staring at and caught a glimpse of a handsome gent all decked out in suit and tie.

"You know him from somewhere, Joline?"

She blushed and I could see she was embarrassed at having been caught off guard.

"Uh, he's just someone I once knew here in Denton. A former beau. We had a short romance."

I glanced around again to see what he looked like, but he was gone.

"Was it serious, Joline?"

She started crying and dug in her handbag for a handkerchief. She pulled out one and dabbed her eyes. It was serious.

"Is there anything I can do?"

I hadn't realized she'd been in love before. She must have known something about men before she met me, but I wanted to think I was teaching her everything about life and that no other man had affected her the way I had.

Joline took a deep breath and looked me straight in the eyes.

"Nolo, I love you very much. I didn't realize how much I loved you until I saw him across the room. I was unhappy with that man every moment I was with him. With you there is life and joy in just living. Even you have changed since I last saw you. I am more in love with you now than ever before. I didn't think that was possible."

The waitress brought our food and we ate in silence, my eyes steadily gazing at Joline. How could my life be any better?

It could be better if I had filed my story with editor Tom back east. My mind returned to business for a moment and I planned out a schedule to send off my stories so the expense money kept coming back from New York.

It was Friday morning and we set the wedding date for Saturday afternoon. The minister of the burned-out church promised to conduct the service at the Grange Hall where he was holding services temporarily.

The local judge issued us a marriage permit. Joline expressed interest in having JDB assist her in preparations for the wedding. There was a new gown to be fashioned and Josie Donna Baines knew a lot about cloth and how to sew it together properly. I wondered what kind of dress Joline would wear at the wedding. But then she had good taste and JDB wouldn't do her wrong.

I got up from my chair in the hotel lobby, stretched my legs, stifled a yawn and looked. Nothing much had changed around here in the last forty years. The wallpaper was streaked with the moisture of a thousand rainstorms. No one had bothered to fix what must be a major leak. The wooden check-in counter showed the boot marks of a myriad nervous cowboys and a string of rowel cuts dotted the floor. I gazed out the front door and made ready to face the world. Soon a new responsibility would be on my shoulders. I'd be married and Joline would need my strength. Like every good western man, I took the job of protecting womenfolk in general and Joline was a whole lot of womanfolk to protect.

I swung open the hotel door, stepped outside and started walking toward the barber shop. It had been ages since I'd seen the inside of one.

Hearing a noise behind me, I turned around. My jaw dropped. Buck Redwing stood just in back of me. A grin crossed his face.

"Buck! What are you doin' in town? Thought I'd never see you again."

I grasped his mighty shoulders and shook him to make sure he was real.

"I came to town for supplies. The man at store told me you were getting hitched tomorrow. Why didn't you tell me? There are many things I must do as a Kiowa before my best friend gets married."

"But Buck. I never thought I'd see you again. You're the first person I'd invite to the wedding if I'd known you'd be around Denton. And what's this about having to do some things Kiowa style?

"Never mind cowboy. I heard what you did stopping that stage. You showed bravery like an Indian. Bravery must be rewarded. Just you wait and see. The biggest bravery is getting married."

With that, Buck turned away and started walking down the wooden sidewalk, his feet making a slap, slap sound on the unfinished wood. I watched him go. Only once did he turn around to look back. There was a wide grin on his face, a grin like I'd never seen before. I wondered what he was planning. Lord, I hoped it didn't include any blood letting.

I continued to the barber shop. Inside was a row of captain's chairs and each was filled. A tall, red-headed man snipped away at what was left of a mostly bald man's hair. Couldn't imagine why someone with so little hair would be getting a haircut. Maybe it was out of habit.

The barber looked up when I came in.

"Greetings, stranger. Ain't got no seats left, but you can drop yourself over there on that butcher table by the window. Grab yourself a copy of Frontier Magazine there. Latest edition just arrived yesterday. Article in it about Sam Bass and Joel Collins. Might like to read that. Everyone around here knows Bass and Collins. Seems like Collins got himself killed up Kansas way."

I grabbed the magazine, sat down on the table top and flipped open to where my article was located. Sure enough, the editor had given me a byline as he usually did. There were a few corrections, but I expected that.

There was a shadow cast on the page as I read. A flaxen-haired gent peered over my shoulder, reading my article.

He looked at me when I turned my head.

"Hey, ain't you that Nolo Blunt who stopped the stagecoach yesterday? You be the same Blunt who wrote this here story?"

The other men turned toward me. It was as if everyone was waiting for me to answer.

"Yup. I'm the same feller. Gettin' married. Need a haircut bad."

That's all it took. The barber whipped the sheet off the gentleman he was working on, dusted off the chair and invited me with a sweep of his hand to sit down.

"Uh, I'd like to get my haircut soon, but there's all these other men ahead of me. I want to take my turn."

Enthusiastic voices greeted my words. Other men said I should go now. I heard someone say it was the least they could do for a poor misguided easterner who stopped stagecoaches with his bare hands and wrote articles for a living.

I slipped into the barber's chair and hoped he would be gentle.

# Chapter 18

Joline wouldn't see me. I knocked on her door early in the morning and all she said was for me to go away. She mumbled something about being superstitious about the groom seeing the bride before the wedding. What a dumb custom. All I wanted to tell her was that Buck Redwing was planning an Indian ritual for our marriage.

Joline wouldn't listen. I finally went downstairs to the dining room and ordered coffee. What I really needed at this moment was a shot of red eye whiskey.

The coffee was hot and it warmed my insides and gave me a lift that would carry me through the day. Where had I gone wrong? Getting married was not my intention when first arriving in Nebraska. But Joline had changed that! The west had changed me and, most of all, Buck Redwing had helped turn me into a western man, capable of all kinds of deeds— even marriage.

I looked up from my coffee to see Mr. Tomkins, the livery stable owner, striding toward me. He looked worried. .

"It's your horse, Mr. Blunt."

I was shocked. Was Big Mama in trouble on my wedding day?

I stammered out something about my concern, but Tomkins just laughed.

"Nah, it ain't nothin' to do with her health. She's just actin' kinda strange that's all. Think you better get on over to the stable and see to her. She's a mighty fine piece a horseflesh. I think she misses you."

I thanked Tomkins and overturned my chair while bolting for the door. Big Mama was acting strange. Never thought anything like this would happen.

She was just standing there. Her eyes were droopy looking and her ears were down. One eye drifted my way and suddenly she lit up. It was too much for me. I rushed to her stall, undid the metal hasp and reached my hand up to console her.

"It's all right, old girl. I'm not going to forget about you just because I'm getting married. You know Joline as well as you know me and you like her. What's the matter, old girl?"

The railing outside the stable was free and I tied Big Mama's rope around it in a hitch knot. Maybe she just needed to be out on the street for a while. I'd have to remember to take care of my horse even though I was getting married.

Noise! What was that noise? All of a sudden the street was filled with pinto ponies. Buck, dressed in dozens of feathers, deerhide shirt, fringed pants, and beaded shoes led the way. It was a sight. Never before had I seen so many Indians all dressed for a special event.

"Buck. You're here. You brought your friends for the wedding."

"We take you now. Come quietly. We prepare you for your mating. Get your horse ready."

Big Mama was saddled and I climbed aboard.

We had ridden about an hour when up ahead I saw a cluster of tepees. Smoke came out of the top of one. It was the same sweat house where I had first sat with the Kiowa clan.

Redwing pulled up now. I bridled back Big Mama. The other horsemen rode on, then as if by plan, halted their horses and dropped onto the ground, dust swirling around them.

"Buck, thought your camp was a day's ride away."

"We move camp just for you."

Redwing's bare arm now encircled my shoulders and he led me toward the open flap of the sweat house.

Inside it was dark, but there was something in the air I had not smelled before. It was a sickening-sweet smell, like burning leaves soaked in sugar.

The others entered the tent and seated themselves around the glowing campfire.

Redwing now pushed me into a buffalo skin-covered seat.

I didn't know what Buck meant but it must be part of an Indian ritual.

My old friend, the fire tender, was busy at his work of pouring water over the hot rocks piled above the red-orange embers. Clouds of steam filled the tepee. Memories of my first encounter with the sweat house returned. Perspiration ran off my brow. I began to feel weak.

As if on cue, the peace pipe was passed. As it reached me, I noticed a difference in the aroma. It mingled with the same sweet smell of the sweat house.

Redwing sat next to me. I turned to him.

"Buck, is this some special tobacco? Will it harm me?"

"You smoke. Can't turn back the ceremony now. If we stop, you die. It's the law of Kiowa. Once the pipe of peace is lit, all must smoke."

Was Redwing telling the truth?

I drew in a large amount of smoke, held it, inhaled, then let it out. Nothing. I took another pull at the pipe, then passed it to the loin-cloth clad Indian sitting on my right.

Although it was morning, it was dark in the tent except for the coals giving out their reddish opulence. Opulence! I hadn't used that word since I was in high school back in New York. What was happening?

I looked around the campfire and observed the others who had used the pipe. Each had a dreamy expression. For the first time I realized that what I had inhaled so greedily must have special powers.

My mind clouded and I passed out on the leaf-covered dirt floor. As I lost consciousness, my thoughts were of Joline.

Someone shook me. A splash of cool water hit my face. I opened my eyes. Buck stared back.

"You slept. You dreamt. I watched you. Your body moved. Now you tell us what you saw."

Could I remember enough to tell the Indians?

I sat up light-headed. Immediately I knew that was a mistake. It took several minutes to shake off a faint feeling. As the blood returned to my head, the memory of my dream became clear.

"Buck, had a vision. Give me a minute. I'll tell you about it."

Buck handed me a drink of water. I gulped it down.

I rubbed my head and then as if a silent hand guided me, I rose and faced the Indians grouped around me.

Their eyes stared back. For an instant I felt important, perhaps as important as their chief. My dream was clear now. I started speaking.

"Sam Bass. My vision was of Sam Bass. He has just robbed a train while I watch and now he's coming toward me. There are two, maybe three or more men with him. He reaches me and slaps me in the face. I fall to the ground and watch as Bass and his men climb on their horses and ride off. I get up, find Big Mama and ride after the men. There's shooting up ahead now. It's the sheriff and his posse. They've been waiting for Bass. As I ride up, the shooting is over. Six men are on the ground. They look like they are dead. But Bass is not one of them. The sheriff mounts his horse and rides rapidly away from the scene. He's trailing someone. It must be Bass. I follow. I ride through underbrush that scrapes against my legs. It's a long time I ride and then I see Bass. He's lying by a tree. He's been shot. The sheriff is standing over him. I approach. Bass looks up at me. He's dying. I bend down close to him. He looks me in the eyes. And then his body goes rigid."

I was exhausted. I sat down and held my head in my hands. Buck's hands were on my shoulders. He spoke to me softly.

"You tell vision. Now we eat."

Raw buffalo liver was set before me. I looked around me. The Indians were tearing into the meat, grabbing huge chunks and shoving it into their mouths. Blood dripped down their faces. They were enjoying it enormously. What was I to do?

I ate the liver. No one was going to say that Nolo Blunt wouldn't go along with the matrimony ritual. There must be something to be gained by eating organs of a large animal. Despite a distaste I had for livers and kidneys, I bit into the raw meat. I didn't like it, but tried to keep my face from showing my disgust. Buck looked at me.

"You do well, Nolo. Buffalo liver will make you strong for being with a woman. Eat all of it. You'll see."

If eating liver was all that was needed, then I would be the greatest husband in the world on this wedding night. When I finished the first piece, Buck handed me more.

I began to wonder when all this would be over so I could get back to town. It was getting toward noon—just hours before the ceremony.

"Buck, when will we leave? Promised Joline to be at the hall."

"You make it on time. You have one more test."

With that, Buck stood up and signaled to an Indian who was standing by the entry flap. He waved to someone outside the tepee. Soon a medicine man entered, looked around at the seated figures, saw where I was sitting and came toward me.

He was tall and ugly with a buffalo headdress that made him seem even taller. The horns didn't match. One went right and the other went left. This design must have a special meaning to this Kiowa medicine man as he danced up and down in front of me, the great horns jiggling on his head. The bells on his legs made loud accompaniment to his movements.

Buck signaled me to lie down. My heart wasn't in it, but this whole ceremony must be important to him. Soon the cavorting medicine man leaped around my outstretched body. Could smell his putrid moccasins he was so close.

The dance ended. I lay still. The medicine man approached me. He held a talon, taken from a fallen eagle.

His knee pressed against my chest. Buck held my right arm to the ground. Lord, I hoped they weren't going to bleed me.

I felt the tap, tap, tap of the needle-sharp object on my shoulder and then the sting of a knife being pressed against my skin. When I tried to look at what was happening, Buck reached up and kept my head from turning.

I thought of everything that had happened to me since I'd been out west. My capture by the gang, the tornado and our narrow escape from the sheriff of Big Springs. But this experience was one for my book.

The pain was intense now and I struggled to get up and away from this madman who was doing something to my shoulder.

"Stay down, Nolo. It'll soon be over. You're a strong man."

Buck's words relaxed me. It was better this way. If I didn't fight it, the pain was less. The process had to stop soon. I would have to bear it.

My thoughts turned toward Joline. It was better to think of her than what the Indian was doing to my shoulder.

The medicine man stopped, stood up and grabbed my hand. He pulled me to a standing position. He took some powder out of a bag and sprinkled it on my shoulder.

"Good medicine. Keep wound clean."

He said something more in Kiowa, jiggled his rattle, danced around me once, then retreated to the flap of the tepee by hopping backwards. The ceremony was over.

I glanced down at my shoulder. Lord, a tattoo. Only the sailors I'd seen on the wharves of New York had tattoos. It appeared to be a young buffalo. It must have a significance.

The others in the tent were up now and making a curving line in front of me. The first one stepped forward, grabbed me by the shoulder, said something I couldn't understand, then let the next man step forward. Buck was last. He reached for my hand, pulled me toward him and clasped his left arm around my back. His mouth was near my ear.

"You are now ready for a wife."

He stepped back.

"Young buffalo knows what to do when he finds a cow in the pasture. You are man to make a bed beside your wife. You'll raise plenty calves."

This Indian humor escaped me, but if it made Buck happy to tell me about how I should be prolific in producing children, I was satisfied. I smiled, then ran my fingers over the buffalo tattoo. I tried to imitate Buck's speech.

"Medicine man do good job. Young buffalo joins his cow. He have fun in the pasture. Now we go."

Buck threw back his head and laughed. The others in the tepee joined him.

He motioned me toward the flap. I could see Big Mama in the distance. She was tied to a tether rope. As I came out into the air, she lifted her head and looked at me. I made my way to her through the ankle-high prairie grass and soon was at her side.

I untied the reins and led Big Mama to a small creek that flowed next to the camp. There were cottonwood trees here and their branches filtered the light from the orange sun high overhead. Suddenly, it struck me. The sun was straight up and I was supposed to be meeting Joline at the hall this afternoon. It was almost an hour's ride back to town. If I hurried, I would just make it. Buck mounted his pinto. He motioned with his hand for me to join him.

The Grange hall was beginning to fill up. The people inside turned to look over their shoulders when we arrived. What a sight it must have been as our group rode down the street. A troop of forty Indians, all decked out in their finest clothing, mounted on matching pinto horses—and me, dressed in only a loin cloth, proudly displaying a tattoo of a young buffalo on my bare shoulder. No other reporter ever arrived at his wedding in a more outlandish state.

Joline was at the entrance. She stood inside the door of the hall and looked angry. I slid off my horse and approached her.

"Joline. I made it. Tried to tell you this morning that Buck was going to take me off. Well, I lived through it and I'm here. Give me a few moments and I'll get properly dressed and return."

Her voice was soft but an undercurrent of something reached my ears.

"*No-lo* Blunt. You get yourself out of here now and return with yourself properly attired for our wedding. I have never been so shocked in my life. And what's that picture of an animal doing on your shoulder?"

I covered the tattoo with my hand.

"Well, Joline. I'm now a member of the Kiowa tribe. We have smoked jimsonweed, eaten raw liver, and the medicine man inducted me into the clan. I've never been so proud of anything in my life."

She stood there glaring at me. There wasn't anything else she could say. I walked back down the path and through the gate to Big Mama. Turning in the saddle for a moment, I saw Joline wave. She stomped her foot, turned and walked away. Would she be there when I got back?

# Chapter 19

Back at the hotel, I dressed quickly and took time to wash my face. Rolling around in the dirt of the sweat house had given me a savage appearance. No wonder Joline wondered what had happened to me when she saw me.

I was about to step out into the hall when I heard male voices.

"He's got to be around here. He's got to die. Which one is his room?"

"Over here, number 9."

My room was number 9. I quickly shut the door and locked it. They must be after me. What had I done now? Couldn't take any chances on missing Joline again. I had to get out.

There was a knock at the door. I pushed myself through the window and launched myself downward toward a shed-like roof just below me. I hit it with both feet and it gave, the entire structure falling away with me riding it like a bucking horse.

I hit the ground running.

No one was on the street at this time of day. Back at the window, two men stared at me. One aimed a gun.

And then I heard the shot. Dust kicked up behind me. For the second time in my life, someone was shooting at me. But why?

I zigzagged toward the wooden sidewalk and took cover using the buildings as shelter between me and my attackers. Something told me to get out of there fast. I ran toward the livery stable where I could get Big Mama and ride back to the hall.

My wedding day was turning out to be the worst day of my life.

I led Big Mama out through the rear of the stable, mounted and headed down the road toward the hall.

Over my shoulder, I could see two riders following behind.

Joline stood at the Grange hall door as I rode past. I waved and pointed behind me. She looked crushed, but when she saw that two men were chasing me, she glanced back and gave me a hurried movement of her hand. In that instant, she understood what I was doing. Life without Joline would be empty indeed, but now I had to worry about life itself.

Big Mama blew easy now. She had her second wind.

I found myself on the road heading toward the Murphy ranch. Where was the sheriff when I needed him? My gun was back at the hotel.

A quick glance back told me the men were gaining. One of them had a pistol. I ducked down on Big Mama's neck as the first bullet whizzed by, spurred Mama and she responded with a burst that carried me around a bend just as he fired again. I looked for cover. There wasn't any. Had to make it to Murphy's and get help.

Big Mama's hooves now made a rapid beat on the rough dirt road. Up ahead was the first outbuilding of the ranch. What a welcome sight. I reined in and swerved off to the lane that led toward the main house.

Jim Murphy saw me ride up. From his ivy-covered porch, he motioned for me to dismount and follow him. I had no argument with that, quickly tying Big Mama's reins to the railing.

Sitting in a wing chair in the parlor was Sam Bass. He had a grin on his face. I couldn't think of any reason why he should be so happy. I was still out of breath. Those two men could still be after me.

The door slammed shut behind me. Underwood and Jackson stood there. They seemed to be out of breath too.

Bass snickered and said, "Told the boys to find you and scare you. Guess they did just that."

Find me and scare me! It had been those two at the door who chased me, shot at me and frightened me half out of my wits. I'd never forgive Bass for that let alone Underwood and Jackson.

I shook my fist at him.

"That was the damnedest thing I ever heard of anyone doing to another human being. Ready to get married and your two gunslingers almost made holes in me on my wedding day. Joline's still waiting."

He just sat there, the grin still crossing his face. He started to laugh.

"Now hold on there fella."

He paused.

"Boys just had some fun with you. If they'd wanted to plug you, you'd be mincemeat by now. Sit down here a spell. I want to talk."

I sat down, but kept an eye on Underwood. He was the shifty one who'd once held a gun at my head.

Bass continued:

"We're movin' and I wanted you here. Maybe gonna pull my last job then settle down somewheres here in

Texas and raise me some cattle. But you been with us on a small holdup. Want you to write about what may be my last one. Gonna be a train."

I couldn't believe it. Bass was finally taking me in on the planning of a robbery. I'd really have something to write about. Needed to know more.

"Where we headed? I've got to tell Joline. She'll worry about me."

Bass eyed me the way he always did, head tilted to the left side, eyelids partially closed, his mouth caught up in a bow shape.

"Hadn't thought about Joline. Guess there's no problem. She knows this gang better than anyone else on earth. I'll send the boys for her. You two can get hitched later. Right now we got business."

Bass busied himself with Underwood and Jackson talking about the Texas and Pacific Railroad and the small town of Mesquite near Dallas. He also mentioned some names of men I didn't know. One was Billy Collins. I remembered he was Joline's younger brother and wondered why Bass would be bringing him in. Sam Pipes and Albert Herndon also would join the gang. Hadn't seen them before.

The excitement of being included in the planning of a train robbery had made me forget about the unsettling experience I had just been through. I thought about Big Mama being sweaty after the big chase. I excused myself saying I was going to walk my horse.

Big Mama was right where I'd left her, still breathing hard. I untied the reins, patted her on the side of her head and walked her slowly down the trail.

A noise at the door made me turn around. Underwood stuck his head out. He was watching. Felt like a prisoner again.

A mile or two of walking would get Big Mama back in shape. Then I'd rub her down and get her oats for dinner.

These times with my horse were the best. Never before had I thought an animal could mean so much to a man. Horses in New York had been objects one used to ride in Central Park. But here in the west, a horse was part of a man, an indispensable part that could mean the difference between success and failure in life. Right now I was glad to have Big Mama by my side.

Underwood was following. He strode toward me, his fingers fondling the butt of his pistol. He looked mad.

"Just want you to know I got my eye on you. Coulda plugged you good back in town, but Sam told me to bring you back without any holes in you. Don't you be gettin' any ideas about ridin' into town and tellin' the sheriff about our train robbin' plan. Be just like you to do somethin' like that."

I just listened. Underwood didn't care too much for what I was doing with the gang. Couldn't really blame him because I'd be thinking the same thing if I was in his shoes.

"No need to worry, Underwood. I'm just walkin' my horse to cool her down, then I'll put her in the barn. Tell Sam I'll be in when I get through."

He turned to go back to the ranch house, stopped, looked back and finally shrugged his shoulders and hurried to the porch.

Joline arrived the next day. Her hair was shiny and curled. She wore a new outfit, tailored brown leather jacket with matching skirt and a blouse of blue silk that set off the patterned scarf she had knotted about her neck. These must be the honeymoon clothes she'd bought at the general store in town.

I'd been working on a story to send my editor, but I stopped in mid-sentence. I threw my arms around her, kissed her neck, then her lips. She melted to me. I knew then that all was forgiven about our delayed wedding. I held her close for a long time, didn't want to let her go.

Still holding hands, I led her to the sofa. We sat close, our eyes meeting, our faces reflecting the joy of love. Joline started to say something.

"...and then I saw you ride by and was angry until I saw who it was chasing you. Then I knew what was going on and waited until Sam sent Jim Murphy for me. What will we do now, Nolo?"

"Let's get married. No reason we can't finish what we started. It may take a few weeks. Sam's planning a train robbery and I want to be in on it. You can help me with my story."

I didn't know how that would set, but she smiled and snuggled up to me, her arm reaching around my waist, her fingertips resting on my ribs. She began squeezing me with her hand. She'd have to stop doing that.

Joline showed no mercy. She moved her head close to my ear and whispered something. Couldn't quite understand. It was something about finding a room somewhere in the house where we could be alone. My answer was what my head told me to say, not my emotions.

"Joline, it's difficult for me too, but I think we should wait. It'll only be a few weeks. Then we can be married and be together like that. I'd feel better about it."

She pushed away from me slightly. There still was a glow about her, a redness in her cheeks that I hadn't seen before. Her eyes twinkled.

"You're always the one, Nolo. You've a sensible head on your shoulders. You're right of course. It's just that I..."

She didn't finish her sentence. She didn't have to.

Bass and his men entered the room.

Sam's bass voice echoed into the rafters.

"Well, look who we have here. Joline Collins as big as life and twice as rosy. Ain't seen you for a while. When was the last time? Let me see. Musta been back at the hideout up Big Springs way. Been a lot a good Texas water down the Brazos since then. Glad you decided to join us."

He walked closer to her and took her by the hands.

"Sorry to hear about Joel. One-a-the good ones. Me and him was just about like brothers. He died brave, I hear. You plant him with a good headstone?"

Tears started at the corners of Joline's eyes. She dug in her pocket and pulled out a handkerchief. The initials J. B. made me think. Of course, Joline Blunt. She already had changed her name.

Her voice was shaky as she answered Sam.

"Joel had a nice burial. Mom and Dad came up from Dallas County to claim the body at Ellis, Kansas. Buried him there. It was a long trip for all of us and not a very pleasant one. Dad Albert had a stone mason make an angel with its wings outstretched to guard over his grave."

Joline was crying. I moved close and put my arm around her. My voice was shaky as I tried to comfort her.

"It's all right, Joline. It's over now. Joel's been laid to rest. We've got to get on with life."

She looked at me and stopped crying. Guess my words helped.

Sam continued.

"Well, glad you're here to keep your newspaper boy company. He does get a bit unsettled without you, kind of like a bull that ain't had no cow rub up against him in a long time. Guess you know what I mean."

Joline smiled. Her mood had changed. She put her arm around my waist.

"Sam, you say the darndest things. But it's true. I need Nolo as much as he needs me and I thank you for bringing us together again. What's this about a train robbery you're planning?"

Bass wiped his mouth with his hand and moved to the massive oak dining table.

"We be getting ready for a little action. Yes, that's right. Got your little brother, Billy, involved too. Sent him down to Mesquite, little burg east of Dallas you know. Billy's goin' to see how the land lays. Sent Herndon to Dallas. Got to know what the train company's doin' about protection."

Bass had a piece of paper in front of him with crude drawings of a train station. I hadn't realized how thorough Bass could be. The details of his planning would go well in my story. Tom, my editor, liked to have as complete a write-up of an event as possible. My hat was off to Sam Bass for letting me join him for this caper.

Bass still talked about his plans.

"And you wouldn't believe what's happenin' here in Denton County. Every lawman on earth's been after me and the boys. Got to be sly as a fox to outwit them. That's part a my nature. Used to play hide and seek when I was a kid up Indiana way. Was good at it too. Ain't nobody could find me if'n I really tried to hide."

He moved to the large window that overlooked the front of Murphy's ranch house. After a while he turned and spoke.

"Got to be gettin' on down the road. Goin' to take the boys with me. You two stay here at Murphy's. Be at the Mesquite station along about ten o'clock in the evenin' on Wednesday. Stay outa sight. You might just get somethin' to write about, Blunt."

With those words Bass motioned to his companions and was out the door.

I felt good that Bass now trusted me enough to let me roam free. Maybe it was because Joline was with me and her younger brother was a member of the gang. Guess Bass figured Joline would have an influence on me if I was to do anything crazy, like telling the sheriff about the train robbery plans for Mesquite.

I knew the ride would be a long one, so I prepared my saddlebags and stuffed in some oats for my horse.

# Chapter 20

Joline and I rode into Mesquite. It had been a grueling trip from Murphy Ranch, but we were together on the trail and that made time pass quickly.

Entering the town, I carefully looked around. Joline told me she'd ridden through the place once. There wasn't much there, one general store where the local people could buy their food supplies and next to it the Mesquite Bar and Cafe. A large sign proclaimed, "Eat here, drink here, and be merry."

Just past the saloon was a stable where a muscular man still worked, even this late, the fire in his forge flaring up and shooting out sparks as he pumped on it with an ancient bellows. Every town out west had a blacksmith.

Beyond was the train station.

"We'll put the horses in the livery stable, over there, Joline. Then we'll find the train station waiting room. All the action will take place near there and we'll have front row seats."

Joline nodded. We rode on in silence.

The waiting room was small. A hand-hewn wood bench stretched from one end of the back wall to the other. The upright beams were rough-hewn, ax marks still visible.

Joline sat near me in a corner. I looked out the open double doors that faced the tracks. From there I could see everything that would take place outside. This was a moment I had waited for and I didn't want to miss it.

"Things should start to happen soon," I whispered. "It's almost 10 o'clock."

She snuggled up against me and put her lips to my ear.

"Nolo, when this is all over, let's get away from Texas. Maybe we can go to New York. I've had enough. My brother's no longer alive because of this kind of life. He'd still be here if he and the gang hadn't robbed that train up in Nebraska. It won't be long before my younger brother meets the same end. Nolo, I want it to stop. I just want a quiet life with you, raise a family, but not here—not in this Godforsaken wild country. I want to be civilized again."

Joline had never talked like that. It took some time to absorb what she had said. Take her back to New York? That was possible, but my career as a writer led me all over the country and I wanted to make the most of it. My place now was in the west.

Joline looked at me with those dreamy eyes. I felt myself melting just a little.

"True, we could go back to New York and we will some day, but for now my job is right here. I've got to finish the story about Bass and then there'll be others to write. We can make a life of it here. It doesn't all have to be train robberies."

Just as I said that a large man with a star on his vest entered. His boots shook the floor. His grey-speckled moustache covered up what once must have been a prominent mouth. He studied us for a moment and moved closer.

"You two lovebirds been here long?"

It wasn't what I expected him to say.

"Been here about fifteen minutes."

The less I said the better.

He reached up with his right hand and pushed back his battered straw hat. At the same moment I noticed a tattoo on his four fingers. The artist had spelled out L-O-V-E just below the knuckle.

"You two see anything suspicious around here, anybody actin' strange-like?"

"Haven't seen anyone, sir. Joline and I were just sittin' here talkin' about our future together. We're fixin' to get married soon and this was the quietest spot in town we could find. We're waitin' for a train. You lookin' for someone?"

He eyed me suspiciously. I could see the furrows in his brow ripple as he pondered what I'd said.

"Might just be somethin' happenin' here tonight. Been some strangers askin' questions 'round town. Bass gang's been robbin' trains in these parts, but I don't think old Bass himself knows about Mesquite or me. I'm Sheriff John Barnes. If he shows up around here, he'll get a warm greeting with my six-gun."

With that he stuck out his chest, reached his left thumb under the lapel of his vest and pulled it forward. I could see something tattooed on his other fingers. It was H-A-T-E.

This man had an ego problem as did most of the sheriffs I'd met.

"We'll keep our eyes open, won't we Joline?"

Again the sheriff looked at me dubiously. I think I'd overplayed my hand, but there was no backing away now. Saying anything more would just make it worse. He slipped through the doorway, his eyes still on me as he walked down the train station platform. I thought that we'd hear from him again.

Joline looked frightened.

"It'll be all right, dear. The man's a blowhard. I've seen his kind before. He may remember us, but we'll be away from here by then."

"I know that, Nolo. It's not that. It's my little brother. If Billy's along on this raid he could be killed and I'd lose another member of my family. When will this end?"

I had no answer. Just sat there and looked at her. She was in a different mood.

"Nolo, I'm so frightened. Hold me close."

She nestled up to me and I put my arm around her.


A faint whistle sounded in the east, bringing us back to reality. It meant only one thing. Sam would be waiting for the train to stop here. I looked at my pocket watch. It was exactly 10:20 p.m. The train was twenty minutes late.

I whispered to Joline.

"Train's coming. Something's going to happen. We better be ready."

She roused herself, straightened her dress, fluffed up her hair and looked at me.

I stood up and went to the door of the waiting room and looked outside toward the platform.

Bass was there with six other men. They were hanging back in the shadows waiting for the train. Each wore a blue patterned handkerchief over his mouth and nose. Only the eyes showed, but I recognized Underwood, Jackson and Bass. The others were new to me.

Then a screen door next to me opened. A station agent dragged a mail sack onto the platform.

A flickering light approached and I heard the sound of a chugging locomotive. The train was near.

Moving behind a wooden post, I watched as Bass dodged along toward me against the station wall. The agent just stood there looking the other way, waiting for the train.

The booming voice of Bass echoed on the night air. There was the glint of moonlight reflected from the barrel of the pistol he held.

"Hold up your hands!"

The startled mail handler looked at Bass, glanced down at the gun and put up his hands. He was scared. Now he muttered something.

"Don't shoot. I'm just a poor farm boy. You can have anything I have. Don't have nothin'. Ain't armed. You can search me."

He moved back against the wall, his hands still raised as high as he could get them, his mouth twitching, his eyes roving from side to side.

Bass waved his arm in the air and soon the other members of the gang rushed to his side. He assigned one to guard the station agent and then he motioned for the others to gather around him.

Joline popped her head out to see what was going on. Bass saw her. He pointed his gun at her and in that movement he caught sight of me behind the post.

"All right, you two. Get over here. Don't want no witnesses runnin' off to find the sheriff. Make it quick."

Joline joined me, took my hand and together we went to stand by the agent. Joline shook. I tried to console her.

"It's going to be fine, Joline. We just should have been somewhere else tonight."

My words were really meant for the man with his hands in the air standing next to me. Bass was pretty smart. He was giving us a way out if anyone should question us. And more than that, he was giving me a chance to watch the entire robbery from the vantage point of the passenger platform right where the action would take place. I had to thank him for that.

The train pulled into the station now and as the steam from the locomotive spewed out beneath it and onto the tracks, Bass was ready.

"On to her, boys. She's ours!"

Jackson jumped up the steps to the engine cab. Within seconds he had the fireman and engineer standing with their hands up. Both men moved quickly to the platform as Jackson shoved the nose of his gun repeatedly into the fireman's ribs. Soon they were standing alongside Joline and me.

There was a disturbance down the track. Just for a moment I caught sight of a man with a lantern as he jumped off the train. In an instant he must have seen what was happening. He extinguished the lamp and without warning he started firing at the gang. I flattened myself on the platform, pulling Joline down with me. Hadn't bargained for this. There were real bullets flying now as Underwood and Bass fired back at the man down the track who crouched next to the passenger car.

In the confusion I saw the engineer take advantage of the situation and try to get back into the cab, but Bass was too fast for him. As the man reached the top step of the metal ladder, Bass grabbed him by the leg and pulled him back onto the platform.

"Where ya goin' there Mr. Train man? Don't pull nothin' like that again lest you want a bullet in the leg to slow you down."

Bass pushed the man toward where the rest of us were.

"You stay put there, Mr. Engineer. No time for you to be a hero."

Just as Bass uttered his words, there came a fusillade of shots from down the track. What a plucky guy down there. He was worth an interview when this was over.

The gang returned fire and one of them must have found flesh with his bullet. There was a disturbing yell from the man down the track and I saw him reach for his left shoulder. He took cover under the train, but even with a wound in his arm he still fired back. Joline and I stayed flat on the platform. Joline had that look about her again, that frightened look.

"Stay down, Joline. That's all we can do now. Keep your eyes open. Want to capture all this in the story. You can help."

"Nolo Blunt! You talk to me about writing a story at a time like this. Our lives are in danger and all you want to do is write. What kind of man are you? Why don't you stop this whole thing now. Run and get the sheriff."

Sometimes Joline made sense with what she said, but this wasn't one of those times.

"Just stay low Joline. It'll soon be over and then we can get away from here."

It wasn't enough that firing was coming from down the track, now someone was shooting at Bass from the train itself. Looked to me like the firing was coming from the car where much of the gold and currency would be kept. The wide wooden door was only partly ajar, but the nose of a pistol poked out through the opening. The man behind the gun aimed his shots wisely, making the bandits hunt for cover. I counted five shots and then the door closed and through the cracks at the bottom, I saw a light go out.

A blast from a shotgun made me turn my head to the right and just as I looked that way a man at the baggage car ducked inside and pulled the big door closed. I thought to myself that Bass had encountered more action than he wanted.

The shotgun blasts got closer now and pellets bounced up from the metal covering next to the track. I nudged Joline and, keeping my head down, pulled her behind me around a corner of the waiting room.

"You're right, Joline. Let's get out of here. We'll crawl to the end of this building, then make a run for it. Sam's too busy to notice."

We made our move and reached the safety of a low stone wall. Then we bent over and raced toward the town.

We stood up as we reached the local saloon. I pushed open the swinging doors and we walked in.

No one was in sight. I went to the bar and looked behind it. A shotgun greeted me. As I slowly raised up my arms, the man at the trigger spoke.

"Boy, you don't know how close you came to gettin' yore head blown off."

The man stood up. When he saw Joline, he backed off.

"Sorry, ma'am, but your boyfriend here ought to have better sense than to go pokin' his head behind places when there's a holdup at the station goin' on. What you two doin' here anyway?"

"The bullets were flyin' back there on the platform and we sneaked out when no one was lookin'. Maybe we can stay here until the shootin' is over."

"Yeh, get around behind the bar over there and keep still. Things should be quietin' down soon."

We took his advice. Bumped against someone as I scrunched down. The man turned his head. I immediately recognized him as the sheriff who had found us in the waiting room. Barnes was his name, John Barnes. So this is how the lawman of Mesquite spent his time in thwarting train robberies. It'd make a great story.

## Chapter 21

More information was needed. Why was this lawman hiding under the saloon counter? I'd have to be blunt.

His head was still turned around toward me. His eyes stared at me like a mountain lion before leaping at its prey.

I spoke first.

"There's a whole lot of shooting going on at the depot, sheriff."

He continued to stare, but now a slight grin started at the corners of his mouth.

"Ya caught me."

That's all he said. He turned around and crouched down even closer to the floor.

I tapped him on the rump.

His head snapped back toward me again. His voice was gruff.

"What do you want? Don't be pokin' me."

"I want to find out, sheriff, why you're not out there tryin' to stop that train robbery."

He shifted his position so he could look me full in the face.

"Ain't none a your business. I got my reasons, but I ain't goin' to tell them to you."

"But sheriff, there's a lot of shootin' goin' on out there. You ought to be organizing a posse or something to put a stop to the bloodshed, unless you're no longer sheriff."

He grabbed my shirt by the lapels and pulled my face up to his. I could smell his beer breath. Every whisker on his pock-marked face stood out. He hadn't shaved in days. His eyes were bloodshot. I'd say he was drunk.

His voice rambled.

"You ain't got no reason to know, but since you're a nosy one, I'll tell ya. Got me a case a that there diree-ya and if you don't get outa my way, you're goin' to be one sad character for scooting in behind me under this counter."

I crawled backward pushing Joline along with me. Sheriff Barnes grunted as he followed me. He stood up, brushed off his shirt and rushed out. The saloon door slammed. I hoped he made it to the outdoor privy.

And then it was quiet. There wasn't any noise coming from the train station. I listened intently. Not a sound.

"Joline, you hear anything?"

"There are no shots. Maybe Sam's gotten away."

I put my finger to my lips and made a hushing sound.

"Don't say that too loud. Someone could hear you. They might think you know him too well if you call him Sam."

She shook her head.

"Nolo, let's get out of here before that sheriff gets back. We can get our horses and ride off before he knows we've gone."

"Good idea Joline, but I want to check the station first. There are people to interview about the robbery. Might not get this chance again."

Joline's voice was crisp.

"Nolo Blunt. You get me back to Murphy's ranch and right now. I've had enough of your writing for an evening."

My heart was with Joline but my brain was with the opportunity at hand.

"Can't do it, Joline. You know the way back to the ranch. No, it's too late. Why don't you get a room in town? I'll saddle your horse and have it ready when we ride. I'll see you at the hotel."

The scene at the depot was all confusion. The train still was in place and there was a little smoke coming out now. The fireman must have banked the coal fire under the boiler anticipating an investigation before they could leave.

The hostages were no longer standing against the wall on the platform. A few people moved around, but there was no sign of Bass and his gang.

The agent was in his office. I stepped through the open doorway.

"Name's Nolo Blunt. Remember me? Joline and I were against the wall with you during the robbery."

The man looked up from what he was writing and stared.

"Sure. I remember you. Had your girl with you. You were lucky. Saw you slip away. What do you want?"

"I'm a reporter for Frontier Magazine. Been in the west here tryin' to get a line on the Bass gang. Looks like I got into the middle of it. Maybe you can give me some information for my story. You'd like to have your name in an article wouldn't you? I heard Bass tell you to hold up your hands. Just wanted to know what went through your mind at that moment. And by the way, what's your name?"

"Name's Zurn, Jake Zurn, and I don't mind appearin' in your story. Just spell my name right. You spell it with a Z. What did I feel? Well, I thought maybe my life was over. Felt jittery, kind of a tingle inside me. Wondered what the bullet would feel like when it went through me. Wondered if I'd live. That's how I felt."

"You come from around here?"

"Nope. Hail from Pennsylvania. My wife was here too. I saw her come out of the station and onto the platform while the robbery was goin' on. One of the robbers threatened her with a gun, but she just turned back and locked herself in the office. You saw the robber fire through the door. That was my wife in there. What a woman. She wasn't hurt"

I'd have to get a statement from his wife.

"You goin' to stick around town now or are you goin' back home?"

"Figure I might as well stay here. Been thinkin' about it, but my home's here now. How many times am I goin' to be held at gunpoint? Sooner or later they'll catch Bass and hang him. He won't show up 'round here again anyway. He'll move on to fresh territory."

Zurn turned back to his writing.

I saw the man who had fired at the robbers when the action first started. He was dressed in a train conductor's uniform. His left arm was in a sling. He looked pale, but he was standing up, talking to the engineer. I interrupted.

"Name's Nolo Blunt. I'm a reporter. Want to get a statement from you two about the robbery. I was one of the hostages against the wall."

Turning toward the conductor, I said, "You're a plucky guy. Don't know your name, but saw what you did. What was that, a derringer you had at first?"

"Alvord. Julius Alvord that's me. Yup. Had my trusty pea shooter with me. Ain't no good for nothin' but close in stuff like poker games and personal protection, but it was the only piece I had on me when the fight started. Gave those bums a good run too. If I'd had me a rifle, it'd been another story."

"Saw you disappear and come back."

"Went back inside the train and got my six-shooter. Can't fight no battles without the proper artillery. Served in the Illinois Eleventh during the war and killed me a few rascals you know. Ain't afraid to be shot at, but I'll get my share when I shoot back."

"The wound. Tell me about it."

"Should never have happened. Got careless. Stuck my arm out to brace myself for a shot. One a them bandits got lucky. Put a hole in my best hat. I figure on sendin' Bass a bill when this is over. Hats ain't cheap."

I fingered the hole in Alvord's hat.

"When you got wounded I saw you drop down under the passenger car. You kept firing."

"I only stopped a minute to tie a bandanna around my wound, but I knew I had to keep pesterin' them robbers until help arrived. Never did see the sheriff. Wonder what happened to him."

Well, I definitely knew what had happened to the sheriff, but I'd keep that to myself. Let Alvord find out later. I didn't want to start any trouble. Again I asked:

"Saw you disappear and not come back. You run out of bullets?"

"Nope. Had me a good supply of ammo, but my arm was bleedin' somethin' awful. I knew I had to get some help. Wounded during the war too and know the pain. Lady on board helped me. Tied a cloth around my arm and stopped the blood flowin'. Don't know what I'd done without her."

I turned to the engineer. He held his striped cap in his hand. Streaks of grime ran down his face.

"You broke away and tried to start the train. Tell me about that."

The man was tall. He had a slight drawl when he spoke.

"J. D. Swearingen, that's my name. Give me your notebook. I'll write it down for you. Want you to get it right. This is the first time any train of mine's been held up."

Swearingen printed his name.

"Knew there was trouble the moment the train came into the station. Saw Jake, the mail agent, up against the wall and all those bandits with bandannas. Tried to heat up the boiler and put on some steam, but the fireman already had started cooling down the fire and before I knew it, there was a gun at my head."

"What did you think was going to happen?"

"Thought maybe I was goin' to die. Never know what them trigger-happy cowboys are goin' to do. Figured it was the Bass gang. They been hittin' trains 'round here. Heard about the Eagle Ford robbery."

Bass and his men had indeed robbed the train at Eagle Ford, a small town six miles west of Dallas. The gang had done this job while Joline and I were settling our marriage plans. I'd heard about it from Bass.

"Did you think about making an escape and finding the sheriff?"

"Nope. Just thought about my own neck. Followed along with what that gun toter told me to do. Ain't no hero. Just a train engineer who wants to retire some day with all my body parts in good workin' order."

"You made an attempt to start the train. If you're not a hero, why did you try?"

He looked at me, wiped his face with his cap and leaned back against the railing of the locomotive.

"Guess it just occurred to me to try to thwart them bandits. Hate it when someone tries to interrupt the lives of others by threatenin' them. Those robbers ain't nothin' more than a bunch a bullies."

I thanked him for his statement and moved on down the track. Some passengers were gathered on the platform near the waiting room door. I approached them.

"Name's Nolo Blunt, Frontier Magazine. Like to get your side of the holdup. Anyone want to start?"

A man stepped forward, shook my hand and started talking. He wasn't a large man and his hair was thinning. I'd say he was in his late 30's. His mouth moved in kind of a funny sideways movement when he spoke.

"My name's Daniel J. Healey. 'J' is for Jonathan. Healey's spelt with an 'e' between the 'l' and the 'y'. Anyway, I stepped off the train when we got to the station. Wanted to stretch my legs in this here town of Mesquite. It's been a long ride and knew we was almost to Dallas where I work. I'm a clerk at the Windsor Hotel there. Well, I saw Jake Zurn on the platform. Know him. Just as I got up to him and started talkin', this gunman sticks a pistol in my ribs and tells me to throw up my props and get over next to the wall. I did, yes sir. I certainly didn't want any bullet interruptin' my peaceful life. Anyway, wasn't long after that the engineer made a break for it and tried to start the train. While the gang was distracted, I shifted a hundred dollars in bills from my vest to my boots. Guess one of the gang thought I was doin' somethin' when he returned. He hit me on the head with his six-shooter. Made me mad. I feigned a faintin' spell, then when nobody was payin' attention to me, I slipped off and hid. Glad I did too. Didn't know whether or not them gunmen was goin' to shoot down all them hostages. Saw you there to, Mr. Reporter. What was you doin' there with your lady friend? Thought reporters only arrived **after** the holdups."

"Normally you're right Mr. Healey. Reporters usually do get to the scene of a robbery long after everyone's gone home, but this time me and my friend Joline were in Mesquite waitin' for a train. The sheriff came by and talked to us and asked us about whether or not we'd seen anyone suspicious around the station. Wasn't long after that the robbers struck and caught us in the middle. Fortunate for me. My editor in New York's been screamin' at me to get a story about a western gang. Guess this is my chance."

I noticed one of the other men listening intently. He scratched his head now and then faced me.

"Blunt, Nolo Blunt. I know about you. I'm Lacy, W.D. Lacy. My mom runs the Lacy House in Denton. I was there in Denton when you came into town after stoppin' the stagecoach. I remember you and your lady friend. She was on the coach when it ran away. You're still somethin' of a hero around Denton. Didn't know you was a writer."

"You live in Denton, Mr. Lacy?"

"Nope. Run a store over in Dallas. Got me a fine little place in that town called Lacy's Livery Stable.

"Where were you during the robbery?"

"Me, I hid under the seat on the train. Had me one of them private rooms and I just scooted under the place where I was sittin' and stayed there until I heard a lot of horses gallopin' away. Nobody knew I was there so I escaped attention. Had me a good bundle a dollars on my person also."

There was an express agent on the train and I wanted to get his story. I went to the baggage car to find the man who'd been inside when the robbery took place. The door was ajar and I pushed it. The man inside jumped and reached for his gun, then saw me and backed off. His voice was shaky.

"You came close, boy. I could have blasted you. Don't be openin' any doors around here without knockin' first. What ya want?"

"Just doin' my job, mister. My name's Nolo Blunt and I'm a reporter. Tryin' to get the facts together on the robbery. Hope you'll tell me about it."

The man sighed and I saw him relax.

"Well, you sure got here fast. How'd you know about the robbery? Happened just now you know."

"Guess it was fate or somethin'. What's your name?"

"J. S. Kerley. That's my handle. Ain't no first or second name. Go by J.S. I was lookin' out the big door there as we come into town. Always do cause Zurn, the station agent, often has a bag a somethin' for me. When I seen them desperadoes on the platform, bandannas coverin' their faces and all, I knew we were in for it. I yelled somethin' like 'Boys, they're onto us,' and closed the door part way. Then I got out my firin' piece and started dumpin' some bullets into the midst a them no good riffraff. Made 'em scatter too. Finally, closed the door tight, blew out the kerosene lantern and waited. Reloaded my gun and got down behind a file cabinet. Scary. Been held up before, but not with so many in a gang."

"What happened next?"

"Just waited. Knew they'd get around to me after while. Then there came a poundin' at the door and a voice yells out somethin' about open the door or he'd burn me out. Well, I thought about that a while. Seen a man on fire once up Nebraska way. Terrible thing. Anyway I pondered a bit more and then I could smell some oil fumes comin' in through the bottom of the big door. Knew those boys meant business. Had 'bout fifteen hundred in bills. Hid it in the cold ashes of the pot-bellied stove. Left a little over a hundred on the desk. Didn't want those bandits searchin' around too deep like. Then I yelled out I was goin' to open the door. Pulled on the hardware and when the door cóme open, I saw one a them boys with a torch in his hand. Guess I did the right thing. Kept everythin' from bein' torched. Anyways they made off with only a hundred fifty in express money. Ain't much when you think 'bout what could have happened."

I had to agree. It wasn't much when there could have been loss of life. It'd been a job to keep up with writing down his story, but I had the gist of it and could fill in the rest at Murphy's ranch.

I headed for the stable to get the horses. It was late, but the owner slept in the building so I could wake him and pay for the keep.

The door was wide open and up ahead a kerosene lamp cast a dull yellow glow over the place.

I grabbed the lantern and entered the tack room where the stable boy would have put my saddle. The tack room was like all of them in the west. Well-worn bridles hung limply from wooden pegs fitted neatly into the rough pine wall. Found Mama's bit and reins. The saddle was over in a corner and as I looked at it I noticed something new. A rope was attached to it and the strand led down onto the floor and back into the shadows. I was puzzled. I stepped forward and grabbed the rope and pulled on it. There was an "ouch" from somewhere nearby and then a familiar voice said something.

"Nolo, is that you?"

It was Joline. Thought she'd be in a nice warm hotel bed by now. I stepped around the saddle and followed the woven cord until I came to her. While holding up the light high enough, I noticed that she had the rope tied around her waist. Clever girl. Couldn't have picked up my saddle without waking her.

I knelt down, sat the lantern on a wooden stool, and took her in my arms. She was soft and cuddly. Her body was warm against mine. I held her face close.

"Joline. You waited for me."

Her hair fell back over my arm and I could feel it against my skin.

"Oh, Nolo. I was so wrong back there in the saloon. I knew you had to do your job but I was too selfish to see it. A hotel room would be too expensive for just part of the night. I knew you had to come for your horse."

I pulled Joline tightly toward me and kissed her.

She had both of her hands on my chest now and she gently pushed me away.

"Back off Nolo. Let's get our horses saddled and head for the ranch."

Joline was right. There would be plenty of time for hugging and kissing once we were married. We had a long ride back to Murphy's to think about.

## Chapter 22

Something was wrong at the ranch. No one was out doing chores when Joline and I rode up late in the morning. The main house looked deserted.

We led our horses into the barn, removed the saddles and bridles and bedded them down. As we entered the back door, one of the hinges squeaked. Within seconds, someone came down the hall to the kitchen where we stood.

It was Sheriff Benson from Denison. He looked mean and he had a pistol pointed directly at my stomach.

"Well, Mr. Blunt. Fine time for you to be ridin' in. S'pose you heard about the train robbery at Mesquite. Maybe you was even there. Mosey on into the parlor. Got me someone in there I'm questionin'. You and your pretty one might just join him so's we can get to the bottom of findin' this here Sam Bass and his gang."

My pulse jumped and I could sense Joline was afraid.

Jim Murphy sat in an easy chair in the middle of the front room. He had on his nightshirt.

The sheriff pointed to a place on the sofa for us to sit. His booming voice echoed in the large room.

"Know you three got somethin' to tell me about the Bass gang. Heard by the wire at Denton about the robbery down Mesquite way. Local sheriff keeps me informed. Been watchin' this ranch just waitin' for somethin' like this. We're goin' to sit here until Bass shows up. Got me a posse scattered out around outside in the bushes. We got signals. Knew who you were, Blunt, before you even dropped off your horse."

He stuck his six-shooter back in its holster, opened his shirt pocket and pulled out a cigarette.

"Sheriff, what right do you have....?"

I didn't get a chance to finish.

"Smart-mouthed reporter. Take a look here at my badge. What do you see?"

It said Benson was a Texas Ranger. I was dumbfounded. Last time he had a sheriff's star on his vest.

"Says Texas Ranger, but I thought you were a sheriff from Denison."

"Been promoted, Sonny Boy. Made my application long time ago and it come through 'cause I been doin' some good tailin' of the Bass gang. Always wanted to be a Ranger. Now I got my chance to do somethin' big. You and your girl and Jim Murphy are goin' to help me."

The reputation that went with being a Texas Ranger must have gone to his head.

"So what do you want from us?"

"Been onto you for a long time. You been slippin' along on the edges of this matter for the last few months. I know all about you and I also know that Joel Collins was this filly's brother."

He pointed his bony finger at Joline. .

"Goin' to use you three to help me catch this here Bass. You're goin' to lead him into a trap"

This I didn't like. I was tired. I wanted to go to bed.

"Benson, I'll think it over and give you an answer tomorrow."

"You ain't goin' to do no such thing. You and the lady along with this here Murphy are comin' into town with me and some of the boys. Goin' to throw all three of you into jail. Then maybe we'll get some action around here. Want to know all about where you were last evenin'. Think maybe you had somethin' to do with the robbery."

There was nothing I could do. We gathered up our coats and Benson followed after us.

The clank of the cell door echoed in the Denton jail. For the first time in my life I was locked up. Not only that, Jim Murphy and I were in jail behind bars and Joline was left with Josie Donna Baines. Benson knew enough to put Joline with another trusted woman figuring that Joline wouldn't escape without me. JDB was the postmistress, and a federal employee.

All was not lost. I took out my notebook, and although it was noon, I began writing my impressions of what it was like to be sitting on a metal bed without a mattress and with the odor of human waste stinging my nostrils.

Murphy stood in the next cell looking out the barred window, his gaze concentrated on the main street .

I put my hand through the bars and touched him on the shoulder. He jumped, then looked at me. His voice wavered as he spoke.

"Got any ideas how we can get out of here, Blunt?"

"No, but I know one thing, Murphy. We must keep our wits about us. Benson's a sly one. He thinks he knows something, but he really doesn't know anything. My being at the robbery scene will be difficult to explain. I'll think of something. We'll be out of here just as soon as Benson decides we aren't part of the gang."

Murphy didn't seem convinced so I continued.

"Look, we aren't charged with any crime. Benson can only hold us a short time without presenting some evidence of our involvement. I know **that** from my days covering trials in New York."

"But Blunt, this isn't New York. This is Denton, Texas, and the laws here are different. We could be locked up forever."

A noise at the door made me turn my head. Ranger Benson stood at the bars, his bushy eyebrows pressing against the metal crosspieces and his bloodshot eyes focused on my face.

His voice sounded raspy as if he'd just quaffed a whiskey or two at the saloon.

"Well, now. Would you look at the jail birds. Isn't that a sweet picture. Goin' to change that soon. Blunt, get over here. I want to talk to you."

I turned away and walked toward the door that Benson had opened. It was a tense moment, not knowing what was going to happen.

"Get on over here and sit, Blunt. Got me some questions to ask. Then I'll question your girl friend. You know Sam Bass?"

"I've met the gentleman."

"Where'd you meet him?"

"Got captured by his gang up Nebraska way. Fixin' to go to sleep out on the prairie one night when I was surrounded by a bunch of masked men. Didn't know at the time what was happenin', but later met Bass at his stronghold."

"You seen him since?"

"Seen him around town here in Denton. Don't recollect that he's been arrested for anything around here lately or even at all."

"Ain't talkin' about Bass bein' taken in. Want to know when you last saw him."

"Saw him last night on the platform of the train station in Mesquite."

"So you were there!"

"Never said I wasn't."

"You helped him rob the train."

"No. Joline and I were in the depot station just sittin' and talkin'. You can verify that with the Mesquite sheriff. His name's John Barnes. He came in and warned us that there might be a robbery. Soon after he left there was a commotion outside. I went to see what was happenin' and Bass threw down a gun on me and lined me up against the wall. One of his men found Joline and she was lined up too."

"Mighty convenient, you two bein' there when the robbery happened. How do you account for that?"

His eyebrows now were raised high. There were deep wrinkles on his forehead. His eyes were wide as he stared down at me. I had to be careful with what I said.

"Joline and I had been to Mesquite to do some shoppin' before our wedding. We saw the train station depot and decided to take a rest before heading back."

"Mighty strange, the two of you bein' in the very place where Sam Bass robbed a train. There's more to this than you're lettin' on. Goin' to ask you a few more questions, but I'm goin' to let you stew a while. Get up on your feet, Blunt. Move on over towards that cell of yours."

What else could I say? He had his six-shooter out again and was jabbing me in the ribs with it.

"Can't we work somethin' out, Benson? You haven't any reason to keep me or Joline. Charge us with somethin' or let us go."

His eyes narrowed and his lips peeled back making a snarly grin.

"You just get yourself back in that cell and just maybe I won't plug you full of holes for tryin' to escape."

The cell door went clank again behind me. Benson turned the key in the lock. There was no arguing with this man.

Afternoon light was just starting to come in through my window. I needed sleep. I sat down on the bed and leaned back, my hands underneath my head for a pillow.

I glanced toward where Benson stood. He had a ladle in his hands. He lifted the lid on the water barrel with his right hand, dipped in, then drank deeply. Some of the water spilled over his shirt front and dropped on the floor.

The jail was brightly lit and I could see Benson as he put the ladle back on its hook. When he opened the front door, a shaft of bright light cast its glow on the rough-hewn boards of the floor. He was leaving Murphy and me alone for a while.

Must have dozed off. When I awoke, the sun shone faintly through the barred window over my bunk. It was late afternoon.

No one was in the sheriff's office outside my cell. I thought that strange.

Glanced over toward Murphy. He was asleep.

And then a familiar voice called from outside. It was Buck Redwing.

I stood on the bed and looked out. Buck was looking up at me.

"You got yourself in jail, blood brother. I'll help you out. You ready? I found Big Mama in the stable. She's saddled and outside here with me."

"But Buck, isn't it dangerous? Benson might shoot me if I try to escape."

When I looked back at the ground, Buck wasn't there. Big Mama was tied to a tree.

Then there was a noise. It was Benson returning. He approached the cell.

"I'm letting you go, Blunt. You and your girl friend. Sent a telegram to Barnes in Mesquite. He confirmed what you told me. But I still think you got somethin' to do with all this. Goin' to hold Murphy though. Got some real evidence against him."

He unlocked the cell. I lost no time in getting out. The feeling of being free was exhilarating.

Buck greeted me outside.

"You're a slick one Blunt. I saw Benson go inside the jail while we talked. You came out. Figured you talked your way out. You're a man of many words."

I grabbed Buck by the shoulders.

"You were ready to help me get out. I'll never forget that. We really are brothers. How can I ever repay you?"

Buck just looked at me, but didn't say anything. He motioned for me to follow him.

Big Mama nuzzled her head under my arm when I reached her.

I rode over to the post office to find Joline. The story of Sam Bass and his gang was warming up. I needed to write in peace and plot my future.

We started toward Murphy's ranch where Joline and I had left our belongings.

Up ahead were some riders. I prepared for the worst. I motioned to Joline to keep to the side of the trail so we wouldn't be seen. It was too late. One of the men let out a whoop and the others responded. Soon we were surrounded by six men wearing bandannas.

My heart beat faster. I could feel a knot growing in my stomach.

One of the men looked familiar. Before he could drop the handkerchief from his face, I knew it was Bass.

"Sam, what're you tryin' to do, frighten us out of our wits?"

His eyes twinkled. I knew Sam had pulled another stunt on me like when he sent his men to kidnap me at my hotel.

"Just wanted to see what you'd do, writer. Had the boys ready to put the drop on you but you recognized me and the game was up. Where ya been?"

"Joline and I were arrested by Ranger Benson and taken into Denton for questioning. He wanted to know all about the Mesquite train robbery and accused me and Joline of being part of your gang. I was able to talk my way out of it."

Bass raised an eyebrow and stared at me in a funny way.

"You talked your way out of it. Sounds strange to me. Did you make a deal to turn us in?"

His hand reached for his pistol. Didn't know whether or not he meant business or was making another joke.

"Lord no, Sam. Just told him Joline and I happened to be restin' in the waiting room. Then you held us hostage."

I doubt if Bass believed me but he cocked his head to one side. He moved his hand from his gun and laughed.

"Blunt, you always take things serious like. Me and the boys were headed to Murphy's ranch for a little rest. You headed that way too? We'll ride along together."

"Danger, Sam. Benson left some men at the ranch. It's surrounded. You'll be a dead man if you go there. Murphy's still in jail back in Denton. Don't know how long Benson will keep him, but he may have enough evidence to keep Murphy a long time."

Bass eyed me again. This time he knew I was telling the truth.

"Owe ya one, Blunt. Me and the boys'll just mosey on out into the cottonwoods for the night and keep outa sight."

Joline and I prodded our horses and headed for the ranch.

# Chapter 23

The place was deserted. There was no sign of Benson's men. Either they were hiding or had been called back to Denton. It looked like Joline and I were alone.

The main house was cold. No one had tended the fire after we left.

Joline had her coat wrapped snugly around her. I could see the outline of her upper body.

"Seems like everyone has vanished."

"Yes, Nolo. Looks that way."

Her voice was warm. I moved toward her, gathered her to me and put my arms around her. She clung to me.

"Joline, I do love you. We should make our love known to each other."

I could tell my words had affected her. She pressed herself harder against me. Her hand found mine. We found the stairs that took us to one of the bedrooms on the second floor.

The oak floorboards creaked under the weight of our steps. I turned the door handle nearest me. There was a stir inside. I pushed the door open. One of Benson's men scrambled for his trousers as a young red-headed girl sat up in bed, holding the sheets to her chest.

I closed the door and looked at Joline.

"This will make interesting material for my next story, but more than that, it'll be a juicy item to throw back at Benson the next time he tries to browbeat us."

The desire we had for each other subsided. I led her to another bedroom and left her at the door. She went inside.

Later that day, Jim Murphy walked in. I was working in the kitchen on my story. He looked tired and there were marks on his face.

He studied me a moment and then he spoke.

"Nolo, you make any coffee? I need some bad."

"Yeh, Jim. Over on the stove. There's a pot brewed. Benson worked you over I see. Anything I should know about?"

Murphy walked to the cupboard, took out a mug and shuffled to the stove. He grabbed a piece of cloth from the sideboard, gripped the coffee pot by the handle and let the hot liquid stream into his cup. He took a swig, found it too hot and put the mug down on the table next to where I sat.

"Had to bargain with Benson. He was goin' to throw me into the federal pen for a long time unless I cooperated. Finally told him I'd see what I could do about getting Bass to give up."

Murphy looked around the room, stepped to the hallway and then returned.

"Want to tell you something. You got to swear to me you'll keep it a secret. If news leaks out from what I'm about to tell you, Sam'd blow my head off in a minute."

I moved closer. This could be my biggest scoop of the entire Sam Bass story.

"I told Ranger Benson I'd help find Bass and I intend to follow through. Only way I can keep from servin' time. Bass is near his end anyway. He can't keep robbing trains and expect to get away with it. You think I done wrong?"

I thought about what Murphy said. He'd been Sam's friend for a long time.

"I heard what you said, Jim. Agreed, Bass can't go on much longer, but I never thought you'd be the one to bring him down. What made you do it?"

"Damn Benson said he'd keep me in jail. Said he'd prosecute me for what I'd done. He had me dead to rights. I like Sam and all that, but it's me or him and it ain't goin' to be me. Now you tell Sam what I said and your life won't be worth a plug nickel, both you and your girl friend."

I'd never heard him talk like that. He'd always been quiet. There was no way I'd leak any information. I wanted to find out more.

"My lips are sealed, Jim. I like my skin and my job and don't see any reason to bring Joline into this. I won't tell her anything. Uh, you know where Sam is hangin' out and when he's goin' to make his next strike?"

Murphy screwed up his face and looked at me kind of sideways.

"Thought you knew. Saw Sam on the way to the ranch. He said he'd seen you. Thought he woulda told you about his next raid. Anyway, he's headed for Round Rock, down Waco way. Goin' to hit the Williamson County Bank. I think it's outa his grasp. He oughta stick to what he knows. Banks are somethin' else. Sam's a great planner when it comes to robbin' trains and stagecoaches, but he's had little experience when it comes to banks."

I had to agree. From what I had learned it seemed Joel Collins had been the smart one of the outfit. But he was gone now and Bass had to rely on himself if he wanted to expand his field of operations.

"When are you goin' to find Sam, Jim? I want to go with you."

"Goin' to get me some clean clothes and a bath, then I'll be off. You better leave your girl friend here. This is goin' to be a rough one if you know what I mean. Both of us could end up dead if anythin' goes wrong. Wouldn't want no girl around to mess up the situation. She can stay here at the ranch."

"Agreed. Joline should stay. I'll be ready when you are."

Joline wasn't too happy when I told her she couldn't go along. She liked the excitement of riding with the gang, but also recognized the danger ahead.

She stood looking at me for a long time.

"Nolo. You are coming back for me aren't you? I need to know you'll be around as the father of my children."

I stared at her. She had never broached the subject of a family with me. It was kind of nice to think that way. Picture me as a father, settled down with Joline.

"Knowing you're here waiting for me will make my job go faster. As soon as I have my story, I'll be on Big Mama and poundin' the trail back or I'll send you word from Round Rock to come down. Wait for my telegram. Then we can make some serious plans."

She moved toward me and cuddled against my body. We held each other and kissed. Her heart beat against mine and her breasts were hard and proud against my chest.

Then it was time to go. Murphy waited for me out by the back door. Big Mama stamped her front hoof in the dust under the big oak tree.

"I must go, Joline. Jim's waiting. It'll only be a week or two that I'll be gone. You make some plans for us, where we'll live, what kind of house you want and I'll be back before you know it."

I grabbed my saddlebags and walked out the door.

The morning was grey when Jim and I rode out from the ranch toward where I'd last seen Sam Bass when Joline and I came from town. We'd be able to search out the gang from there. Murphy was one of the best trackers in Denton County. No wonder Benson wanted him on the side of the law.

"You think Sam will suspect anything, Jim?"

Murphy moved his head closer to mine as if to whisper.

"Don't talk like that, Nolo. There are ears everywhere in these woods. Sound travels far in this country, especially on a morning like this."

He made a motion of silence across his throat. He was right. Being a nosy reporter did have its drawbacks. I'd opened my mouth once too many times before.

We rode lazily down the trail. The early morning dew fell from the trees that lined our way, the drops making a splattering noise as they reached earth and stirred up the nearly dry oak leaves that littered this woodland path.

Jim held out a hand in caution. A lone rider on a black horse appeared ahead. The man wore an all-black outfit and cradled a shotgun in the crook of his left arm. It was Underwood.

He challenged us, held the gun barrel in the air and then lowered it. We were close enough now to talk.

"Get down off that horse, Murphy. I'm goin' to blow your brains out."

Murphy cringed. Then slowly he dismounted, keeping his hands free to reach his weapon. I wondered what would become of me if Murphy were shot. Underwood wouldn't want any witnesses.

But before anything happened, horses approached. Sam Bass rode up beside Underwood.

"Put the gun down. We ain't goin' to murder one of our boys and Murphy's one of our boys."

Underwood lowered the gun. His voice was raspy.

"But Sam, this man's been in the Denton jail and he's been talkin' to that ranger Benson. I know he's made a deal. Just ask him."

Bass looked at Murphy and smiled.

"Well, Jim. Did you make a deal with Benson 'cause if you did, you're a dead man and you been too close to me all these years to see you go that way."

Murphy had a problem in answering. He had to convince Sam that everything was all right. His voice shook slightly, but I didn't think Sam would notice.

"Hell, Sam. You know me and we been through a lot together. Sure, Benson wanted to make a deal, but I turned him down. Ain't no way I'm goin' to join up with the rangers. Hate their guts. They arrested me in my own house two nights ago and threw me and Nolo here in jail. I got out 'cause Benson didn't have anything on me. Me and Blunt were ridin' out to find you and join up for your next job."

Sam was no fool. He studied Murphy's face and looked at me.

"Blunt, you wouldn't be fool enough to be ridin' with this man if he'd turned me in. I may not know some things, but I know a lily-livered eastern pen pusher like you wouldn't risk his skin by bein' with a turncoat."

With that he turned his horse, motioned to his men and shouted over his shoulder at us.

"Come on along, you two. We're headin' south and you're part of our gang now. Got me some plans. We'll talk about it at supper tonight."

Once again we were on the trail and there was dirty work to be done in the next few days.

Not far from Waxahachie is Bardwell Lake. Sam must have liked the tree-covered plain that lay between the two. Night was coming on. I was hungry and hoping we would stop somewhere nearby when someone yelled ahead. It was Underwood's sidekick, Jackson. He'd found a good place to camp.

"Runnin' water, fish jumpin' and plenty of cottonwood trees around. Sam, this is a good place to spend the night."

Bass looked satisfied. He loved Texas and his heart was here now.

Setting up an outlaw camp took lots of work. Guards had to be posted and relief schedules figured out. Then there was the cooking. Sitting around a campfire waiting for the coffee to boil gave the gang time to talk about the day's ride. Big Mama came into the discussion.

"Mighty fine animal you got there Blunt. Been meanin' to ask you what you paid for her. Whatever it was she's worth it. Ain't never seen an animal respond to a human bein' the way she does to you."

I sat back against my saddle.

"You're right, Sam. Big Mama's been a good horse for me. She answers when I call her. Feels to me like we got one mind at times."

Bass chuckled.

"Think you're right there son. You and the horse got about the same amount of sense when it comes to thinkin', although I ain't too sure but what the horse might win out."

He laughed again. The other men looked at me. I had to respond or be laughed out of camp.

"You're right, Sam. Big Mama sure knows human nature. Just the other day I asked her what two times two was and she pawed the ground four times. It shocked me no end. Goin' to try her out with bigger numbers later."

Bass eyed me suspiciously and then he laughed again.

"Boy, that sure does top all. A horse that can do arithmetic even though anyone knows two times two is five."

Again he laughed. I decided to leave it at that.

The pot boiled now. I found my trail cup near the top of my knapsack and rubbed it with a rag, then poured some coffee.

Murphy sat beside me. He acted uneasy.

"Get some coffee, Jim. It'll make you feel better."

He filled his cup, took a sip, burned his tongue and sat his mug down on the ground next to me.

"Tell me, Nolo. Do you really enjoy bein' out here in Texas when you could be back in New York where there are trolley cars?"

Had to admire Murphy. Although he'd been raised near Denton he knew a lot about the big cities back on the east coast. I'd told him quite a lot myself.

"No, Jim. I like it here. It's peaceful. Like the idea of takin' care of myself, livin' my own life without any interference from some uniformed policeman. This country suits me fine. But writin' is my life and wherever I am, I'll be puttin' down words to describe something. You ever do any writing?"

"Naw. Runnin' a ranch is about all I can manage. Then I met Sam and life got a little more complicated. You know where we're headin' in the mornin'?"

"Heard talk we'd make Waco tomorrow night. Shouldn't be more than another night or two until we reach Round Rock."

Murphy looked at me. I could tell he was troubled. He leaned close and whispered.

"I got to find an excuse to leave the gang in Waco. Got to get word to Benson. You got any ideas?"

Murphy must have been desperate. Otherwise he wouldn't have tried to tell me about what he was planning. Underwood got up and moved our way. His voice was threatening.

"Stand up, Murphy. You look to me like a man who's goin' to turn us in. Got my ideas about you. Goin' to plug you now and on this spot."

Underwood's hand reached for his gun. He had it out of his holster and the trigger pulled back in one smooth motion.

"You been plottin' here with this pipsqueak of a writer. Never thought Sam would let you join us. But this here's too much. You and Sonny Boy sittin' there whisperin' to each other. We ain't got no secrets in this gang. Only someone like you'd be whisperin' behind our backs. Where you want it, front or back?"

Bass was on his feet now. He had to act quickly to stop Underwood from shooting Murphy. Bass snatched the pistol out of Underwood's hand and dropped it on the ground next to his boot.

"Henry, you do that again and you ain't goin' to be livin' long. Like I told ya back on the trail, Jim here's one of my friends and he's part of the gang just as much as you. Now get on back over there and sit down and be quiet. That's the end of it."

Underwood mumbled under his breath, but he obeyed. What a relief. If something should happen to Murphy, I'd be the next one to go. Had a lot of writing to do when this thing was all over.

I spent the night with one eye open.

## Chapter 24

We broke camp after a few days of bad weather and left before the sun finished rising over the mesa to the east. I was worried that Texas Ranger search parties would spot us, but Bass had instincts that told him when lawmen were close. He knew when to be on the move. We were on the move now, a ragged group of horsemen strung out over hundreds of yards. However, Jim Murphy stayed close to me.

Most of the men were up ahead. Underwood and Jackson led. Bass and the others followed. Altogether there were eight of us. Billy Collins, Joline's younger brother, was along. Seab Barnes was a mean one who I'd met earlier in the woods outside Denton. Then there was Charles Carter, kind of a timid fellow who was seeking a way to raise his image by being a member of the gang. He was worth watching. I'd seen him lurking in the background and acting as if he were waiting to strike out. He was keen with a knife. He'd sit and whittle, hours on end, or throw his knife into a tree maybe fifty feet away. I'd hate to have him mad at me.

Murphy moved even closer. His knees brushed mine. He leaned toward me.

"I've got to get away from the gang in Waco. Got to contact Benson. I need your help."

Help him in Waco. But how? Still forty miles to think of a way.

The countryside was boring. Grey-colored sagebrush was scattered across the prairie as far as I could see.

We followed a dirt trail, a wagon's width wide. Tracks of many carriage wheels had made ruts in the bright red soil. We passed abandoned covered wagons, their skeletons shadowed against the morning light, the metal ribs rising in a pattern almost as if they were the bleached bones from a buzzard-picked animal. A story was entombed in each wreckage.

Up ahead Bass motioned for me to join him. Big Mama responded to my nudge.

"What's on your mind, Sam?"

"Wanta talk to you. Might as well get some things off my chest while we ride along here. You know why we're headed for Round Rock?"

"Well, I suppose you're goin' to do some business there, Sam."

"Goin' to be my last holdup. After this is over, goin' to find me a spread around Denton. Goin' to find me a spunky gal like JDB and settle down. Maybe even do some dirt farmin', but mostly, I'm goin' to raise horses. Love these animals. Been thinkin' about buyin' your horse there, Blunt. She's a mighty fine one."

My heart sank. Give up Big Mama. The thought was painful.

"Well, Sam. About my horse. There's no way we would ever be parted. She's like a member of my family. Depend on her to get me around this big country. She's never let me down. Must be thousands of better horses for you to find."

Bass reached up and took off his hat and slapped it against his leg. He smiled. He'd done it to me again. When would I ever learn?

He kept talking.

"We get to Round Rock, two days more at the most. Want you to write down everything that happens there. Since it's my last job, goin' to make it my best. The world needs to know about me. It's not the money I'm after, Blunt. It's makin' a name for myself before I take that last rustlin' ride up into the sky. Been thinkin' a lot about that lately. Think time's runnin' out for me. Best I should get my last job done."

Couldn't agree more. He'd been lucky. Maybe he was smarter than I thought. No man could evade the law forever. The odds were catching up. Before long, every Texas Ranger south of Dallas would be looking for him. And with the help of Jim Murphy, they'd find him and gun him down with the rest of his gang. Had to think of my own skin.

For now, we were all riding along peacefully. A casual observer would probably think we were just a bunch of cowboys.

I spotted Billy Collins and waved. Then I guided Big Mama over his way so we could talk. Still didn't know why he was on this caper. His blond hair blew in the wind. His matching blond eyebrows shaded a pair of the bluest eyes I'd ever seen. I'd never seen Billy close up but now I stared. My children could resemble him one day.

"Hey, Billy. That's some horse you've got there."

He rode a spry pinto stallion. Collins had been friendly enough.

He knew about his sister loving me. He also knew I'd been in Kansas just after his brother had been killed.

Now he showed off his horse.

"Yeh. Got him in Denton. Paid good money for him too. He's a fine animal. Couldn't ask for better. I can ride him into the ground and he still comes up snortin'."

"Your sister know you're along on this ride?"

"Nope. Didn't tell anybody. Goin' to get me some quick money and buy me a few more horses. Start a herd of my own. Means a lot to have a good horse under you when you're herdin' mangy cow-critters. Ever run a herd?"

"Can't say as I have. Been out here only a few months. Met your brother Joel in Nebraska. Liked him a lot. Sorry about what happened."

A tear started at the corner of Billy's eye.

"You really miss Joel, don't you Billy?"

"Yeh. He taught me everything about growin' up. Learned about horses from him. Never forget him. You see him after he died? Lot of bullet holes?"

"Saw him, Billy. Back of the barber shop in Kansas. Joline doesn't want you to end up the same way."

"I know that, but I got me a job to do. I'm my own boss and I'll take my chances like anybody else. This bank deal's goin' to be over quick and then I'll have some real money. What you goin' to do when it's over?"

"Haven't thought about it much. Got a lot of writing to do. I'll join up with Joline again and we'll be married. Don't quite know where we'll live yet. I know it won't be in Denton."

For the last few miles, a meandering river ran by the trail. Seab Barnes rode alongside.

"Hey, Seab. You're a Texan. What's the name of this river? I need it for my notes."

Barnes scratched his bare head, looked at the sky, then back down at the gushing water.

"Must be the Brazos. We be close to Waco now. Up ahead is a big lake. Used to go fishin' in it. You need a boat to get to the middle where the big ones swim. Maybe we got time for wettin' a line 'fore we get on the trail again. You ever been fishin' in Texas?"

"Can't say as I have. Saw the Indians fishin' up Buck Redwing's way. I've tasted Texas bass though and might add, they're real tasty. Why don't you catch a batch for supper? Tired of them beans Underwood's been cookin'."

Barnes rode closer.

"You be an educated man, Blunt. You think Sam knows what he's doin' on this job? I got my doubts. Only reason I come along is to get a few greenbacks to pay off my land back up Denton way."

"Sam's smart enough to rob a train up in Nebraska and get away free. Saw that one myself. Watched him run from a sheriff's posse. Followed him down here and was at the robbery down to Mesquite. Sam'd be a lot better off if Joel Collins hadn't got himself blown apart up in Kansas."

Barnes fussed with the blue bandanna around his neck before he spoke again.

"Yeh, but this is a solid stone bank we're goin' after in Round Rock, not one a them trains. Sounds to me like Sam may be swimmin' in deep water. We pull it off, there'll be plenty a cash for all of us. How do you figure in splittin' the loot? You in on this with the rest of us?"

"No, Seab. I'm just a reporter tryin' to get a story. Don't want any part of a holdup. Just writin' Sam's story for the folks back east. My editor in New York is a mean one. He wants a story each week or he breathes fire and threatens to cut off my pay."

Barnes laughed.

"Had a boss like that once. After the war 'tween the states. Finally told him to keep his job. Ain't never been sorry about tellin' him that neither."

"Well, I can't really do without my writin' job. Guess I'll just have to put up with the man back east. At least he ain't out here in the west. He only hears from me when I want him to. Got to send a story by wire in Waco. You know where the telegraph office is?"

Barnes evidently had heard enough. He waved me off and rode up ahead to join Underwood and Jackson. He'd probably pass on the information about my sending a story back east. That would be just fine. Maybe also I could send a wire to Benson in Denton so he'd know where we were. I had decided to help Murphy.

Waco was a bustling town with its own university. The campus ran right along the river.

What I needed was the telegraph office. The gang had ridden on ahead just as planned. Told Sam that my horse was feeling tired and I'd just take it easy. Bass told me to join up with them just outside of town near Cottonwood Creek. He'd be setting up a camp for the night.

In time I found the telegraph place.

It wasn't much. An operator sat, punching the key. I waited so as not to disturb him for the moment.

The sun was about to go down. I was anxious to get the job done and join the gang at supper. I made an "ahem" and the green-visored man turned his head toward me.

"Just a minute, young feller. Got to finish this here message. Be right with you."

His hand moved slower and then he signed off with his signature.

He rose from his desk and walked to the counter.

"Now then, what can I do for you?"

"Got a couple of messages to send. One's a story to my editor back in New York. Want to send that one collect. The other's to Ranger Benson in Denton. That one I'll pay for."

I handed the operator the story I had prepared back at Murphy's ranch and then I wrote out a few words on the note pad to be sent to Benson.

> **Ranger Benson**
> Denton Jail
> Denton, Texas
> BASS HERE STOP ON TO ROUND ROCK TOMORROW STOP WILLIAMSON COUNTY BANK STOP BLUNT

I read the note again and handed it to the operator. He read it over, counted the words and looked up.

"That'll be forty cents payable now. I'll get your longer piece on the wire later tonight when there's an opening on the line back east. Short message should be in Denton in no time. You some kind of lawman?"

"Nope. I'm just a reporter doin' a job. Thanks for gettin' my messages out."

I counted out four dimes and dropped them into his waiting palm.

The door slammed behind me. I didn't even look up, but then I felt something hard jammed into my ribs. I turned my head quickly.

Underwood stood next to me, a revolver in his hand. It looked like the giant face of death. Then I thought about the message I was sending to Benson. Underwood's gruff voice broke the silence. He kept the gun in my ribs and turned his head toward the man behind the counter.

"Let me see them messages."

The operator wasn't going to argue. I could see that. He handed the sheets of paper over.

Underwood grabbed them and held them up to a kerosene lamp that hung on the wall. His mouth moved as he read the words of my wire to Benson. He folded that sheet of paper and stuffed it in his shirt pocket. After scanning the longer message, he handed it back to the operator.

"Slight change Mr. Telegraph man. Mr. Blunt won't be sendin' the short wire. You go right ahead and send the longer one. And as for you, Blunt, you're comin' with me."

Underwood jammed the gun deeper in my back and pushed me with it toward the door. He stopped and looked back.

"Now you, little man. You better not be sendin' anything to Denton. I hear about that, I'm comin' back here and drag your tongue outa your head through your nose."

With those words, he pushed me through the door and onto the porch.

"Well, Mr. Reporter. You finally showed your true colors. Sam's goin' to be proud of me for outfoxin' a man such as you. We'll be havin' a necktie party this evenin' I think. Now get up on that horse a yours and don't make any funny moves. This here piece a mine has a hair trigger and I might just have to blow your head off 'fore we can hang you."

My knees trembled. It wasn't easy to get on Big Mama, but I settled in the saddle. Didn't want to do anything that would set Underwood off. Maybe I'd have a chance with Bass. Holy mother of mercy! Where was Buck when I needed him.

# Chapter 25

Underwood pointed me in the direction of Cottonwood Creek. My time had come. I could feel it in my bones. Nothing could save me now.

I rode along dejectedly, my head on my chest and my shoulders slumped. What did I do to get in such a jam? What a dumb idea!

I wanted to help Jim Murphy. Now he'd go free and I would end up buried right here in Texas.

Underwood guided me on a trail through the underbrush. He picked a different way out of town just in case that telegraph operator alerted the law.

I rode along the narrow path with branches scratching my face, brushing them aside as best I could. My arms were bleeding by the time we got through the worst of it. I used my neckerchief to blot up the blood. Then I heard a familiar voice just loud enough so Underwood couldn't hear.

"Duck down, blood brother."

I lowered my head and wrapped my arm around Big Mama's neck. I could detect rawhide stretched across the trail. It would catch Underwood unawares behind me.

I prodded my horse to speed up. As she did, Underwood cursed out loud. He spurred his horse to catch up. As he did, the rawhide bit into his neck. He clutched his throat, lost his balance and fell to the ground on his back. His horse skittered off into the brush. Buck Redwing came out of the woods.

He turned the stunned Underwood over and tied his hands with more rawhide.

Buck pulled the revolver out of Underwood's holster and handed it up to me.

"You shoot him if he moves. I'll get the horse."

With those words he was gone.

I dismounted, stuck Underwood's gun in my belt and felt in Underwood's belt for my pistol. I'd shoot him without question.

Underwood revived and gagged. The rawhide had cut into his throat. A fine line of blood oozed from the wound.

Buck came up leading Underwood's horse.

"We'll put the man across the saddle and take him to the sheriff's office."

We managed to thrust Underwood onto his horse. His head and shoulders hung down limply from one side and his feet from the other. He was unconscious again.

Buck retrieved his own horse. We went back to town.

We left Underwood at the sheriff's office, no questions asked. The sheriff knew all about the Bass gang. Underwood was no stranger. The lawman dug out a wanted poster of Underwood. It described him as a stagecoach robber near Denton. He'd been spotted by a female relative and she turned him in.

The sheriff thanked us for bringing in the outlaw and said there might be some money coming to us.

Now to find Sam Bass and the rest of the gang.

Buck Redwing had been with me in the office, but now he had disappeared again. Didn't get a chance to thank him.

I was on my own to find the gang and brazen it out with Bass if he asked me about what had happened to Underwood. First I had to return to the telegraph office and send that wire to Sheriff Benson.

Woods were ahead of me. No problem. Buck had taught me how to follow a trail. I nudged Big Mama in the ribs with my knees and she stepped up the pace.

The country south of Waco featured low mesquite bushes dotting the landscape. The soil was red, much redder than around Denton, and the land was flat. It was easy to see my goal, a heavy stand of cottonwoods that drew closer with every hoofbeat.

Yellow-green prairie grass covered the approach to the trees. It would be good fodder for my horse. I slid off her back.

A sound at the edge of the trees ahead made me turn. A horse and rider emerged. It was Buck Redwing. He rode faster now as he approached.

He was even with me now. He hastily reined in his horse.

"Bass isn't here. Maybe he caught wind of what happened to Underwood. You, me, we'll travel together now. We'll make camp not far out of town. Lone camp. It's not safe to see the gang again. We'll go to Round Rock on our own."

Didn't argue with Buck. It felt good to be together again, riding the trail. I caught Big Mama's reins and swung into the saddle.

Our camp was next to a rocky overhang. Water ran nearby. We had made good time to reach it. I was ready to rest both me and my horse.

"You get firewood. I'll look around. I want to make sure no strange eyes are here."

My muscles ached as I stood, but maybe a little exercise would be good.

Buck had disappeared again!

Trees were few and far apart in this region. I saw some scraggly ones in the distance. If I didn't find some dry limbs, I could always fall back on bushes.

Reaching the edge of the trees, I realized I'd have to hurry to do my job. A thin slice of daylight in the west told me it would soon be sundown.

There were enough dry twigs and branches on the ground to gather for a good fire.

As I reached for some branches, I heard the frightening sound of a rattlesnake. I pulled back quickly. It was too late. The snake bit me.

I could die. Had to find Buck. He would know what to do.

I walked back to camp, my hand aching. I was about to panic. I heard that you could cut the wound and suck out the poison, but Buck would have to do that. I couldn't. I was a goner.

My vision blurred. Up ahead Buck came running toward me. I fell.

Then Buck bent close.

"What happened, brother?"

"Snake, hand. Help."

That's all I could get out. Buck picked up my purple hand and ran his finger over the puncture marks. He put my hand back on my chest, stood and walked rapidly away. Here alone, maybe dying, and my blood brother walks away.

A cool cloth was on my brow. My hand felt better, but when I moved it, pain shot from my neck to my forehead.

What had happened to me? All I could remember was the snake biting me and Buck leaving. Now he stood over me, his hands at his sides, looking grim.

"You came close, white brother, but the Great Father watched over you and brought you back. Mixed a potion. Drew out the poison. Breathe deeper, Blunt man. Get air into your body."

He bent over me and lifted my head, readjusted the blanket he had put under me.

My voice was weak.

"You saved my life, blood brother. Once again I owe you much."

There was a scratching sound. It was Big Mama, her nose close to my face, near my head causing me to turn to see what was making the noise. She snorted. The spray flew out of her nostrils. I turned to Buck.

"You feed her? You give her water? Forget me. Take care of Big Mama."

My head suddenly felt very heavy and I lay back on the blanket. My eyes closed and I could feel myself dropping off into a deep sleep.

Days must have passed. I still was weak, but I knew now that the worst was over. Buck had taken good care of me. I must have spent a lot of time sleeping. Where was Buck? He was nowhere in sight. I sat up. My head started reeling.

Big Mama was tethered and munching prairie grass not far away. When she saw me sitting up, she whinnied and started toward me. Even though she strained at the rope, she couldn't break loose to reach me.

But where was Buck? I studied the camp. There was a fire burning. He must be around. A coffee pot simmered on a hot rock next to the fire. The odor of stew met my nostrils. I was hungry, maybe for the first time in a week.

Toward the woods, I saw a figure in the distance. It was Buck. He made big strides, kind of a lope, and soon he was beside me.

"Blunt man. You're sitting up. Good news. I'll give you some strong broth. It will help you."

Buck ladled out some into a bowl and handed it to me. I grabbed it and let the liquid slip down my throat. Nothing had ever tasted better.

"You cook good, Buck. Just right."

When I finished, I looked at him.

"Any word about the Bass gang? You've been to town?"

"Went back to Waco. Found out Bass is still in woods south of town. He waits for Underwood, but Underwood doesn't come."

My heart started beating rapidly.

"Can they find me?"

"No, they can't find you. You're here with me. Texas is a big country. It's easy to hide."

I appreciated Buck's confidence, but would have liked to get farther away from the gang.

"Any word on when the gang will be going to Round Rock?"

"Maybe they'll start soon. We get you well, then follow."

Bass would get to Round Rock to rob the bank and I would still be on the prairie recovering from a snakebite. I'd have to get moving. With some effort, I stood up slowly. Buck rushed to me.

"Easy, Blunt one. You're not steady yet. More time is needed."

He held me by the shoulders and I stood erect. My legs were weak. As I moved them, the circulation returned.

Getting myself in shape to ride again was another challenge. Buck and I worked daily on strengthening my body. What had seemed like a simple task, now loomed as a major effort. I had to get to the Williamson bank, perhaps Bass' last robbery before he quit. My writing career depended on it. Though my body was not up to strength, I knew I must get there.

"I'm ready to ride, Buck. Let's go."

"You stay. I'll get your horse."

Buck untied Big Mama, brought her to me and put on the saddle.

# Chapter 26

It would take a good ten hours of hard riding to get to Round Rock. I looked off to the east and saw a cloud of dust in the distance. I shouted to Buck. He looked at the cloud.

I pulled alongside.

"What do you make of it, Buck?"

He squinted in the early morning light.

"Maybe seven or eight horsemen. It could be Bass. We'll watch. If we see them, they see us. If the cloud comes our way, we'll ride like the wind."

Buck studied the horizon and turned his attention to the trail.

If it were Sam Bass and his gang, we could be in serious trouble.

The trail wasn't much, wheel ruts in the rusty-brown soil.

Buck speeded up now. By the time I realized it, he was far up ahead. I touched Big Mama in the ribs, but there was no way I could catch him. What was he trying to do? He had disappeared before, yet always for a good reason.

I soon found out. The dust cloud we'd been watching only moments before was now heading my way. I could just make out the riders and horses. It didn't look good.

Buck was out of sight and my horse was breathing hard. The cloud of dust grew larger. I had an inkling of what was about to happen. I wanted to delay it as long as possible.

Big Mama was riding hard, but the horsemen drew closer. So I stopped.

Seab Barnes was in the lead. I could make out his eyes. They were filled with hate. I knew Underwood was Barnes' best friend. The gang must have found out how Buck and I had turned Underwood in to the sheriff back in Waco.

Barnes jumped off his horse. He headed straight for me, fighting mad.

He was on me in a flash and pulled me off my horse. I hit the ground with a thud. The blow knocked the wind out of me. He stood over me, his right hand coiling a leather-braided rope and his left balled up into a fist. Drops of perspiration formed on his forehead.

"Get up, you measly dog. I want to knock you down again and when I finish that, I'm goin' to string you up to the next tree we pass for what you did to Underwood. Nobody gets away with that in this gang."

I cringed, and curled up into a ball and awaited his blows, but none came. The voice of Sam Bass reached my ears.

"Hold on there Barnes. He means more to us alive. Get back. You ain't goin' to hang anyone."

I straightened myself out and prepared to stand, but before I could get my legs under me, Bass reached down and pulled me up by the shoulders. He glared at me.

"You tried to send a wire."

My mind flashed back to the telegraph office.

"Yes, I did. It was for your own good. You're better than a common crook. Someone had to stop you before you made a fatal mistake. It was my duty."

"May be fatal or otherwise, but we're headed for Round Rock and there's no way we're goin' to turn back. You'll come along as a piece of baggage. If there's any shooting goes on, you'll get the first bullet in the head. Now get your note pad out and start writing. You got to earn your keep around here."

I dusted myself off and looked around. All eyes focused on me. I'd never felt so small in my life. Ahead of me was Jim Murphy. His eyes met mine for an instant. Then he looked away. I had to talk to tell him about the second message to Benson.

I grabbed Big Mama's reins and stepped into the stirrup with my left foot. It was Barnes who grabbed my shoulder.

"Listen, scribbler. I'm goin' to be right behind you all the way to Round Rock and beyond. Ain't nothin' you can do without me seein' what it is you're doin' so don't try anythin' fancy. I'd just as soon part your hair with a bullet as swat a fly."

He took his hand off my shoulder. I swung into the saddle. Sitting on Big Mama once again felt good, but I was still weak. It would take some time before I felt like myself.

A glint of silver near a grove of trees caught my eye. Something made a reflection. No one was there. Buck Redwing. Could he be watching over me like a guardian angel?

We were moving and I spurred Big Mama to keep up with the other riders. Barnes was right behind me.

We had just crossed the river south of a town they called Belton when Jim Murphy rode up alongside me. Barnes had ridden off to talk with Bass, leaving me unguarded for a moment. Murphy's voice was hushed.

"I got a note off to the Rangers back in Waco. You really sent a wire?"

"I did. Don't know if the agent actually sent it. Underwood scared him something awful and took the original. I sent another one after he was arrested. What's going to happen?"

"We'll meet again in Georgetown. We should be there by tonight. Look sharp. Barnes is riding towards us."

As Barnes rode up I switched our conversation to Joline.

"Haven't seen her since I hit the trail to join up with the gang. She's going to join me in Round Rock. We're still going to be married, but it may be a while."

Murphy nodded his head and drifted away.

We made camp that night on the outskirts of Georgetown. We still had about fifteen miles to go to reach Round Rock. Bass probably wanted to rest our horses for a day before making the final leg.

Conditions had not improved between me and the rest of the gang. Jim Murphy would be on my side if anything should happen. I hoped I could count on Buck Redwing, somewhere in the bushes, watching and waiting for the right moment to get me out of trouble.

Didn't trust the rest of them. Any one of them would like to stick a knife between my ribs, especially Barnes. He kept dogging me.

Removing the saddle, I rubbed down Big Mama and found a place for her to munch and used my hat to bring her spring water from the nearby stream.

I spread my blankets on the bare ground not far from her.

The campfire was still aglow. Dinner had consisted of canned beans and fried bacon. I was the last one allowed to eat. The coffee was so hot it burned my throat.

My thoughts turned to Joline. I hoped to see her again and soon. After the Round Rock robbery, I'd be through with my assignment with the Bass gang. Then I'd have to make up my mind about marriage and staying in the west. My editor back at the magazine would have a lot to do with my decision.

A chilly wind whistled through the trees. I covered myself in the dim light of the campfire. A coyote howled in the distance. Once again I felt at home on the prairie.

The first rays of the morning sun hit my eyes square, waking me up. My horse was still there, dozing.

The others were up and about. I reached for my boots and checked to make sure no critters had crawled inside. One snakebite was enough for me. I'd heard stories about them curling up in a cowboy's boots during a cool evening.

Murphy was rolling up his blankets. He came over to me. Barnes was nowhere to be seen.

"How're you going to send your second message? There must be a telegraph office in Georgetown."

"Speak softly, Nolo. If anyone's listening, we could be shot. I'll find a way. Bass has confidence in me. You do what you can to keep him busy while I go into town."

Bass drank a cup of coffee. He saw me looking at him and waved at me to come over. I stood up and walked toward him. He ran a hand through his black hair and his eyes drooped just the least little bit.

"Mornin' Blunt. Been thinkin' about what you said to me yesterday, part about wantin' to stop me 'fore I did somethin' fatal. You really think that or were you just tryin' to save your own hide?"

"Sam, let me put it this way. Without you I don't have a story to write and I'd have to catch the next train back to New York. With you alive I can keep my editor happy. That's what I meant."

"Makes sense. But Barnes is goin' to have your hide if I'm not around to keep him reined in. You better not get in his way. If anythin' should happen to me, you better high tail it out of the country. That trick your injun friend played on Underwood left Barnes as testy as a mother bear with a sore paw."

"I'll be careful. When are we ridin' into Round Rock?"

"We'll break camp early come this evenin'. Want to get into Round Rock, scout out the Williamson Bank, and rest the horses. Gotta have fresh legs under us if we want to get away without some lawman catchin' up to us. After another two days, won't need you anymore. May not see you again for a while. Don't want you ridin' out of town with us. You stay and write your story. Make it good. Soon it'll be my birthday. Be twenty-seven years. Goin' to make my biggest holdup on my birthday."

I smiled. Maybe Bass was human after all. He didn't seem like the rough kind of man it took for this job. I'd never seen him kill anyone. He did have qualities that made him likable. I'd be dead by now if it weren't for him.

"Sam, why not give it up? Let's head back for Denton or somewhere else. You can make a livin' on a ranch. You've got a good horse and you know cattle."

"Not a bad idea, but I've gotta get to Round Rock. Everythin' in my life leads me to that bank. Goin' to hit it big, then maybe I'll settle down."

He looked away. I could tell he was thinking again. I left him sitting there and went back to roll up my blankets.

A coyote howled. I thought nothing of it except it was still morning. I'd never heard a coyote call to his mate this early in the day. My mind returned to Buck Redwing. He had used a coyote howl to communicate when we'd been separated. I looked along the horizon. There was a smattering of cottonwoods off in the east. Then the sound came again from that direction. It must be Buck.

Barnes had been sent into town with Murphy. No one else was watching. I untied Big Mama and led her toward the trees as if I was taking her to water at the creek.

As I neared the grove, there was the shape of Buck crouching down. I pulled up on Big Mama's rope, turning her around so she would be between me and the camp.

"I watch. You're still alive. When do you go to Round Rock?"

"We leave at sunset. Buck, it's good to know you're watching. I'm safe until after the holdup, then Bass will turn me loose."

Buck didn't answer. He'd slipped off again without my knowing it.

I led Big Mama back to camp.

An argument was going on when I got within earshot of the men. Barnes was making the most noise now. Murphy was alongside where Bass still sat.

"I tell you he was tryin' to send a telegram to the Texas Rangers. He claims he was just tellin' his men back at the ranch what to do. But when I looked at the order blank, he had written in 'Headman, Murphy Ranch, Denton.' I tell you he's got a code and was sendin' a message to Ranger Benson. His words said, 'Round Rock tomorrow...stop...Return in two days...stop...I pay bills...stop.' Now if that ain't some kind of code I don't know what is."

Bass scratched his head.

"What you got to say Murphy? Thought we had this thing straightened out. You're the one who set us up for the bank in Round Rock. We go, you go and we all hang together. If Barnes is tellin' the truth, you might hang a little early."

Murphy perspired. If he lost his head, I would be next. The gang knew that Murphy and I had been in jail together and questioned by Benson. Probably Josie Donna Baines had told them.

Jim's voice was deep and confident as he spoke.

"Barnes is right. I did send a telegram, but I had to tell my bossman where I'd be and when I'd be home. Taxes come due on the ranch next Tuesday and no one but me knows how to figure out what to pay. Didn't want the man I left in charge to worry about it. He'd just foul things up if he tried to pay them. Runnin' a ranch ain't easy. You know that Sam. You've stayed with me many times."

Bass made up his mind. He looked at Barnes.

"Seab, don't blame you for snoopin'. We all got to snoop. But you got somethin' stuck in your craw about Murphy and you won't let it go. Murph here found us the bank to rob and he's goin' to be along on the job. Seems to me if he was so anxious to tell the rangers about it, he'd be settin' himself up to get killed in a crossfire. Ain't no man goin' to do that without gettin' paid highly for it and the rangers don't pay that much. No, Murphy here is tellin' the truth. Seen him at work at the ranch and he does all the bookwork. Man's got to make a livin' and pay his taxes. Now let's hear no more of it and that's an order."

Barnes could do nothing but sneer and turn away. Sam was the boss.

# Chapter 27

I'd heard stories about Round Rock. I'd even read one in my own Frontier Magazine. The Great Northern Railroad ran its line through the place and caused problems for the citizens, forcing them to split in two. New industry developed in the southeastern part where the Great Northern train station was located. The old part remained Round Rock. Businesses like the grain and feed stores stayed.

The bank was in the new section and Bass was eager to check it out. He and Frank Jackson rode there when we reached town.

Texas summer twilight made seeing easy, even though the sun had just set. Fireflies skittered about my head. They bothered Big Mama and she twitched each time they flew by. I patted her neck and she quieted down.

We were to make camp west of town on the road to San Saba. Bass figured we'd be far enough away from Round Rock so we wouldn't attract any attention from lawmen. He wanted to rest the horses a day even though we'd only come eleven or twelve miles from Georgetown.

Seab Barnes built a fire. The coffee pot was filled with fresh creek water and bubbling on a rock next to some blazing mesquite wood. Barnes broke out the bacon and beans and soon we'd be gathered around the campfire. I'd be busily scraping up the last bit of food out of my tin plate. Just thinking about it made me hungry. I'd tied Big Mama to the picket line that Jim Murphy had stretched out earlier.

My saddle rested at the head of my bedroll. Next to it were my leather saddlebags. I dug my hand into the bag where I kept my eating gear. There was a piece of paper. It hadn't been there before. I pulled it out along with my plate and utensils.

Jim Murphy's initials were scrawled at the bottom.

"Wire was in code. Benson knows. Watch out tomorrow. Chew this up and swallow it. Anyone gets this note we're dead."

The taste of yellowed paper wasn't what I had in mind when I dug into my saddlebag but Murphy was right. The evidence had to be destroyed.

I'd swallowed the last bit when Bass and Jackson rode into camp. Their horses were blowing hard so I guessed they had ridden fast from town.

Bass was out of breath as he dismounted.

"Well, boys. We got ourselves a sweet one. That bank's ready for pluckin.' Soon we'll all be countin' those greenbacks by the thousands. If we had fresh horses we'd get that bank first thing in the mornin' and be on our way back to Denton before noon. But it appears to me we'll take a few days, rest up our ponies and keep our eyes open for any lawmen."

Jackson, Barnes and Murphy gathered around Sam. I hung back. This wasn't for me. I was a prisoner and it was better if I didn't know the details of the robbery.

Who would help me prove I wasn't an outlaw? Murphy's the only one, but he could be shot at any time if Bass found out he'd sent a message.

The bacon made my mouth water. A cast iron pot held brown beans, not just ordinary beans. They were pintos soaked overnight then put on to boil when we'd arrived in camp. Later molasses had been added. It'd take another hour or two for them to be done. Sam had brought back sourdough bread with him from town and there's nothing better than a strip or two of bacon stretched across a fresh piece of bread with all the drippings soaking into the middle. Again, I'd be the last to eat.

I sat down on my bedroll, got out my pad and pencil and began writing about the events of our journey. After many days of collecting notes, I had a thick file that could be used when I wrote my final story.

Two days we rested. They went by quickly. We'd moved our camp to a grove of oak trees near the town cemetery. Bass figured lawmen wouldn't care to nose around tombstones. I had to agree. It probably was the best place for the gang to hide until the robbery.

Bass had spent the morning in Round Rock. He'd returned at noon to say that he'd seen men who looked like they might be rangers. He wasn't sure. He called Jackson and Murphy over.

"I want you two to get your hides into town. Look around some more. If you see anyone who looks like he doesn't belong with the townfolk, high tail it back here and tell me. Can't be too careful these days, not with the money pilin' up in the bank and our hands gettin' itchy."

Murphy and Jackson returned to camp after a few hours and told Bass they hadn't seen anything unusual. Bass seemed reassured.

I'll say one thing for Bass. He had made careful plans for this job. Barnes would go in the bank first and try to change a greenback for silver. Then Bass would rush in, leaving Murphy and Jackson to guard the door.

Bass also had made a list of provisions they would need when they made their score. The list included tobacco and coffee. He decided it was time for all of us to go into town.

We rode along a narrow trail. A light rain had fallen in the early morning, but the ground was drying out enough to create dust. I was near the end of the pack with Barnes behind me, Murphy, Jackson, and Bass spread out ahead of me.

We reached the outskirts of Round Rock. A feed store was just ahead. Some old timers were outside, probably just passing the time. They all didn't appear to be all old timers. Some had shine on their boots. Could they be lawmen? Had Bass noticed, too?

Evidently he had. He called Murphy to ride up. I wanted to get closer and hear what was going on.

"Murphy, you get on over there and mingle with those cowboys. Maybe you can find out if any rangers are around. Wouldn't want anyone givin' us a surprise once we get started on the bank."

Murphy cut his horse out of our pack and headed toward the store. He pulled up, dismounted, tied the reins to the post rail and stepped up onto the wooden platform where the cowboys lolled.

We now headed for the new part of town.

The Texas sun beat down on my back. I was thirsty and knew Big Mama needed water, too. Up ahead was a hitching rail and a trough.

I pulled back on the reins and as I did, Bass looked at me. I pointed toward the trough. He nodded his head up and down. Guess he figured I couldn't get into trouble watering my horse. I dismounted.

Big Mama drank her fill. Bass, Jackson, and Barnes halted their horses just up ahead. They entered a store on the corner. The sign over the door read "Henry Koppel's Tobacco and Dry Goods Emporium."

My attention shifted to two other men on the other side of the street. One was wearing a badge on his vest. The other was dressed like an ordinary cowboy, but there was something recognizable about him.

Then I knew. Ranger Benson. I was sure he hadn't seen me yet. Big Mama walked next to me toward Koppel's store. When I reached it, I tied her to the rail, keeping her between me and the two men, making like I was rubbing down my horse.

Now they crossed the street toward me. Maybe Benson had recognized my horse. As he neared, he passed right by without looking my way. He headed for the store. When he got to the door, he looked around and saw me. For an instant the expression on his face froze and then he nodded toward me, his hand reaching down to undo the strap that kept his pistol tight in his holster. The man with the badge entered Koppel's. Benson stayed by the door.

Horses with riders came toward me now and Murphy was among the group and waved. He saw me and shouted to the others. The group halted in the street. They dismounted and pulled their horses to where I was standing. They tied off their mounts at the rail and then scattered out along the wooden sidewalk. Two of the men had rifles.

Murphy got off his horse with the others and walked up to me. He looked out of breath. His voice was no more than a whisper as he spoke.

"Rangers. Found them back at the feed store. Bass inside?"

"He and the others. Deputy just went in. That's Benson at the door."

Before I could say anything more, the sound of gunfire echoed on the street. I flattened myself on the ground and kept my eyes on Benson. His gun was out. He opened the door and fired at someone inside. Then he stepped back, his left hand grasping his shoulder. Blood flowed down his shirt. He went to his knees, but kept on shooting.

Bass burst through the door first, his right hand bloody. He shifted his pistol to his left hand and fired at Benson, but missed.

Jackson and Barnes ran out, Barnes firing his pistol one more time toward someone inside the store.

I heard the crack of a Winchester rifle behind me. Chips of stone flew off the store wall. The bullets hit right where Barnes had been standing. Others joined the battle and I was right in the middle. And Big Mama was in the line of fire. I had to do something.

Keeping low, I reached the hitching rail and untied Mama's reins. I led my horse along to an alleyway where we'd be protected. I could still see what was happening.

Bass and the two others went for their horses. A bullet caught Sam square in the stomach. He bent over, dropping his pistol, but he inched closer to his horse and crouched there, perhaps waiting for help.

Meanwhile, Barnes and Jackson made their way to the horses, firing toward the rangers, covering each other as they edged closer to where Bass waited.

As Barnes pulled a second pistol out from under his shirt, he was shot in the forehead. He was dead before he hit the ground. He lay in a crumpled heap near where Bass crouched.

Jackson still fired his weapon. His shots slammed against the building near me. A ranger ducked down to reload.

Jackson made it to his horse and helped Bass into the saddle. They galloped off down the street.

I breathed more easily. Barnes was dead, Bass was wounded and I was free.

I had to find out what happened in Koppel's store. I stood up and led Big Mama back to the main street and tied her in front. A crowd had gathered at the entrance. I pushed my way through until I stood inside the doorway. Gunpowder smoke made me cough.

On the floor was a dead man, bullet holes in his body and head, a pistol still gripped in his right hand. His eyes were open.

Still another man crouched in the corner. I walked over and reached out my hand. He took it and I helped him stand.

"Tell me what happened. I'm a reporter for Frontier Magazine."

His eyes were glazed. I touched his shoulder. He shook his head and looked at me.

"All he did was ask if the man had a pistol. A reasonable request in this town. We got a law against carrying concealed weapons. Then everything broke loose and all three of those thugs emptied their guns into Grimes. That's A.W. Grimes, our deputy sheriff. Never gave him a chance. Who were they?"

"That was Sam Bass and two of his gang."

"Sam Bass! Hell, I waited on him. He's the one who had his hand blown off? I'd just sold him a bag of tobacco when Grimes came in. Never know who you'll meet these days. Lucky I wasn't in the line of fire."

He walked into a back room.

I went outside. Benson sat against the wall of the store. A man with a black bag bent over him, tending to his shoulder. I assumed he was a local doctor.

Benson looked up at me as I neared.

"Nolo Blunt. I'd never be in this fix if it hadn't been for you. But we got him. We got Bass, didn't we?"

"Don't believe Bass'll make it too far. Murphy's wire reached you?"

"Sure did. Set up that code while I still had him in jail a few weeks ago. You remember. You were in there with him. Pretty smart of me. Rode straight through to get here. Doc here says I'll make it, but it was close. Bullet must have grazed my lung. Hard to breathe."

Benson bent over and coughed.

"That hurts. You see Bass 'fore I do, tell him I'm comin' for him. Goin' to string him up. Personally goin' to whip his horse out from under him. Leave him swayin' in the breeze with his neck stretched."

I pictured Bass hanging from a rope. When I last saw him, there was a doubt that he'd make it that far.

I felt a hand on my shoulder and turned around. Buck Redwing stood behind. His eyes were on Benson.

"Same ranger who put you in jail. Why do you talk to him?"

I stepped away from Benson, grabbed Buck around the shoulder and led him to where I'd tied up Big Mama.

"Buck, a reporter talks to everyone. I've got to write a story. Want to get my facts straight. Where have you been?"

"See it all. You were smart to move away from the crossfire. Taught you that myself. You're one big western cowboy now. Where did Bass go?"

"He rode out of town with Jackson. I need you to help me track them."

"I've been ready. What are you doing? We waste time."

Before I could think about what Buck said, he was on his pinto riding away. I quickly mounted and Big Mama headed after him.

# Chapter 28

Following Bass and Jackson wasn't that hard. We knew the direction they'd gone when they left town. I had a hunch they would head for our camp near the cemetery. We'd left some of our gear hidden away there.

Buck followed their trail. Blotches of blood mixed with hoofprints were on the ground. Sam wouldn't get too far before he would have to rest.

Ahead was a grove of trees. I could make out the figure of a horse grazing. We got closer. Sam was lying under an oak. Jackson wasn't around. Sam's head was propped against the tree. He was breathing hard. His right hand hung limply by his side. Sam was in deep trouble.

I jumped off Big Mama with my canteen. Sam watched me.

I held a canteen to his lips and he took a few sips.

"Didn't even get to rob the bank. It was a good one too. Have to wait until my wounds heal."

His eyes closed. Didn't know if he'd open them again, but he did, a few seconds later.

"You saw the whole thing?"

"Sure did, Sam. Sorry to see you in such a shape. Tried to warn you about what could happen. We'll get you to a doctor and patched up. Buck's here and the two of us can get you back to town."

Bass looked up.

"Where's Buck?"

I spun around. Buck wasn't there. I was left alone to take care of the wounded man.

"Well, he **was** here. Helped me find you. Good tracker. The best."

Bass had stopped bleeding. I got an old cotton shirt out of my saddlebag, tore it into strips and set about to bandage Sam's hand. The hole in his middle looked terrible. I pulled away his shirt, but the cloth stuck to the wound. I wrapped a portion of the shirt around his body and tied it in the back. He groaned.

"Can you ride, Sam?"

His lips formed words, but no sound came out. I offered him another drink of water. He pushed the canteen away with his good hand.

"Nope. Can't ride. Too much pain. Just leave me here."

His eyes closed. There didn't seem to be much I could do for him. I put the canteen next to him where he could reach it, got his blankets from his horse and put one over him.

The best thing for me was to get back to town and find a doctor.

The main street of Round Rock was quiet. Business was going on as usual. Koppel's store was open and customers entered and left. Blood stains were still visible where Benson fell.

Inside Koppel's I found the clerk I'd talked to after the shooting. He was busy with a customer. I waited until he finished.

"Where can I find a doctor? What happened to Benson?"

"He's over in doc's office. Up the street, second floor. You'll see his sign."

I headed in the direction he'd pointed out, found the sign, "Dr. C. P. Cochran, General Medicine."

I ran up the flight of rickety wooden stairs and knocked.

"Hold on out there. Be there in a minute. Got a patient in here."

I looked out over the rooftops and false fronts of Round Rock. One town in Texas looked like any other. The Honky Tonk Saloon was on the other side of the street. Next to it was the Williamson County Hotel.

The doctor opened the door.

"What you want young feller? I'm busy. Oh, yes. You're that nosy reporter. Come on in."

Benson lay on a surgical table near an open window at the side facing the street. A pair of tattered lace curtains drifted lazily in the early evening breeze.

I faced the doctor.

"Need your help. Sam Bass is dying. Found him lying under a tree a few miles out of town. All I could do was give him water."

Benson turned his head as I spoke.

"You say you've been with Bass? Tell me where he is. I'll get the rangers after him."

"He's out on the Georgetown Road. A few farmhouses, then the trail dips off to the right. Your rangers can probably follow the tracks in the morning. Not much chance in the dark. I'll lead them come first light."

Benson grunted. He put his head back down on his pillow, but his voice still rumbled when he spoke.

"Doc, you got to get me patched up. I want to be in on the arrest. I trailed that man too long to let some other lawman get all the credit. You got to fix me up."

The doctor walked over and stood beside Benson.

"There's no way you're going to get off this table. You've got a bruised lung and there's still a bullet rattling around inside of you. You move now and you're dead."

The doctor turned.

"Young man, you get on over to the Williamson Hotel. Plenty of rangers over there. See Major Jones. First name's John. He's in charge."

I crossed the room and stood next to Benson.

"No matter our differences, I hope you get better. I've always been on the side of law and order. Only reason I was with Bass was to get a story. Don't worry. I'll see that the lawmen find him. You'll get your credit in my article."

Benson looked up at me, but didn't say anything. He looked unhappy. Maybe he had the reward on his mind.

The doctor walked me to the door. He whispered:

"That lawman's going to need plenty a rest and care before he walks again. Don't even know if I can save him, but I'll give it a try. Bass'll have to take care of himself. I'm not going to leave a wounded ranger to treat some no account train robber. Not any other doctor in town either. Might just be an herb healer out in the shacks by the cemetery who would treat him for the right price."

With that, I left.

I headed across to the hotel.
The lobby was filled with lawmen.

I walked up to the front desk. A deer head stuck out from the papered wall. The clerk saw me standing by the counter.

"You needin' somethin'?"

"Yes. I'd like to find a Major Jones. You know him?"

"Sure do. That's him over there with the big stogie stickin' out of his mouth. He never lights it, just keeps chewin' on it like it was his good luck piece."

I walked toward him.

He was talking to Jim Murphy. The major turned his head, looked startled for a moment and then shook my hand.

"Nolo. Haven't seen you since the excitement this afternoon. Where you been?"

"Got information for Major Jones."

As I said Major Jones, the others looked my way. I felt like an actor must feel when he first steps on stage in the opening scene.

"Are you Jones?"

The man took the cigar from between his teeth.

"Sure am. Who might you be?"

"Name's Nolo Blunt. Reporter for Frontier Magazine. I know where Sam Bass is."

The major's eyes got wider. He put an arm around my shoulders and pushed me through the crowd to an empty place near the stairs.

"You've got some information about Bass?"

"Sure do. We tracked him and Jackson out of town. Found Bass under a tree a few miles up the road to Georgetown. He's wounded bad. Needs medical attention. I checked with the doc, but he was busy treating Benson. Said he wouldn't leave his patient. Told me you were in charge."

"That's right. You think you could find Bass in the dark?"

"I doubt it, not without my blood brother, Redwing. He's the tracker. But I can sure find him in the daylight."

"Then you be here in this foyer in the mornin' come six o'clock. We're goin' to get us a train robber. You say he's wounded. How bad?"

"He's got a bullet through his middle and his right hand is useless. He must have lost a lot of blood. May not make it through the night. Left him some water. Only thing I could do."

"Can't fault you for that, young man. You did right comin' here to tell me about it. Now get yourself some sleep. We'll have a busy day tomorrow."

I walked to where Murphy had been standing, but he was gone. There was nothing more to do but get Big Mama to the stable and find myself a room in the hotel.

As sunlight streamed through the second story window, I reached for my railroad watch, flipped open the cover and saw it was 5:30 a.m. I had a few moments so I splashed some water on my face. .

As I dried off, there was a knock at the door.

I put on my trousers and shirt and answered in my bare feet.

It was Murphy.

"You ridin' out with the rangers this mornin'?"

"I plan to. Jones told me to be downstairs at 6 o'clock."

"I'll be goin' along too. If you see Bass first, don't tell him I'm along. I'll stay in the background. Could be trouble if Bass sees me and finds out I turned him in to Benson. Some of Sam's old gang will hold it against me."

"All right, Jim, but I got something you can do for me. You tell Jones how I was a hostage from Waco here and had no way to escape."

"It's a deal. You heard from Joline? Is she still at my ranch?"

"Far as I know. Goin' to send her a telegram as soon as Bass is in custody. Want her to come here to Round Rock on the next stage."

Murphy turned and walked down the hallway to the stairs.

On the road to Georgetown, there were a dozen rangers and Milt Tucker, a local deputy sheriff, riding beside me. Jones decided to stay in town to investigate the shooting at Koppel's Store.

I found the fence where the trail had turned and waved an arm at the others to indicate we would turn.

When we reached the tree where I had left Bass, he was gone. So was his horse.

Tucker rode up.

"Where is he?"

"He's not here. He was right under that tree there. There's my canteen. Lid's off. Lots of blood on the ground. Blankets are gone."

We guided our horses to the oak. Tucker and I dismounted.

"He was lyin' right here. You got somebody who can trail him?"

Tucker called one of the rangers over.

"Nevill, help me find Bass. Plenty of tracks around here."

Nevill waved everyone back, dismounted and studied the ground.

"He went that way. Still was bleedin' from the looks of it. Can't be far, not with all the blood he's losin'."

Nevill picked up his horse's reins and led the animal behind him as he followed the trail on foot. Confident he had the right track, he mounted and waved for us to follow.

Sam hadn't gone very far. We went over a rise and there he was, sittin' under another tree. He looked like he was in bad shape. Tucker approached him cautiously, his pistol drawn and cocked.

"Don't shoot me boys. You got me dead to rights. Don't want to die out here."

The lawman kept his weapon on Bass while another ranger jumped down and searched the wounded man. He just lay there, scanning faces in the group. Jim Murphy wasn't among them.

Tucker was off his horse now and standing next to Bass.

"End of the road for you mister. Have to get you back to town."

A ranger found Sam's horse nearby and led it back. Bass was lifted into the saddle. His good hand was tied to the pommel. Bass slumped over onto his horse's neck. I thought he was going to fall off, but a ranger straightened him up and grabbed the reins to lead the horse. It would be a long ride for Sam back into town. I doubted he could make it alive.

## Chapter 29

We took a back way. The alleys connected in a kind of maze, but Round Rock wasn't that big. We rode to the rear entrance of the Williamson Hotel. Tucker got off his horse and went inside and before long he returned. He had a blanket, sheet and pillow under one arm and a portable cot under the other. The man headed for a nearby shack.

Bass was in no condition to be moved. The lawmen lifted him down. He moaned as he hit the ground.

His stomach wound had opened up on the trip to town. A red stain spread on his shirt over the dried marks of the day before. His right hand was of no use to him. A rag tied around it oozed blood.

Two men carried him, one at the shoulders and the other at his feet. They managed to get him inside the shack. I walked in after them.

There were no windows. The morning light peeked through cracks in the wood strips of the hut. The floor was rough timber, unfinished, and still covered with patches of sap that gave the place a turpentine smell.

The men laid Bass down on a cot in the corner, placing one blanket under him and a sheet over him. Bass gave a long sigh and passed out. He was limp. His arms hung down over the sides of the bed, his hands almost touching the wood floor.

Dr. Cochran was there. He stacked some strips of white cotton cloth on a small table. He pulled back the top sheet and with a pair of scissors, cut away Sam's shirt from around the belly wound. He dipped the strips of cloth in some kind of liquid and laid them across the place where the bullet had entered. He added some wider pieces of cloth, placing them over Sam's middle.

The doctor took Sam's right hand in his own and looked it over. He cut some more strips of cloth, soaked them and wrapped them around the hand. I noticed the thumb and middle finger were missing.

When I left him, Bass was sleeping. The ranger on guard duty acknowledged my leaving and closed the door after me.

Round Rock was buzzing. Citizens gathered in front of the telegraph office. I listened to what they were saying about the capture of Sam Bass.

"Did you hear? Wounded something awful. They got him hid out in town."

"Some nosy reporter from back east turned him in."

"I heard it was Jim Murphy, one of the gang."

"Heard he's goin' to die. No way he can live."

I entered the telegraph office and walked to the counter. The clerk, looked directly at me, smiled and reached out his hand.

"You must be Nolo Blunt. Saw your picture in the latest edition of Frontier Magazine. You been writin' them stories about Sam Bass. Especially liked the one about the death of Joel Collins up Kansas way. So you're goin' to marry his sister. Said so at the end of the article. Saw you hidin' behind that building across the street during the shooting yesterday. Recognized you right away from the picture you had in the magazine. You really hugged the earth when the bullets were flying. What can I do for you?"

"Want to send a wire."

I wrote it out on note paper.

> **Joline Collins**
> Murphy Ranch
> Denton, Texas
> JOLINE I LOVE YOU STOP COME TO ROUND ROCK STOP MARRY ME STOP

I signed it, **"Your Nolo."**

The clerk counted the words, wrote something on a pad and looked up.

"That'll be fifty cents. You goin' to be married here in town? Sure like to see that. I can see the heading now, *'Famous writer weds sister of Bass gang member.'*"

I hadn't thought about that, but it was true. Never thought of Joline being related to a robber.

I gave the clerk his money and left.

The guard at the shack recognized me when I returned and let me through the door. It took a few minutes to adjust to the dimness. Major Jones stood over Bass asking him questions.

"Who were the others in your gang?"

"Ain't no way I'm goin' to tell you that. Mighty good ridin' partners them. Wouldn't want to rat on 'em and get 'em hanged."

"You're dyin' anyway. What difference does it make. Let me know who they are so they can be brought to trial for their crimes."

"Ain't goin' to tell ya. Rather die than tell on my pals."

Bass turned his head away from Jones and stared at the wall. I walked over to the major.

"I can fill you in on the details. Was a prisoner of the gang for the past week. I know everything about every member. Be glad to testify in court."

"You'll get your opportunity young man. But I want to hear it from Bass. A dyin' statement from him will be good evidence."

Bass was listening. He turned his head back toward us.

"Never meant no harm to you Blunt. You're my last chance for fame in this world. I know I'm dyin', but your words about me are goin' to live forever. Now get on over here with your note pad. Got something to say."

I got out my paper and pencil, then sat next to Sam.

"All right, I'm ready."

He cleared his throat.

"Ain't never meant to harm a livin' soul, even yesterday. Over in Koppel's Store, just mindin' my own business. Sheriff wanted to know if I had a gun. Knew he had me dead to rights. All three of us drew on him and shot him. If I'm the one who killed him, be the first time. Never killed anyone before."

Bass closed his eyes, but kept talking.

"Had me a fine horse back in Denton a long time ago. Denton Mare she was called and that horse could run. Won me a few sporting dollars on her. Met Joel Collins in Denton. Me and him went together in the races. Got together a pretty good poke too. Enough to get us some ridin' stock. Then we busted outa Denton.

Went on a cattle drive up Nebraska way. Took Redwing along. Sold the herd for the boss and lost the money gamblin'. Guess I been tryin' to make it up ever since. You understand?"

"I do, Sam. Remember, I met you up in Big Springs. You kidnapped me out on the prairie. It was all a game for you, but not for me. Thought I was goin' to die."

Bass tried to laugh. It was too much for him. He choked and coughed. I reached for the canteen by his bedside, uncorked the lid and held it to his lips. He took a long sip, wiped his mouth with his good hand and laid his head back on the pillow.

"You sure were a sorry sight young feller when I first saw you up top that big horse a yours. What you call her, Big Mama? Still remember the look on your face. You thought we'd kidnapped Miss Joline and you were goin' to be one of them there knights like in old times. Rescue the maiden. You were so green I could see the leaves growin' outa your ears."

There was a sadness in his face now. Maybe it was fear of dying. Tears formed at the corners of his eyes.

"We been through a lot together. Kept you from bein' shot a few times. Guess you owe me somethin' for that."

"I really do, Sam. You did that. Barnes and Underwood both wanted my hide more than once."

"What happened to Barnes?"

"Buried him yesterday. Bullet hole in the middle of his forehead."

"And Jackson?"

Sam's voice became soft. I had to lean close to hear him.

"Jackson's still at large."

"And Murphy. What happened to Murphy?"

I had to be careful. Even though I knew Bass wouldn't live, I wanted to keep him thinking that Murphy was his friend.

"Murphy's around town. Saw him yesterday."

Bass scratched his head.

"How come he's still runnin' around?"

Before I could answer his question he attempted to sit up straight on the cot.

"So that's what happened. Murphy was the rascal after all. Turned us in did he."

The strain was too much. He lay back down on his bed.

"And he was my friend."

Bass closed his eyes. He had passed out again.

I sat next to Bass for the next two hours. Didn't want to leave his side. He could go at any moment and I wanted to be there when he did. Not only did I want to write the story of his death, but I really had become fond of Sam. Somehow I knew he would be remembered in history as a kind robber.

Sam's eyes opened. He blinked a few times. It was noon. The sun beat down on the shack which was unbearably hot. We were both sweating.

I found a cloth and soaked it in water, folded it and put it on Sam's brow. He looked over at me.

"You're still here. Thought you'd be off somewheres by now."

"I'll stay with you Sam."

He tried to sit up and I helped him.

"Ain't got a cent to my name. You imagine that? All the work I did, plannin' and schemin' and takin' all them risks. All I got is my horse and I liberated **him** from a farmer back up Waco way. Good horse too. Woulda got me outa town after we sprung the Williamson Bank. Woulda liked to have seen some stacks of greenbacks stickin' outa my saddlebags. Still remember those gold pieces from the robbery up in Big Springs. Counted them over and over. Feel them goin' through my fingers now."

The fingers on Sam's good hand moved as he spoke.

A hand touched my shoulder. Major Jones stood over me. He motioned for me to get out of the chair so he could sit down. I moved to one side but close enough to hear any conversation. Didn't want to miss a word.

"You mentioned someone named Jackson when you were talkin' with this here reporter. Where is Jackson now?"

Bass puckered his mouth like he had just been eating something sour.

"Told you. Don't rat on my friends. Don't even know where Jackson might be. Left me under a tree near where your boys found me."

"You must have had a plan for getting together when you got separated. How did you do it?"

"Usually just listened to what people told me."

"What people?"

"Folks what knowed me."

"Who are these folks?"

"Ain't goin' to tell ya. Don't rat on my friends."

A look of pain crossed Sam's face. He dropped back down onto the cot from his sitting position.

"You got to help me, Mr. Ranger."

"Ain't nothin' I can do for you. Doc's here. You wanta see him?"

"Guess there ain't much he can do for me. Feel like an angry bull's been standin' on my stomach."

Sam stared at the ceiling. He moved his left hand to his forehead and wiped away the pad of cloth.

"You boys playin' a joke on me? This here room ain't stayin' still."

Bass closed his eyes. There was a silence about him. His breathing was irregular, then it stopped. His head twitched once and he was gone. I opened the cover of my watch. Three fifty-eight in the afternoon. I wrote it down in my notes on the page where I had written the date, Sunday, July 21, 1878.

July 21st. It was Sam's birthday. He was twenty-seven years old.

Next day I saw Sam's body. He was stretched out in the back of the barber shop. A woodworker was putting together a casket made of old pine boards.

The scene reminded me of the barber shop in Kansas where Joel Collins was taken. He and Sam were pals who met the same fate.

Who was the more fortunate?

Out here in the west funerals came soon after deaths. Embalming was for rich people. Robbers and no-gooders usually were put under ground as soon as possible before their bodies decomposed. Bass fell into the latter category.

When his coffin was finished, two workers lifted him and put him inside the box. The lid was nailed on and they carried it to a small cart hitched to a single horse.

I followed as we started toward the cemetery, the one where the gang had camped. A strange thing happened. The procession grew as we passed through town. By the time we went by Koppel's Store, there was maybe a score of men walking behind the coffin. Some may have been curious but others probably wanted to tell their grandchildren they witnessed the burial of a train robber.

Jim Murphy was one of the crowd, walking at the back.

"You headin' back to the ranch soon?"

"Soon as we get Sam under ground. Got my horse ready. It's in the stable. You?"

"Goin' to wait here for Joline. Expect tomorrow she'll be comin' in by stage. You know, Jim, Sam knew you turned him in."

Murphy's face didn't change expression.

"Knew he'd figure it out before he died. He say anything about me?"

"Didn't say anything much. Maybe even expected it. Said you were his friend and then didn't say anything more. You did what you had to do."

"Know that, but it still bothers me. People in town are callin' me a hero, but I don't know quite how to take that. Feel guilty somehow for Sam bein' in that pine coffin up ahead."

We walked along silently as far as the edge of the cemetery. Then Jim split off to walk with two of the rangers. I continued on straight behind the cart.

Our burying party arrived at an open grave, one dug by the prisoners from the local jail. That was a way for getting drinkers to sober up, digging a six-foot hole in the tough Texas earth as part of their sentence.

Sam would be buried in the pauper's section. There was no tombstone for him, not even a wooden cross or stake to mark his resting place.

A preacher had turned up. He was directing the workmen placing the coffin in the grave, lowering it down with ropes slung underneath. The box made a crunching sound as it hit bottom.

The reverend's voice resonated across the cemetery. "We come to bury a man of Texas. He was a thief and a robber, but he was a man, a God-fearin' man no doubt 'cause he always left his victims a little something to get home on. He was not a wanton man. His tastes were narrow. He hated no person and never killed no one until his last days on earth. He's atoned for that killin' now and we bury him with solemn ceremony for his redeemed soul. God have mercy on this sinner who lies now in a state of perpetual forgiveness."

The preacher gathered up soil, crumbled it and dropped it on the casket. Soon the grave was filled with earth. When the job was finished, a deputy sheriff headed toward town with the prisoners.

Out of the corner of my eye I saw a figure next to a horse at the top of the hill. For a second I thought it was Jackson.

# Chapter 30

The walk back was a lonely one.
 I reached the outskirts of old Round Rock and stepped onto the boardwalk that ran past the feed store. A row of men sat on the chairs out front. They leaned against the wall. They all wore boots, except one. The fellow in moccasins was Buck Redwing. He tilted forward in his seat and stood up as I approached.

"Been waitin' for you. I'll walk with you to the hotel. Come on."

Buck put an arm around my shoulder and pulled me toward him.

"You're a western man now Blunt one. Bass is gone. Stay in Texas. Raise a family like Buck Redwing. Join our tribe. Miss Joline will be your squaw. We'll have a big wedding in my Kiowa village. You'll write stories. I'll take them to town to the telegraph office. You'll teach me and my tribe to read the words you write. That's all I ask."

I listened to what Buck said.

"Let me think, Buck. Joline's coming in on the stage tomorrow. I'll talk with her. She may not want to do that."

He looked crushed. He stepped back while still looking at me. His eyes moved from my head to my feet and back.

"You're a western man. You tell the woman what you want. She'll obey."

"Buck, that may be what it's like with your tribe, but Joline is an independent woman, not a squaw. She has a mind of her own."

He looked down, then slowly raised his head until our eyes were level.

"No matter. You know what Buck wants."

We arrived at the hotel where his pinto was tied. Before I could say anything more, Buck was at his horse's side, his foot in the stirrup. In one smooth continuous motion he was in the saddle and headed down the main street. Wondered if I'd ever see him again.

My room at the Williamson Hotel was at the rear of the second floor. It was small yet it seemed like a castle after living on the prairie so much of the time in the past months. There was a bed in one corner with a straw mattress. The sheets were coarse yellow-colored muslin, but they were clean. Feeling them next to my bare skin was better than sleeping with my clothes on outdoors.

I got ready for bed and was just pulling off my boots when there was a rap at the door. Opening it, I found Jackson there. He pushed his way into the room, closed the door, locked it and looked straight at me.

"You were with Sam when he died."

"Sure was. What do you want? How'd you get up here without anyone seeing you?"

"Back stairs. No one watches the back stairs. You told the rangers about me?"

"Your name came up. Bass wanted to know where you were. He whispered his message to me. Major Jones overheard, but Bass didn't know where you were."

He stepped back. His right hand dropped to his holster.

"You told the rangers how to find me didn't you?"

"No, how could I? I didn't know where you were. You're takin' quite a chance comin' here."

I had to think of something.

"You need money, Frank? I've got some. Get you outa town and you can head away from here."

I moved toward my saddlebags, but he reached across my chest. He grabbed my shirt and yanked me to him.

"Don't try any tricks, scribbler. Gettin' some money from you did cross my mind. Now be gentle about it and pull your poke over here by me."

He released me. I picked up the bags.

I laid them on the bed and with one hand loosened the strap. Jackson's eyes watched me, his gun drawn, the hammer cocked.

I dumped the contents on the bed. My wallet fell out onto the blanket and I picked it up, pulled out the money and handed it to Jackson.

"Here, Jackson. Almost a hundred dollars. Should get you outa town and as far north or south as you want to go."

He uncocked his six-shooter and put it back in his holster. He took the bills and flipped through them quickly.

"Right nice of you to do this, Mr. Reporter. You may have saved your own hide. Now I'm leavin', same way I came up. You ain't goin' anywhere."

There must have been a look of amazement on my face as his fist found my chin. All I felt was a solid blow.

Morning came and light streamed into the room from a jagged tear in the dirty curtain that covered the open window. I felt the warmth of the sun's rays on my swollen jaw and rubbed the place where Jackson had hit me. Moved my mouth back and forth. There was pain, but not like my jaw were broken. Wouldn't be eating any steak for a while. However, I was alive and Jackson was gone.

Though my legs were wobbly, I managed to get to the wash basin, pick up the water pitcher next to it and pour its contents over my head. It felt good.

There was the sound of a stagecoach, creaking wheels, horses' hooves pounding, drivers shouting and the like.

And then it struck me. Joline. She'd be on that stage.

Had to get myself together. Pulled on my boots, then stood up. I was dizzy and my head ached. I sat on the bed and lay back with my head on the pillow. My eyes closed and I felt myself drifting off. Didn't know for how long.

There was a rap at the door. I struggled to sit up. If Frank Jackson had come back, he could shoot me if he wanted. I was ready to die. I yelled, "Come in," and the door opened slowly.

Joline looked down at me. She was dressed in her favorite denim skirt. She wore the white blouse I'd bought her for our wedding. She smiled at first, but then could see something was wrong.

"Where's Billy? You must know. You were with the gang."

"Billy's all right. Bass sent him to Georgetown to get supplies. He missed the shootout at Koppel's Store. Bass is dead and so is Barnes. Others got away."

"Thank God, Billy's safe. I'm going to talk him out of being a gang member. He and Henry are my only two brothers left. Haven't heard from Henry in Salt Lake City, but I wrote and told him he'd have to get along without me. Nolo, you're hurt. What happened?"

Her hand was cool on my brow. I tried to smile.

"Frank Jackson. Hit me last night. I've been unconscious. Jaw hurts something fierce. Get a cool cloth, please?"

I rubbed the spot on my chin where Jackson's fist had landed.

Joline left the room and I presumed she was going to get something to make me feel better. It was nice having her around to take care of me. Just her presence in the room had raised my spirits and I began to feel much better.

She returned, noticed my look and blushed.

"There's a minister in town. Met him at Sam's funeral. He'll marry us if we want," I said.

Joline leaned over and kissed me softly, a kiss that wouldn't hurt my jaw.

She sensed I was thinking about something else. She broke off our kiss and moved her head away.

"Nolo Blunt. You don't care anything at all about me."

She dropped her hand from my chin.

I sat up half way in bed.

"Joline, my love. I do care about you. It's just that I'm still feeling the effects of that blow. Have patience. Let's talk."

I reached for her hand and held it.

"Joline, Buck wants us to come and live with him in the Kiowa village. He wants me to teach the Indians in his tribe how to read. It has something to do with survival of his people. He knows they'll be left behind when civilization reaches the west. He wants them to be prepared to meet the future."

She looked puzzled.

"You owe Buck a lot. However, that's a lot to ask of me. I'm not someone who could live very long without being in a town. Maybe we could spend some time with Buck and his friends in the future. Right now we must get you well. What's the name of that minister?"

I went to the stable, saddled Big Mama and led her out. We headed for the telegraph office. I had sent a wire to my editor to let him know Bass was dead and also that I was getting married. Now I wanted to see how he answered.

Big Mama snorted in the early morning air as I tied her to the rail.

The clerk was behind the counter. He looked up when I entered, recognized me and reached for something in a basket.

He handed me the message. It read:

**Nolo Blunt**
Frontier Magazine Reporter
Round Rock, Texas
FINISH UP WITH BASS STOP MARRY YOUR FILLY STOP SPEND YOUR HONEYMOON IN SOCORRO, NEW MEXICO STOP MAN THERE TO WRITE ABOUT STOP ELFEGO BACA STOP

I'd heard stories about Elfego Baca. He was a fearless lawman in the western part of New Mexico. He'd have a great story for my magazine. I could hardly wait to get started. What a difference. I'd spent the last months writing about a cowboy gang. Now I'd be writing about a sheriff.

I folded the telegram and put it in my pocket.

The morning Texas sun blazed away. My horse needed water. Joline would be waiting back at the hotel. I wondered what she would say when I told her about going to New Mexico for our honeymoon.

# BIBLIOGRAPHY

Sam Bass by Wayne Gard. 1936. Houghton Mifflin.

A Treasury of American Folklore. Ed. B.A. Botkin. 1983. Bonanza Books.

## ABOUT THE AUTHOR

Sid Hoskins is a graduate of the University of Southern California and received his master's degree from California State University at Long Beach. He spent thirty-four years in the Los Angeles Unified School District and was a principal when he retired in 1984 and began his writing career at the age of fifty-seven. He has published over sixty articles and short stories and has been involved in television news work. Currently, he produces and appears in his own cable TV show, Long Beach Forum. He and his wife, Leslie, live in Long Beach, California, and have two children and one grandchild. This is his first novel.

**Daniel Defoe**

HOW I COVERED SAM BASS is one of a series of novels being published by Senior Press which has been established to promote creative writing by the mature.

Senior Press seeks fictional works representing the efforts of those fifty years of age and older. Novelists who have never had a book published are given priority.

Daniel Defoe, pictured above, is a symbol of achievement for all mature writers. He was almost sixty in 1719 when he completed his first novel, LIFE AND STRANGE SURPRISING ADVENTURES OF ROBINSON CRUSOE. It became one of literature's first bestsellers.

For further information on forthcoming books, write

SENIOR PRESS
P.O. Box 21362
Hilton Head Island, SC 29925